Telepathic Super-spy

"What I tell you now, Professor Madderly, is in strictest confidence, understood?" Wills, the special assistant to the President, began. "We have good reason to believe that Golchov and the Soviet government have made the single most important intelligence breakthrough of all time."

"Intelligence?"

"Military, top-secret, cloak-and-dagger. That's why we need you, Professor."

"What can I do?"

"You've had three years in Special Defense Projects. Solid research in psychic phenomena. We think the Soviets have found a way to acquire top-secret information from us by using a highly advanced form of telepathy. We want you to find out how they're doing it, even if we have to send you to Moscow. . ."

Also by William Doxey:

DEAD WRONG
BYE, BYE, LONESOME BLUES

ESPionage

William Doxey

LEISURE BOOKS NEW YORK CITY

For Lyndall

A LEISURE BOOK

Published by

Dorchester Publishing Co., Inc.
6 East 39th Street
New York, NY 10016

Printed in the United States of America

If the reports of the Soviet breakthrough in parapsychology, resulting from their remarkable experiments at the Pavlov Institute, are even half-true, then the Russians are sitting on the biggest news story since the Crucifixion.

—Ivan T. Sanderson

TO THE READER

Although a work of the imagination, this novel is based upon extensive investigation of ESP research, psychic phenomena, charismatics, faith healing, and witchcraft. An accurate description of ESP experimentation in the Soviet Union is given.

ONE

Winter in this latitude. Maples and dogwoods picked clean of their fleshy leaves. A cool blue sky staring down through gray branches, reminding one of death.

But close by pines were crisp and green with life. And there were moments when the north wind shifted and blew promises from the south.

Life, death, renewal. The Great Wheel of all things turning on the pivot of the universe, casting the glitter of its spokes even here.

James Madderly, aged 32. Above average height, athletic build. Brown hair and mustache. Green eyes.

Professor James Madderly, Ph.D. Specialty: very special, the unknown, but not undreamt.

Madderly, a man standing on the far edge of psychology, peering into that darkness beyond spoken of in whispers by every generation. In his eyes lurked a gift, or a curse, a something extra unsought by him.

It was there even now, on this mild winter day in Georgia.

Madderly gripped the steering wheel of his green MG and tried to be analytical.

The feeling had plagued him for more than a week. Something would happen—to him, this time. In moments of clarity he almost saw through to the event. But always, just when the radiance was brightest, someone or something shattered his concentration and, like a shadow, the ordinary world and its usual, predictable occurrences came between him and *it*.

Now as he turned into Sunset Hills he felt that whatever it was it would happen soon. At the gun club earlier in the day, his perception was so intense he broke fifty targets without missing and won the pool. But he *knew* that would happen before he stepped to the line. Shooting expertly was very fine, and it was satisfying to know the other skeet shooters both admired and hated you for being so good. But what was the real fun when you knew the outcome before the first target zipped across the sky?

Precognition.

There were as many explanations for the phenomenon as there were explainers.

But all agreed that something did happen, that in many cases persons did see events before they took place.

Did this mean another time-dimension, a parallel universe containing all the elements of this one, each and every atom, running moments ahead in time? Two identical clocks, but one slightly faster than the other?

Madderly frowned. He'd been over this ground before, with the same lack of results. It was enough perhaps that such things happened. Still, as a man of science he had to ask questions.

And even now he saw in his mind's eye a car, a blue Buick sedan.

He concentrated. He saw the rear of the car, the bumper, the license tag. The numbers were—the first several were blurred—but the last two were crisp and clear: 9-7.

Some persons were seated in the car. Two men

and a woman. They—

A passing truck blew its horn and the image faded.

Madderly looked through the windshield at the bright winter day. The sky was so deep, so blue, he fancied he might see into the very heart of the cosmos.

He passed the country club, came around the sixth tee, and turned down his drive.

The blue Buick sedan was there; the tag numbers were 4-2-3-9-7.

Three persons.

They got out of the car and approached him.

The one who had been driving was tall and slender. His pale cheeks showed a stubble of reddish beard. His tie was loosened. The fingers of his right hand were stained with nicotine.

The man in the passenger's seat was short and heavy. He wore a severely tailored blue suit. His eyes struck Madderly as being those of a man who likes a little joke, so long as it is not on him.

The third person was a woman. Her hair was gray. She wore a dark gray suit accented by a green brooch.

Madderly recognized her.

Week, Sylvia Week, a witch of great reputation.

And suddenly in his mind he knew that she knew he recognized her.

The slender man said, "Dr. Madderly?"

Madderly nodded. "That's right. What can I do for you?"

The heavy man laughed. "A great deal, we hope!"

"My name is Wills," said the slender man. "Can we talk?"

Madderly hesitated. There was worry in this

man's eyes. But again he was aware of a communication from Mrs. Week and he knew he had nothing to fear.

He showed them into the house. They seated themselves in the living room. The terrace, rose garden, and lawn were visible through sliding glass doors shut now against the wind.

"Some brandy?" asked Madderly, gesturing to a decanter and glasses on a nearby table.

"That would be nice," said the heavy man. "It's a bit chilly and we've come a long way."

"Help yourself," said Madderly.

"Anyone else in the house?" asked Wills.

"No."

"Better take a look, Stan," Wills said to the heavy man.

"Now wait a minute," said Madderly.

Wills held up his hand. "Trust me. Can you show some identification?"

"But this is my house!"

"I've got good reasons, okay?"

Madderly shrugged and gave the fellow his driver's license. He studied it for a moment and handed it back, then removed a leather folder from his pocket and flipped it open for Madderly's inspection.

Gordon Arthur Mills was a special assistant to the President of the United States.

"Satisfied?" asked Wills.

Madderly nodded. "And curious."

The heavy man came back into the living room. "All clear, old boy," he said.

Wills said, "This gentleman is Stan Porkowski. He's an associate. The lady is—"

"Mrs. Sylvia Week," said Madderly.

"By god, he *has* got ESP!" cried Porkowski.

"Perhaps," said Mrs. Week, "but in this case I rather suppose he recognized me from the photos in my books."

"Correct," said Madderly. "Sylvia Week is the world's most famous practicing witch."

Mrs. Week smiled gently. "Only white magic, Professor."

"Of course," said Madderly. He turned to face Wills. "But you said talk. About what?"

Wills took out a cigar. "Do you mind?" he asked. "Some psychics claim the aroma disturbs them."

Madderly shook his head.

Wills blew a cloud of smoke across the room. "Now that I'm facing you," he said, "I don't quite know what to say, so I'll be blunt. I was ordered by the President to find a very special man for a very special job. We think he's you."

"Mrs. Week found you for us," said Porkowski.

"In the Yellow Pages?"

The humor escaped Wills. "National security is involved, and perhaps the destiny of our country."

"Professor Madderly is an excellent shot," Mrs. Week said. "I see him breaking clay pigeons. He shoots a perfect score and now he collects wagers from his companions."

"I don't know what qualifications you want," said Madderly, "but I'm no assassin."

Wills replied urgently, "No one claims you are. Sylvia's demonstrating her 'gift' for you."

"I'm already aware of it," said Madderly.

"And are you also aware, as you put it, of our business?" asked Porkowski.

Madderly groaned inwardly. "Thought transference—or mind reading—isn't a phenomenon that can be switched on and off. Sometimes it happens, sometimes not. Let's stop playing games. Tell me what you're after."

"What we want," said Wills, "is help. Does the name P. I. Golchov mean anything to you?"

"The Soviet psychologist? Sure. I know about his work at the Pavlov Institute."

"What of it?"

"You want a critique? All right, in general Golchov seems to jump to conclusions. However, his note last year on psychokinesis was fascinating. He's done considerable research in telepathy, too."

"Is Golchov capable of pioneering radically new territory?"

Madderly frowned. "Who knows for certain? He's been in the field at least thirty years. And the Soviets have put a great deal of money in his programs."

Wills nodded. He lowered his voice. "What I tell you now is in strictest confidence, understood?"

"Yes."

"We have good reason to believe that Golchov and the Soviet government have made the single most important intelligence breakthrough of all time."

"Intelligence?"

"Military, top-secret, cloak and dagger. That's why we're here. We need you, Professor, desperately."

Madderly laughed. "I'm only a student of psychology. What can I do?"

"Some student!" Wills chuckled. "We know your record. Three years in Special Defense Projects. Solid research in psychic phenomena. Excellent professional reputation, both here and abroad. They say you're on a par with Dr. Rhine, if not his superior. The South must specialize in psychics."

Sylvia Week's eyes found Madderly's. She

whispered, her voice barely audible above the moan of the winter wind outside, "It is a matter of eternal importance, Professor. Trust him."

"Suppose I do," said Matterly, "what then?"

"You'll take a little trip," said Wills.

"To jolly old London town," said Porkowski.

"But I'm involved in several projects here," said Madderly. "I can't—"

"Independent research, Professor," said Wills. "We checked. You have assistants qualified to cover. One phone call is all it'll take."

"And if I refuse?"

"It's for the good of your country. How can you?"

"But suppose I do?"

Wills attempted a smile. His thin lips curled back slightly to reveal surprisingly white teeth. "Don't be cute, Professor. You know the facts of life. You know where research money comes from."

Madderly shut his eyes. Wills' mind was open to his. He was cautious, not evil. What he said was true.

After a moment Porkowski said, "Is he in a trance?"

Madderly opened his eyes. "Nothing so arcane. Just trying to straighten out my thoughts." He glanced at Wills. "You know, my work here *is* important. It involves psychic healing. There's a possibility I may eventually be able to prescribe mental techniques to cure certain so-called diseases."

"Pack a bag," said Wills.

The hour's ride to the Atlanta airport was uneventful. Mrs. Week sat beside Madderly in the back seat and made small talk about the beauties of nature. She was quite taken with the dense southern forests and asked Madderly questions about the Indians who once inhabited them. In her lifelong study of magic she had read much of the Shamanic powers of Native Americans. As the miles passed she cited case after case, all fascinating, all based on hearsay.

When at last she paused for Madderly's reaction, he was tempted to remind her that in the long run those powers came to naught because the white men had very little trouble dealing with the Indians.

But he said nothing of the sort. He smiled and told her the subject was interesting.

"Professor," she replied, touching her fingertip to her forehead, "you forget who I am. It is well you are a gentleman; but you are also a scientist. Always be honest with me."

It was not until the government jet was an hour from London's Heathrow Airport that Wills laid his cards on the table.

"'The Other Side' is Washington's designation for this project," he began. "You're familiar with the term?"

Madderly was and was not. A nation's enemy was sometimes called "the other side." But there was another use for the expression. "The Other Side" was the world of the dead, of the spirit, be it heaven, hell, or something in-betwen.

Porkowski said, "We use it in the spiritualist sense. The Other Side is the land of the soul."

Wills said, "All right, souls or whatever. These are the facts which cause us to wonder if Golchov has—well—broken through and made contact."

Madderly said, "But you don't believe it's happened, do you?"

"What I believe is of no importance."

"That's right," said Madderly. "But don't be ashamed of your skepticism. It's the healthiest approach."

Wills scowled. "Let's get one thing straight, Professor," he said. "I'm the guy responsible to the President. I'll do my things my way and you do yours your way."

"Fine," said Madderly.

"Good. Now here are the facts:

"Seven days ago a high-ranking diplomat met secretly with the President. The gist of their business was that the President instructed him to assure the chief of state of one of our allies that very shortly new covert aid would be sent."

Porkowski said, "A virtuoso performance on the President's part. Neither State nor the Joint Chiefs were consulted."

"Even CIA was in the dark," said Wills. "Moments after the meeting the diplomat died. Bad heart. The very next morning the President learned such aid would be disastrous, because it would upset the balance of power in that part of the world and give our opponents damn good reason for increasing their involvement in the area.

"You can well imagine the President's relief when he thought his plan died with the diplomat. But it didn't! Two days later a story was leaked to news agencies antagonistic to our side. It quoted *verbatim* the President's conversation with the dead man!"

"World opinion swung one-hundred-eighty degrees, and now we are the villains," said Porkowski.

Wills continued, "Security went over the President's office with a fine-toothed comb. Nothing. The President himself submitted to extensive interrogation. He told *only* the dead man of his plan. We carefully reconstructed the diplomat's last moments before his heart attack. He died in the White House before the ambulance arrived. There were no last words."

Porkowski said, "It is impossible his secret was revealed, yet it was."

"Nothing is impossible," said Mrs. Week, "except the impossible."

"I don't see that you have a problem," said Madderly. "Since there aren't any witnesses, the President can issue a flat denial."

"Which he's done," said Wills. "But what about next time? The Soviets *did* find out. They can do it again."

"The President suggested a psychic explanation?" asked Madderly.

Wills shook his head. "What does it matter? We have to consider all possibilities. Here. Read the details."

He gave Madderly a manila envelope.

Madderly scanned a dozen typed pages bearing strike-outs and changes in at least two hands.

To begin, the notion that the supernatural was involved did not come from security. On the contrary, they were convinced of a leak at highest level. When they could turn up no clues, the President gave Wills the green light to try other angles. Here Porkowski entered the picture. He was nominally attached to the State Department as an Eastern Europe expert. He and Wills shared an interest in psychic research. They were aware of the creation in 1967 of the parapsychological laboratory at the Pavlov Institute in Leningrad. Through interrogations of several defectors, Porkowski determined that Golchov was the beneficiary of a KGB roundup of mystics, mediums, and clairvoyants—those suspected of extraordinary powers. Porkowski's report estimated no fewer than eighty had vanished into the Leningrad labs.

Of course, Madderly knew similar research was being carried on in this country. Dr. Rhine was at Duke University, Stevenson was at Virginia, and there was a small group operating secretly at a closed down airfield in New Jersey. Some projects were funded through HEW grants. No telling what the CIA was into. But there seemed to be no central control, no coordination. Madderly's own work appeared minute, but he was in association with gifted persons. On two occasions they led him to states far exceeding the telepathic. In those moments he glimpsed the other side—or at least felt he might have.

Might have.

That was the problem in psychic research. A calculus of the extrasensory had not yet been developed. Results were random. It was an exploration that worked more on intuition, on feeling, than on analysis and reason. And there were cheats, frauds, who preyed on the weak and the sick.

The seat-belt light flashed. A disembodied voice announced: "Landing in fifteen minutes."

London.

Madderly looked out the port. Clouds. In the seat across from him Mrs. Week was napping. Madderly tried to experience her thoughts. Nothing. Either his powers were taking a rest or she was blocking him out.

Yes, an ordinary person would object to another reading his mail or scanning a newspaper over his shoulder. If anyone knew how to secure or infiltrate a person's consciousness, she would. As one of the main personalities in the ESP scene, Madderly was not too surprised to discover she was involved with Wills and Porkowski.

"She's your go-between with a contact who has first-hand information regarding Golchov's work," Wills had said earlier to explain Madderly's trip to London. "She's been working on our side for some time."

Madderly studied Mrs. Week's peaceful face. She was about fifty or fifty-five, he estimated. Her gray hair was pulled back severely from her high brow and she wore no makeup. Her mouth was thin, no more than a line. With eyes closed she was as commonplace as someone's maiden aunt. But when she opened those eyes. . .

After they passed through customs, Wills said, "We split up here. You go with Sylvia. She knows what to do. Later we'll meet at the embassy."

"Don't let them catch you, old boy," Porkowski said, as he moved away down the concourse with Wills.

"*Them*?" said Madderly.

Sylvia looked both ways. "The game has begun. Follow me."

"Wait a minute. What game? And who are *them*?"

"The watchers. We're being observed now."

"By whom?"

"Really, can't you guess?"

Madderly glanced over his shoulder. A large man in a dark suit seemed to be looking in his direction, but then so did an attractive blonde at the magazine stand.

Mrs. Week steered him through the crowd. They found a cab and she gave the driver a scrap of paper and said, "Take us to this address, please."

Madderly concentrated upon the cabby as he read the note. The fellow's lips moved somewhat, but Madderly still fancied he received distinct mental impressions. They were bound for the Hotel

Europa, Grosvenor Square.

When the cab was in the flow of traffic, Madderly asked, "Why didn't you tell me we're staying at the Europa? Afraid I'll tell *them*?"

"Because we aren't. A car will meet us at the hotel. Enjoy the ride. Do you know London?"

Yes and no. He'd never actually walked the streets, yet he found he possessed a mental construct of the city, a sort of expectation that he would see certain things on certain streets.

"You've never been to London?"

"I was always too busy."

"That's a shame. But I imagine you have a sense of *déja vu*. Most Americans do. Some suppose it's because in previous lives they lived here." She smiled. "Who knows, perhaps they did. On the other hand, much English history, culture, and literature is taught in public schools."

"You are skeptical of reincarnation?" Madderly asked.

"My thoughts on the subject are not important. Nor is your lack of travel. I fear this trip will afford little time for sightseeing."

"Time is relative," Madderly said.

Hotel Europa stood close by the United States Embassy. As they waited on the walk before the foyer, Madderly noticed the Marine guards and the flag.

A double-decker bus stopped down the block, then crawled away. Madderly checked his watch, then remembered he was still on States' time. Here in London it was already another day. Thousands of miles separated him from home. Yes, and it might be interesting to conduct an experiment. Telepathy. Why not focus on one of his assistants—say Wilson. They'd succeeded in making contact at a distance of two hundred miles.

This was much further, but why should that be a problem? Cernik in Prague had partially established communication with a colleague in Cairo.

Madderly called Fred Wilson's smiling face into his mind. He focused all his energy. There was some obstruction, however, another force—

Mrs. Week had taken his arm. As her presence came into his consciousness, Wilson's image faded.

"Yours is a powerful gift," Sylvia said.

Had she read his thoughts? He shook his head and replied, "I was daydreaming."

"Certainly. Get into the car."

A Rolls. The driver was a dark-complexioned man who spoke with an accent so thick Madderly could understand little of what he said. Sylvia called him Stephan. Twice he mentioned someone named "Katya."

He drove with an abandon that terrified Madderly. They raced into Park Lane, turned sharp right at Hyde Park Corner, then quick left down Grosvenor Place. Another hard left took them up Victoria Street, and as they passed Westminster Abbey and sped across the bridge, Madderly called out for the driver to slow down.

Mrs. Week laughed and said, "Do you fear crossing into the other side?"

Madderly braced himself for a crash. "No, but I'm in no hurry to make the trip."

"Relax, Stephan is an accomplished driver. Who knows but that, in another life, he may have been charioteer to Xerxes the Persian?"

From Westminster Bridge Road they slid through Borough Road, down High Street, passed over London Bridge—Madderly saw the Monument flash by—went down Gracechurch, and stopped with a scream of tires that tossed him against the front seat.

Sylvia pointed to a street-level door. "Home again."

As they got out she told Madderly to leave his bag in the car since he would not be staying the night.

She also looked up and down the street.

It was empty, save for a single car parked down the block. Madderly could not be sure, but it appeared two men were slumped low in the front seat.

"Madame has been away too long."

"In body but not in spirit, Marie," Mrs. Week said to the dark young woman who opened the door. "This is Professor Madderly. Are the others assembled?"

"Yes, Madame. They are ready."

"Good, we shan't waste time, even though," she looked in Madderly's direction, "time is relative."

"Madame?"

"Nothing. We shall have tea when we finish. Now, Professor, if you will follow me."

They went down a flight of stairs and along a corridor to a massive door fixed upon huge iron hinges that opened soundlessly to Sylvia's touch.

The room was illuminated by a single small bulb which pushed the darkness back from an area purhaps fifteen feet in diameter. Madderly's eyes quickly became accustomed to the dimness. Three walls were painted white. The fourth, opposite the door, was red. A small, unadorned wooden table stood against it. A circle some nine feet in diameter was drawn on the floor.

As Sylvia bolted the door, persons in the room greeted her. Including himself, Madderly counted thirteen—six men, seven women.

One approached him and asked, "You have

formed the circle before?"

Her accent was as difficult as Stephan's, but Matterly understood. He nodded. During the course of his research he had read the literature of The Golden Dawn and had participated in similar ceremonies.

"Professor, this is Katya," Mrs. Week said. "And this is my coven. Shall we disrobe and get to work?"

The stone floor was at first cold and clammy to his bare feet. A damp odor stimulated his senses. Upon the table was a single small candle. The lightbulb flickered and went out.

The coven joined hands and formed a circle and moved slowly to the right, stopped, moved to the left. Katya began humming, softly, then louder and louder. Now the sound from her throat brought similar tones from the lips of the coven, as though their bodies were tuning forks emitting sympathetic vibrations after having been struck by a great force.

Madderly moved in harmony with the group, his bare flesh gleaming as theirs in the candleglow. Before and behind him women glided in the same sure motions, their ripe bodies releasing forces he recognized and acknowledged. Their hands intertwined, moistly, hotly, and always the candle beckoned like a living eye out of the death of darkness.

He knew what to expect. He watched as he moved. He tried to be objective, scientific. He knew the bodies, the chanting, the ritual movement were a means to an end, not an end in themselves. Energy was being generated. It would be focused, utilized.

The candle wavered. A cold wind moved catlike about his legs. And now Katya spoke but no longer with her voice. Another voice chanted a language Madderly did not know. But he held fast to the hands holding him so the circle would not shatter and all be lost.

The voice spoke on and on. Katya's face trembled, her flushed breasts shook as the words spilled forth. Her body shifted, turned, twisted, as though there were something deep within her being that must come out.

"One lump?"

Madderly tried to hold the cup and saucer steady, but his fingers shook. "Better give me two."

Sylvia lifted her silver tongs and deftly deposited the cubes in his tea. "One for me," she said. Now she settled back on the sofa, smoothed the green velvet robe she'd put on after the ceremony, and told Madderly he looked very tired.

"I am. It's been a long day."

"Yes, days have a way of stretching themselves out if we allow them." She sipped her tea. "What do you think of my coven?"

The tea was scalding. "It's a bit premature for a judgment. I haven't seen any results. In fact, I'm not sure what you were trying for."

"Katya was communicating with her sister Natasha in Leningrad. It isn't generally known, but our coven has been doing odd jobs for British Intelligence since the repeal of the Witchcraft Act in 1950. We've always worked for our country, however. You've heard how we confused Hitler's invasion plan in 1942?"

"I've heard the story."

"It's more than a 'story.' That was a combined effort of forty covens."

As Madderly listened, he looked at the cup in his hand. The liquid was releasing energy in the form of heat. Soon it would be cool enough to drink. It was a perfectly normal physical process.

Katya and the other so-called witches functioned normally too, when they utilized the circle's power. An energy exchange took place between her and her sister. The principles were not yet understood. But physicists were working on the phenomenon, attempting to find a scientific basis for the incidents that occured in conjunction with rites generally associated with the crude, the superstitious, the primitive. It was amusing to know that for many years the leaders of psychic research were not Hollywood witch-types, but rather greatly esteemed men of science, several of whom were Nobel Laureates.

He tried the tea. Not quite.

Mrs. Week said, "Katya's sister is in a position to know what is happening in Leningrad. Some of the sensitives taken to Golchov's laboratory are her friends."

"When will we know?"

"To translate the message takes time. As you are aware, telepathy is not always verbal. Images, pictures, and sensations are often exchanged." She put her cup and saucer on the silver tray beside the pot. "It will be best for you to go to the Embassy. As soon as the communication is readable, I'll have a copy sent over. Drink your tea now, and Stephan will drive you."

Even with two sugars the tea was very bitter. But Madderly drank it down, hoping it would brace him for another wild ride.

But the return trip to Grosvenor Square was smooth. They came by way of Threadneedle to the Embankment, and from there to Trafalgar Square. Tourists were poking about Downing Street. They turned right into Piccadilly, left down Bond Street, and a hard left to their destination.

When Madderly realized Stephan did not plan to smash the car, his mind began to wander. Sylvia Week was a remarkable woman. Wouldn't Golchov love to get his hands on her? He frowned. He was leaping to conclusions. What did he really know about Wills, Porkowski, Week—the whole matter?

Nothing, except he was drowsy. He yawned, rubbed his eyes.

He knew the Russians were deeply involved in ESP and other parapsychological research. Raikov in Moscow was inducing what he called "reincarnation" in art students with the idea of bringing to life long-dead talent. There was a girl who "knew" she was Rubens. Raikov claimed her work could not be distinguished from the Master's. The Popov Group was working with *psi* as a source of energy, and exploring telepathy as a foolproof communication system for space exploration. Soviet cosmonauts were trained in precognition. In 1968 Madderly urged a friend in NASA that astronauts at least be tested for sensitivity. The fellow laughed.

But the last laugh was mine, thought Madderly. On an Apollo mission one crewman conducted an ESP test with a subject in Chicago. The results were encouraging.

The car stopped. Stephan said, "The Embassy, sir."

Madderly tried to stir himself. He was so sleepy. He shook his head, whispered, "I. . ."

Two marine guards brought him up a back elevator to a bedroom on the top floor of the Embassy and put him on a bed. Porkowski closed the curtians and turned on a soft light.

"Which potion did she give him," he asked,

smiling, "bat wings or frog fur?"

Wills checked Madderly's eyes. "Don't know, but it did the trick. Get Chambers up here on the double."

"Really, old boy, do you think we should be doing this?"

"Don't tell me *you've* got second thoughts?"

"The professor is an American citizen, and you have his dossier. Must we resort to drugs?"

Wills lit a cigar and thoughtfully killed the match in an ashtray on the table beside Madderly's bed. After a moment, he said, "This is the big-time, Stan, remember? We do what we have to."

"Perhaps, but ask yourself—what else is there to know about Dr. James Madderly, 32, single, BA, University of Florida, MA, PhD Duke? Would you like a list of the courses he taught at Chapel Hill and Berkeley?"

"Get Chambers. I'm the one responsible."

Porkowski sighed and picked up the phone. He asked to be connected with Dr. Inez Chambers, the embassy physician. As he returned the phone to the hook, Wills said, "Afraid of the prof, Stan? Worried he'll get inside your head and tell all your deep dark secrets?"

"My life is an open book."

With lots of interesting reading, thought Wills. What do I know about him, *really*? That during the war he collaborated with the Nazis till an opportunity presented itself to escape? That he went west instead of east because of the collaboration? The United States picked him up in Paris and used him for a time as an operator, then sent him to Vienna as a translator. He had a talent for spending more than he earned, which necessitated additional employment. For years he had been paid to slip worthless information to the Reds. He had also been working for the Reds, feeding the allies equally phony material. His being a double agent was what made him valuable. Though totally corrupt, he was ironically trustworthy up to a point.

Porkowski watched Wills and thought—although at times he feared Wills could read his mind. A man could not help thinking! You could hold your tongue, but thought? It was the human condition: *I think; therefore, I am*. Right now Wills was tuned in. Very well, give the smug pig something to gloat over. *You snoop. May a wart grow upon your nose*!

That would hold him for a while. Americans. Bah! Working for them was playing with amateurs. Did they believe he did not know the "Top Secret" material they let him read was fraudulent? Was he born yesterday, or the day before? The Reds were just as naive, though. Even the Chinese. He'd be seeing Ch'en soon. It was all a man could do to make ends meet.

He looked at the man sprawled on the bed. Madderly was a wild card, the joker in the deck. That damned Sylvia! What was she up to? Psychic—bah! A hoax! If not then, why hadn't *they* haunted him? He tried to forget them, but the memory was like a spider web which held fast to the dry bodies of consumed insects. Was it his fault anyhow? Nazis would've caught them. They were too stupid. A man must survive! All five were hanged slowly. They would've strung him up too, but the devil of a Gestapo man in charge said no, might be valuable, and besides, they could always do that. Not always! He escaped. Now he worked for all sides, trusted none. He kept some things secret. It was like money in a numbered bank account, for sooner or later every bubble bursts. Yes, and even Wills was dangerous, what with his hired gunman, Relling. A man alone had only himself.

"Let her in, Stan," said Wills.

"Eh—what?"

"The door. You in a trance?"

Porkowski questioned the word *trance* as he turned the knob. Was Wills intimidating him?

A tall, slender woman paused in the doorway. "It's snowing, or did you know?" she said. "Coming down so thick you can't see the park."

"We'll build a snowman tomorrow," Wills said.

"You make that happy thought sound like a threat," said Dr. Chambers.

A marine sergeant looked in from the hall.

"Yes, Towers, what is it?" Wills asked.

"Sir, we got an ID on that car following Mrs. Week and the professor."

"KGB?"

"Yes sir. They trailed the professor back from Mrs. Week's and they're parked across the street now."

Wills puffed his cigar. Then, "Hope the bastards don't have a heater. Okay, sergeant, that's all for now."

"What about little me?" asked Chambers. She gestured toward Madderly. "He the victim, this time?"

"This is Professor Madderly, *Doctor*," Wills said. "I want to know what he knows."

"And you always get what you want, right?"

Wills's eyes narrowed. Smart bitch! Had all the facts on her, how she carried on with a certain big shot. The info was enough to get her involved in "Embassy" work. She was a pain, but there was no one more knowledgeable when it came to drugs.

"I'm too tired for games," he said. "Just do your job."

Chambers felt Madderly's wrist, looked at his eyes. "What did you give him?"

"I don't know—something to put him out."

"You don't know? Why, that's naughtier than prescribing without a license."

Porkowski said, "Sylvia administered a magic potion."

"Look, work on him! Or do I have to—"

Chambers said, "Mixing drugs is dangerous—can be fatal. Are you willing to accept the responsibility?"

Wills glanced at Madderly's placid face and nodded. Everything was a risk, so what was one more?

Ouch!

Something stung him.

A bee? But that was impossible. It was snowing—he touched the wet flakes with his tongue—bees didn't venture out during snowstorms. Had more sense, even if they were only insects.

Who—who—who—?

Owl?

That was more like it. There were snow owls, big fluffy white creatures with saucer eyes. Crouched on gnarled tree limbs, and even though there was no moon, they saw all and their grey talons were as sharp as their yellow beaks.

—who—?

Yes, even now they see me! thought Madderly. He was a strange little animal. If it weren't for his tail the snow would swallow him up.

Swallow up!

Yes, the owls were screaming towards him, talons set, beaks open. Their mouths were blacker than the night and he was such a tiny thing they would finish him in one terrible gulp.

Only of course they couldn't because he would not let them. There were ways to change your identity. A wolf taught him.

Wolf—?

Madderly giggled. Owls weren't so smart! Wasn't a real wolf. That was his name—Wolf—*the* Wolf Messing. He was a Polish psychic—and I hope you dumb owls know what *psychic* means, thought Madderly, because I will not explain everything.

Wolf Messing could influence the thoughts of others and make them believe he was whatever he wanted to be. Once when he was a little cub—Madderly laughed—the wolf slunk aboard a train and influenced the conductor into accepting as a first-class ticket a piece of torn newspaper he held in his paw.

And, owls, that's not all. Listen to this and eat your feathery hearts out. Another wolf—Joseph Stalin—was very interested in Messing. Only like an owl, he was skeptical. Wanted proof, wanted to put his hands in the wounds, so to speak. So he told Wolf to visit him at his dacha near Moscow, which was only the most heavily guarded place in the Soviet Union. Messing strolled in unchallenged by the sentries. How? Simple. He influenced them into accepting him as head of the secret police.

Madderly turned himself into a huge gray bear, and the owls flew back to their gnarled tree.

He could see them from the window. His arm was on fire. A cloth touched his face and the owls cried "Who?" Only now he was not sure they were really owls.

He shut his eyes—opened them again.

He was in a bed and the snow had turned into sheets and the trees were people looking down at him. He was dying—they did not say he was, but he could tell. He had died before. It was nothing new, but still he was rather sad because those who lived on never understood, until it was their turn, and then it was too late.

He turned his face. He was in a hospital ward

and there was a window through which he saw the water. Now he knew—it was the Black Sea.

The ladies in the ward were very kind. British. That was not strange because he was from Liverpool himself. The Mersey—would be good to see that river again. But he would set his eyes upon it never more. No, thought Madderly, I will die here in this bloody hospital in the Crimea, and all because some bloody fools kicked up a ruckus!

A lot of good lads were dying with him. You could smell death. The hospital was an ancient fortress, and the thick walls were wet with the moisture of centuries. Many men had died here. Spiders lived in the stones. He watched them catch the buzzing green flies that feasted upon the dirty bandages covering his wounds. Saber slashes were nasty. The surgeon—a fat man with a ginger mustache—took one look and said, "Oh, mother of God!" The nurses were kind. He would get well very soon, they said, with their sweet rosebud smiles.

And he did. He died there in the hospital in the Crimea. It was far far from home. How bitter to pass on among strangers! He was just a lad. And his mother longed for him. He knew her grief, for when he passed out of life he fell down down down into England and saw her, sitting there at the window, knitting socks by candlelight for him. It was bloody cold in the Crimea and they were woolen socks. He showed himself to her—a quick flash as though the candle flame leaped at a draft, and she knew she saw and felt him gone, though she continued working the needles and did not drop a stitch.

Porkowski said, "Well, old boy, are you satisfied?"

Wills looked with puzzlement at Madderly's

sweating face. What sort of trick was this? All drug interrogations produced a great deal of loose talk. But reincarnation? He reached for another cigar.

"He'll sleep now," said Dr. Chambers. She removed his shoes and spread a blanket over him.

"What do you make of it?" Wills asked her.

Chambers thought for a moment, then, "It could be a reaction to the mixture of drugs. On the other hand, he could be telling the turth—as he knows it."

"Don't make me laugh! Reincarnation's no 'truth'."

"Half-a-league, half-a-league, half-a-league onward!" Chanted Porkowski. "Into the valley of death rode the six hundred!"

Chambers said, "More than half the world lives as though reincarnation's a reality." She closed her medical bag. "Any more dirty work?"

Wills said no. After she left the room he lit his cigar, went to the window and parted the curtains. Snow, falling soft and white, like sleep, like forgetfulness. It was possible someone programmed Madderly to respond as he did under interrogation. But nothing in his dossier suggested that. Records could be changed. *Everything* could be changed.

"I think I'll get some rest," Porkowski said.

"Yeah, good idea."

As Wills left the room and passed the marine on guard in the hall, the idea came to him that at least Madderly would hold up under questioning should the other side get their hands on him.

TWO

Someone was moving close by. Madderly lay still and tried to orient himself. It was very quiet. He felt a certain constraint, as though he were shut off from light. Something covered his body—a blanket? Yes, he was upon a bed in a darkened room.

But where?

He tried to remember. Stephan—they were in the car driving from Mrs. Week's to the embassy. An accident? Good God, was he in a hospital, injured, paralyzed? He moved his feet, his hands.

No accident, no. He was very tired. Yes, must've fallen asleep. In the car?

"Sir? Good morning."

Madderly opened his eyes and saw a square black face marked with a friendly smile

"You slept round the clock, sir. It's morning."

Madderly rolled onto his side, then swung his feet to the floor. His head ached. He was thirsty.

"I'm Sergeant Towers, sir. Mr. Wills told me to wake you. Breakfast is ready, if you are."

Madderly stood up. His knees were a bit wobbly, his left arm numb. Must've slept on it. He rubbed his eyes. Breakfast sounded good. Wash and shave first, though.

"Which way's the bathroom, Sergeant?"

"Door to your right, sir. I unpacked your bag

and stowed your gear in the locker."

As he lathered, Towers asked what he wanted to eat. Madderly ordered eggs and bacon, toast and coffee, a large glass of orange juice. By the time he came from the shower and slipped into his robe, breakfast was served on a table beside the bed. On the tray was a vase containing a single rose, an American Beauty.

Madderly smiled and sat on the edge of the bed and tried the coffee. To Towers he said, "Have a seat, Sergeant. Hungry?"

Towers took a chair by the window. "No sir, I've had chow."

As he ate, Madderly studied the marine. He judged him to be in his mid-thirties. He was a little over six feet and would go probably one-ninety. There were four rows of ribbons and two marksmanship badges on his chest.

"Still snowing, sir," said Towers.

"Where are you from?"

"L. A., sir. Los Angeles."

"Not much snow out there. You know Atlanta?"

Towers smiled. "Atlanta's a good town, sir."

"What's your duty here at the embassy?"

"I'm one of the guard detail, sir. Pretty routine, not very exciting."

"By the looks of those ribbons you've had enough excitement."

"They pass 'em out with the uniforms, sir."

The door opened and Wills came in followed by Porkowski. "Well, glad to see you up," he said. "You must've been exhausted."

"I'm not accustomed to jetting across time zones. What's new?"

"A couple of things. You finished eating?"

Madderly nodded, and Towers took away his tray.

"Here, try this first," said Wills, handing him an envelope. "Sylvia sent it over a few minutes ago."

Madderly withdrew several sheets of paper and read the typescript:

> "A face. Lips, curving—a smile. Natasha. A second face. Male. A tombstone. 'Papa' is carved on it and underneath 'Monday.' A train. Two figures wave from a window. Emma and Joseph. Emma holds a book. They are going away to school. The title of the book is 'English Literature in Translation.' A young man in uniform. Red Army. He smiles. Cousin Ivan. He points to the rank on his tunic. A captain, and so young! No wonder he is happy.
>
> "Landscape. Snow. Bare trees, their branches bright with ice. A river. The Neva. People are chopping a hole in the ice. Now they strip off their coats and leap into the freezing water.
>
> "Leningrad. A narrow street. A house. It is Dostoyevsky's. People enter and pass down a hall to a room in which there is a glass case containing sheets of paper. A manuscript. *The Brothers Karamazov*. A small woman, frail. Mother. She shakes her head. Behind her springs up a forest of tall pines made white by moonlight and snow. Wolves. She stoops and writes in the snow with her hand. 'Sixty years.' And then, 'Siberia.'
>
> "A face. A man. Across his forehead letters appear, red as blood, spelling, 'Vincent.'
>
> "A telephone operator at a switch-

board. She—no, it is the man whose face is marked 'Vincent.' He dials a number. He smiles and offers the phone.

"He drops to his knees and clasps his hands to his breast. He bows low, touching his forehead to the floor. The telephone cracks apart, goes to pieces.

"Nothing."

"Buildings. Leningrad. The university. A bus with thick wire mesh over the windows drives up the steps. People in a room, at desks. Students. Men in uniforms give them examination booklets. The pages are blank. The men wave whips and demand answers. A student shakes his head and holds up his booklet to show the men there are no questions to be answered. He is beaten.

"A man in a black gown enters. The men with whips bow down to him. He eyes the students. He speaks but they cannot understand his words. He writes on the board behind him: G-O-L-C-H-O-V.

"Nothing. A face. Natasha. A smile. Sad. A wave.

"Nothing."

End of Report was typed in red below the last line.

Madderly looked up. "We drew a blank. Now what?"

"Read the next page, old boy," said Porkowski.

"Certain phrases are code," Wills explained. "Looks like the Soviets are into something big."

Madderly scanned the attached sheet. "People are chopping a hole in the ice" meant a breakthrough of some kind had been made. "Vincent" stood for psychic phenomena. His operating a switchboard indicated that some advanced psychic discovery had been attained. His begging attitude was taken to mean that some direct action should be quickly taken. "Sixty years" meant that sixty sensitives were now held against their will in the Pavlov Institute. Many phrases were pure nonsense designed to confuse anyone who, by chance or design, might intercept the message.

"Briefly summed up," said Wills, "it seems we're on the right track. Golchov's our boy."

It appeared so, but Madderly wondered if they were jumping to conclusions. How reliable, after all, were telepathic communications? The Greek Lachnos was satisfied with a twenty percent result, and that pertained to simple card patterns, not complex language. On the other hand, Natasha and Katya were sisters, and Douglass had demonstrated experimentally a strong psychic affinity between subjects of the same genetic makeup. Besides, when all was said and done, it was the only lead to the Soviets they had.

"Where does this leave us?" he asked.

Wills took the message and stuffed it in his coat pocket. "In view of what's happened, I'm not sure," he replied. "There's been another incident."

"*Incident*?"

"Yeah. Like at the White House. At noon yesterday Fred McNeal, and Under-Secretary of State, was in a car accident. Badly injured. Comatose. He died this morning. But listen to this: approximately two hours after McNeal's accident, our code men cracked a Soviet communique dealing with information only McNeal knew."

"You're sure?"

"What does *sure* mean? I'm telling you what was told me."

"My point," said Madderly, "is if only McNeal knew something, then how can we know he knew? It's like the story of the man who fell asleep in church and dreamed he was dead, and when the service was over he *was* dead. If he died without waking, then no one could know what he dreamed."

Wills said, "I don't know about sleeping in church, but this time you'll have a chance to question a witness. Oscar Miller, the Secretary of State, is scheduled for a conference in Paris this evening. I convinced him to stop in London for thirty minutes. Get dressed, Professor, and we'll take a ride to the airport."

The Air Force 707 taxied to a restricted area removed from the Heathrow terminal complex. As the jet engines died, an unmarked embassy car sped down the tarmac and stopped by the nose section. A boarding ramp was rolled into position by a crew of marines in airport maintenance uniforms. After the marines fanned out to form a guard perimeter, Wills and Madderly hurried up the ramp.

The Secretary's staff were congregated in the compartmentway. Wills pushed through and said, "All right, where's Abe?"

A bluff voice replied, "Where do you think?"

"With you there's no telling," said Wills, guiding Madderly aft toward a small, dark man.

"This is Abe Galt. Abe, Dr. Madderly."

Galt's eyes were underlined with heavy shadows. He needed a shave. As Madderly offered his hand, Wills said, "Don't be conned by Abe's name. He's about as honest as Porkowski. Where's your boss?"

"Back there," said Galt, thumbing to the door behind him.

Wills opened the door without knocking. The

Secretary of State held a half-full glass in one hand and looked over the rim at Wills. The young woman beside him started to rise.

"Hi, Oscar," said Wills. "What's new?"

"Sit down, O'Connell," the Secretary told the young woman. "O'Connell—ain't that a hell of a name for a pretty little thing?"

"It's descriptive," said Wills. "Oscar Miller, this is Dr. Madderly."

"That so?"

"Yeah, that's so. Oscar, you drunk?"

"Who wants to know?" He sloshed the glass, the ice clinked. "That's my business, *Mister* Wills. It's no damn affair of State."

"Me and Oscar went to different schools together," Wills said. "He married a Chicago pork heiress and contributed a lot of ham and bacon to the party."

"Ha-ha," said Oscar.

Wills turned to Abe. "Scram and take this O'Connell with you."

As the young woman passed, Madderly read her facial expression and made himself receptive to her state of mind. She was quite smitten by Wills, and at that moment visualized him snug in the Secretary's place in another compartment.

"Now, let's get to business," said Wills.

"What business?"

"Dammit, Oscar, the McNeal thing! Professor Madderly needs information. I told you about it!"

"*You* asked me to put down here on my way to Paris." He rose and lurched to a small bar across the compartment. "While I fix a little drink, suppose you explain."

As Wills told him the facts, Madderly watched the Secretary's face, his gestures, and attempted to attune himself to his consciousness, expecting to find little besides alcoholic fantasies.

But Miller was not drunk. His mind functioned rationally, clearly. He paid close attention to Wills's words and, at the same time, sized up Madderly. The glass in his hand was a prop, calculated to disarm his interrogators.

For a moment Madderly was confused. But then he understood. Oscar Miller was a man alone surrounded by factions. The best offense in his game was a good defense. The false front ruse worked because Oscar realized time was the determiner of destiny. Delay long enough and good would come to pass without necessitating the use of force. While he fixed another drink, a crisis resolved itself.

But he never missed a trick. Madderly got the feeling that Oscar *almost* had a gift.

"So cooperate!" said Wills.

"Why sure, ol' buddy. Anything in the world for you and the Pres. Okay, Matterly, shoot."

"Madderly dammit!" said Wills.

Oscar grinned and waved his glass. "Don't get mad, Madderly," he said. "You might end up like Wills—no sense of humor."

Wills started out the door. "I'm gonna talk to somebody interesting, like O'Connell!"

Now the Secretary of State put down his glass. His voice was steady, serious. "Madderly, I don't know whose team you're on, if any. But I'll lay a few of my cards on the table. First, I know something about you. In my racket, epistemology is everything. Abe Galt dug up a few facts—doctorate in psych from a reputable school, published a few solid articles, did good work in Special Defense Projects, whatever the hell that is. You specialize in ESP, right?"

"We call it parapsychology."

"I call it hogwash, but so what? You're a mind-reader, a mystic, Wills got to do a job he thinks is connected with the death of a pal of mine, Freddy McNeal. Freddy was as fine a fellow as gets tangled in politics and diplomacy—which means he was an S.O.B., but he was *my* S.O.B. and I liked him. Card two: there's something big in the breeze. Of course, since I'm just Secretary of State, nobody tells me. But I got a feeling it concerns you, professor, and I'm very interested."

Madderly sensed the Secretary's thoughts matched his words. He was telling the truth, for the moment at least. The thing to do was assay his psychic ability. Some subjects, though not receptive to psychic forces, were unconsiously telepathic and had power to broadcast their thoughts unwittingly. If Oscar Miller were of this nature, then it was possible he leaked information which fell into enemy hands—if the psychic were indeed involved. If such was the case, then perhaps the death of the White House aid and the injury to McNeal, resulting in coma and death, were coincidental. There was a chance the President also possessed a similar unconsious telepathic power. Was the time coming when those having a "gift" would automatically be excluded from positions of trust? The future can take care of itself, thought Madderly. To Miller he said, "Who besides McNeal had access to the information?"

"Just me. We were the only two who knew."

"How did you feel yesterday?"

"Before or after Freddy's accident?"

"Both."

"Now as I look back I didn't feel one hundred percent. Tired. Planned to sleep late—in Washington nobody gets enough sacktime except the whores—but Abe buzzed with news that Freddy had to see me. He came over and we had our talk. He had just left my place when he cracked up.

Felt damn sick then—still do."

"That's a normal reaction."

"Tell that to my enemies!"

Madderly smiled. "Now I'd like to try an experiment."

He held up his hands, fingers spread. "I'll put my hands behind my back and indicate a number from zero to ten. You tell me the number."

"All the way across the Atlantic at taxpayers' expense to play guessing games?"

"It's important," Madderly replied. "Close your eyes. I'm wiggling my fingers. Picture them moving. Now I indicate a number. Visualize it."

Madderly saw the heavy wrinkles upon the Secretary's brow. He was making an honest effort. Time to make an dishonest one. He switched the number from four to nine.

"What do you see?"

"I—three—no—seven, yes—*seven*!"

Madderly opened his mind to Miller's. There was a suggestion of power, but at this uncultivated stage it was hardly more than that of an excitable child.

"Are you certain it's seven?"

The Secretary set his jaw in a determined line, as though he had suddenly remembered ESP was hogwash. "It's seven," he declared.

"Very good. You may open your eyes."

"Well, have I got ESP?"

"To a certain extent we all do," Madderly said, standing up. "You're no exception."

The Secretary stood and shook his hand. "That's a politician's answer. Want to run for office or for your life—or both?"

"It's bad enough being a professor," Madderly replied.

Miller laughed and reached for his glass. "Good luck, Doc. I think you'll need every scrap you can lay your hands on—pun intended." Then, all laughter gone, "Get to the truth, quick. We may joke, but inside we're serious—dead serious."

Madderly rejoined Wills, who was entertaining O'Connell by sitting beside her and saying nothing.

Madderly appreciated Oscar Miller's allusion to the laying on of hands. The Secretary of State, he decided, was a good man to have on our side.

Captain Ivan Petrovich Gouzenko was late.

The bus crept up Gorky Street. Gouzenko peered out the frosted window at Moscow. Behind was the great Dynamo Stadium; ahead rose the Kremlin walls. Venerable landmarks passed: Mayakovsky Square and the Puppet Theatre, the Moscow Soviet Building, the Bolshoi.

The bus stopped to discharge passengers, then started off once more. What excuse can I use today? Gouzenko wondered. The snow? Impossible—a horde of old women had swept it away. The bus was late? That would never wash—Comrade Driver kept one eye on his watch, which was synchronized with the dispatcher's at the main garage.

Oh well, Gouzenko told himself, when all fails, there is but one thing a KGB man can do: tell the truth.

Meanwhile he would enjoy the ride.

Gouzenko came to Moscow for the first time six years before. When he was eighteen, the district Komsomol selected him for "further training." He left his mother in Irkutsk and journeyed to the capital.

He did not see much of the city then, though. For four months he attended the Marx-Engels school at Gorky. All the other Komsomol members said it was a fine assignment. They were picked for the intelligence service, the KGB. Gouzenko's opinion was not quite so positive. Four months behind thick walls reading and rereading *The History of the World Worker's Movement* and *The History of the Communist Party of the USSR* was not very exciting.

After Marx-Engels, however, life brightened. He was "graduated" to the Lenin Technical School near Kazan in the back-country of the Autonomous Tatar Soviet Republic. Here Gouzenko spent a year studying KGB tactics. He was one of the leaders of his group, but by choice not *the* leader. Top men were rewarded by more extensive training for work in the English-speaking world. They went to Gaczyna, the 400-square-mile preserve southwest of Kuibyshev where complete English and American communities existed. A man might spend as many as ten years in this environment, and when he went on assignment overseas, in heart and soul he was no longer a Russian. It was a necessary branch of KGB operations. After all, the British and the Americans had such programs which supplied agents for work in the Soviet Union. But it was not what Gouzenko wanted, so he held back just enough and left Kazan with a good recommendation which guided him into the Second Directorate of the service.

His assignment dealt with internal security. His small stature and Oriental features suited him for duty in the East. And so he embarked for Khabarovsk, on the Amur River three hundred miles from the Pacific Ocean and four thousand miles from Moscow at the terminus of the Trans-Siberian Line. The Chinese border was twenty miles away. Officially he served with the border guard; in reality, he investigated the officers and sounded out their feelings about the Chinese.

When hostilities with China broke out,

Gouzenko was wounded. He was a captain now, but he thought his KGB career ended with the steel plate in his skull. He was examined and reexamined by specialists, one of whom, he later discovered, was doing research on brain damage as a way of understanding normal brain functions. But the gray matter within his skull was not injured. Still, he was surprised to be ordered back to Moscow for reassignment soon after he recuperated.

When he presented himself at the Lubianka building at Number 2 Dzershinsky Street, he was attached to the First Directorate, which dealt with foreign intelligence. He would join the First Division as an undercover operative in the Moscow area. "Let your hair grow long, Comrade," a deputy minister said. "Buy some fashionable clothing; and above all, strengthen your liver."

Which was precisely why he was now late for work. His duty was to go from café to café, from bar to bar, and mingle with the patrons. His cover was the head wound. He was a discharged officer undergoing special treatment at Moscow University Hospital. After the Chinese trouble, the assignment did not seem serious, but he was a KGB man, so he followed orders.

The bus turned left on to Kirova Street. The next corner was his stop.

He started to signal the driver—and didn't.

He dropped his hand, pretended to rub his nose. A man needed to affirm his independence periodically. He wouldn't shout such reactionary ideas in the lobby of the National Hotel, but he could think—they could not enter his mind!

He frowned.

Or could they?

Those examinations by the so-called brain experts. The operations, the plate.

What if—

Gouzenko called out to the driver, "Where are we, comrade?"

"Turgenev Square, and on time."

"Open the door, please."

The driver shrugged and pulled to the curb. Gouzenko jumped from the bus and almost slipped on the icy street. Disregarding traffic, he plunged across Kirova Street, hastened through Novaya Square, and turned right. The Lubianka's grim facade loomed before him.

Towers was no charioteer but he still drove too fast for Madderly's liking. Wills seemed not to mind. He looked intently at Madderly and said, "Well, what about Oscar?"

Madderly shook his head.

"No ESP?"

"Everybody's got some power, even you. But I don't believe it's possible that he passed information telepathically."

"So where does that leave us?"

"Well," Madderly replied, "let's continue to assume the White House and the McNeal events are part of the same syndrome. In that case we can rule out the President's unaware participation. No need to test him."

"Good," said Wills. "If the media even suspected he was linked with—well, reporters hang around the White House like buzzards around the last water hole."

"But something *is* happening," said Madderly. "Maybe a worth while clue is the fact that McNeal's information was known to the Russians before he died. You said he was in a coma?"

"From which he never regained consciousness."

"Consciousness," whispered Madderly.

"What?"

"Consciousness," he repeated, louder. "We still don't understand what it is. Theoretically, there are levels. Perhaps one of them, activated under stress, opens the contents of the mind to another person's consciousness."

"Ghosts?" said Wills, as if it were a challenge.

"I don't know. Perhaps a presence of some kind."

"Same thing. So now what? Golchov?"

"I guess so."

Towers swerved into another lane. Madderly looked with shock at Wills, who said, "He's just doing his job. We're being tailed."

"By whom?" asked Madderly.

"Who knows? Could be MI5—our British cousins. Or KGB. Maybe Social Affairs—Chinese intelligence." He laughed. "Sounds like a singles club, doesn't it?"

"But why are they following us?"

"*Us*?" said Wills. "Professor, don't be so modest."

Tamara Rostov came to Moscow the year before from the Lenin Institute and was assigned to the Second Directorate. At first the comrades on Dzershinsky Street made fun of her because she was so tiny. "You are such a little girl," one said, "we will hide you among the dolls at the GUM department store. And who knows? You may apprehend the revisionist criminal who's been stealing them blind in women's lingerie!"

Tamara smiled sweetly, as she always did when angry, and asked the boor his bra size. That ended the matter, but she could not forget it. It was not because they laughed at her smallness. She was used to it. But that they should, even inadvertently, link her with those thefts! The truth was that she occasionally took items from stores, but only to hone her skills, she reassured herself. She spent days surveying the locale before she struck, and besides, they were only trifles—a lipstick, a pair of hose, or panties. And furthermore, she thought, was not the basic rule of Communism "From each according to her ability, to each according to her need?" Yes.

She slowed as Gouzenko hurried into the KGB building. What a funny fellow! One moment he sits peacefully on the bus, the next he is off and running as though something were after him.

Tamara was reminded of her grandmother. The dear old lady claimed she could stare at the back of a person's neck and make him turn around. Once she went so far as to declare she could cause a person's ear to tickle so he would swear a bug had taken up residence inside.

Perhaps someone on the bus had done this to Gouzenko?

Tamara shook her head. Of course not. Such thoughts were unscientific, silly. In dreams—but no, the Revolution did away with superstition once and for all.

When Tamara reported to her superior, Colonel Bazarov, he asked, "How goes it with our war hero today?"

The Colonel's attitude toward Gouzenko did not amuse her. In her heart she felt the Captain was indeed a hero. He was also handsome. And his Oriental eyes were —well, mysterious. Occasionally she observed him charming young ladies in hotel bars, and invariably she was jealous.

"He was late for work today," she said. "Too much vodka perhaps."

"Oh?" said Bazarov.

"Yes, he was riding on the bus and all of a sudden he threw his hands to his head and cried out for the driver to stop. He jumped off and ran here."

Bazarov laughed. He bore Gouzenko no ill will. Tamara he found a positive delight. But business was business.

"Please have a seat," he said. "I have news for you. The First Directorate is sending our friend with the hangover to London. You will accompany him."

"London?"

"Correct. It is rare than an agent from the Second Directorate is sent abroad. Your case is special. Frankly, I opposed your new assignment because I think you best suited for work within the Soviet Union. However, others believe it more advantageous that you stay with Gouzenko because you know him thoroughly."

Tamara nodded.

"You will present yourself immediately to the duty officer. I wish you a pleasant journey and," his voice hardened, "a speedy return."

Porkowski sipped the jasmine tea and tried the chop suey. Not half bad, he decided, patting his lips with a paper napkin decorated with red and gold dragons. The plastic Oriental lanterns cast rosy shadows across his table in the rear of the Canton Chinese Restaurant. Porkowski chuckled when Ch'en told him this was to be their rendezvous. Of all the places in London for the Social Affairs Department to choose! But there was a bit of Eastern logic to the ploy. Charlie Chan, perhaps, but who would suspect Chinese in a Chinese restaurant? KGB was more highbrow. They got together at the Tate Gallery or the British Museum.

"Hey, Buddy, this seat taken?" asked a voice at his shoulder.

Without turning, Porkowski replied, "You

know it isn't, Ch'en. What's new, old boy?"

Ch'en sat down. There was little Porkowski knew about him. He was in his early thirties, and he had enough authority with Social Affairs to pay small sums to keep his contacts interested. He was above average height and spoke English with an American accent. That was rather confusing, but the Chinese had as elaborate a training program as the Russians, and accent was simply a matter of seeing to details, which the Chinese were very good at. Ch'en wore his slick black hair long and dressed modishly. Shades of Chairman Mao—today he was wearing a purple shirt and tie, a green jacket, lavender trousers, and fringed boots.

"You look simply marv," Porkowski said.

"You mean groovy."

"I do? Well, so be it. Have some chop suey? It's finger-lickin' good."

Ch'en signaled the waiter and ordered a ham on rye with beer. To Porkowski he said, "You won't catch me eating that swill, man. It's bad, bad."

"Everyone to his own taste. This is still a free world."

"Sure, baby, sure. Only let's can the bull and do some business. What happened at the airport?"

"Airport?"

"Come on, man, time's money. Heathrow. Restricted area. Air Force 707." He glanced at his Accutron watch. "Hour ago."

Porkowski made some rapid calculations. Time factor made it doubtful Ch'en was at the airport. More than one Chinese agent was involved. That necessitated communication and coordination. The Social Affairs people were very interested indeed. But how much could they know about the total situation? The Russkies and the Chinks were shooting hell out of each other in the East, but they would still play ball when it was advantageous, and each could quote Marx in justification.

"Are you dead?" asked Ch'en.

"I'd love to be of help, really, but my memory—it's not what it used to be. I had a most unfortunate experience during the war which requires weekly medication."

"Okay, okay." He tossed an envelope on the table. "There's your loot. Get your head together."

Porkowski opened the envelope and thumbed the bills. Ten twenties, old, worn. The kind that leaves no tracks.

"Don't you trust me?" asked Ch'en.

"Why, of course. But if people don't count every once in a while, it would become a lost art, and then where'd civilization be?"

"Very funny. But I want facts."

"I feel something coming into focus. Ah—the airport. By Jove, it *is* Heathrow, and there's Wills boarding an Air Force jet."

"Come on, I've got other fish to fry."

"Patience, patience. I thought you Oriental chaps were long-suffering."

"You got it backwards. We like to make others suffer long. One of these days I might give you a free home demonstration, baby."

Porkowski sipped the tea. Napoleon's injunction never to wake a sleeping tiger crossed his mind. He put down his cup and said, "Mr. Wills was called to the airport for a brief meeting with a visiting dignitary."

"We know that. Which one?"

Porkowski tried the tea again. Those slanting eyes—they never leave your face. Strange thing, that shape. Anthropologists said it was due to the harsh climate of that part of Asia where the race originated. The fold of skin kept out cold and dust.

Sounded like science fiction—men made to order! Or bred to order.

Ch'en caught his wrist. "I'm busy, man. You got info or not?"

Fellow has a nice grip, thought Porkowski, feeling his own eyes narrow with rage. That was a mistake. Must always be the jovial fat man, devoid of courage. Yes, that was the rational way.

He put a tremble in his voice, pulled weakly against Ch'en's grip, and whined, "Good heavens, don't be physical! It's such bad form. The dignitary was Oscar Miller, the U.S. Secretary of State."

Ch'en released him and made a fist of his hand. "What was the meeting about?"

Porkowski shook his head. "There's a limit to the confidence Mr. Wills places in me."

"We want to know what."

"And so do I. It's not every day the Secretary flies the Atlantic to spend thirty minutes with Mr. Wills."

"When can you find out?"

"Oh, that depends."

"On what?"

Porkowski patted his lips with the napkin and settled back in his chair. "I am a simple, uncomplicated fellow. My life is essentially low-key. Still, I must live like everyone else, and that requires substance. So. . ." He made an open-handed gesture.

"You got your money."

"And you got your info."

Ch'en's voice broke with anger. "We have a saying—even a swine knows the difference between enough and too much!"

"Well said. I assure you this swine will recognize enough when—and if—he ever sees it. Now, old boy, if you will excuse me, I really must be on my way."

Porkowski flagged a cab. He knew the long walk back to the Embassy would be good for keeping the legs and wind in shape. But snow made the streets slippery. One had to weigh possible gains against possible losses.

The cabby drove cautiously. Porkowski eyed his thick neck. Flesh was loose, and the chap had lost most of his hair. But he was still functioning, was still among the living.

Yes, that's the ticket, he thought. He had no death wish. Ch'en was different. He harbored dangerous illusions. Why, the young fool—for all his Oriental "wisdom," he was prepared to die for The Great Cause, whatever that might be!

You could always die, so why hasten the event? He opened the window a crack and sniffed the cold air. Ah! It tickled the nostrils, stirred the lungs. Even now as he thought about it, the membranes of his body were drawing off the life-supporting oxygen and rushing it through his bloodstream to his brain so he might be aware that he lived and savored life.

Of course, his lungs also had to deal with noxious fumes—exhaust, dust, germs—agents harmful to life. Sooner or later those destructive forces would. . .

He signed. Why spoil present delights with future terrors? Thing to do was live well as long as possible. When the end came. . .Porkowski closed his eyes.

Darkness. Nothing.

A flicker of light. Was that hope?

No. He knew it was simply the mechanism of the eye. Had something to do with pressure on the nerves.

But suppose this business about the psychic were indeed true? It was not impossible that life continued in another form. Science had accumulated much knowledge through the centuries, but still there was more unknown than known.

He opened his eyes, turned, and glanced out the rear window. What he had to do now was find out the facts about the McNeal affair. Oscar Miller was no fool. Suppose he sided with Madderly?

That would be proof?

A car trailed the cab. The winter light was dim but Porkowski plainly saw the angular face and pale hair of the driver. It was Relling, Wills' hired gun.

The cabby said, "Anything wrong, sir?"

Fellow was watching in the mirror. Porkowski faced front once again. Relling was a slick operative. Did he have an arrangement with the cab driver? No, that was absurd. Relling was a loner. And, besides, here was the Embassy.

He paid the driver and hurried past the guards into the foyer. Relling's car continued toward Hyde Park and was lost in traffic.

An Embassy officer signaled Porkowski. "Sir, Mr. Wills wishes to see you in his office. Dr. Madderly and Mrs. Week are with him. It's urgent."

All three together, thought Porkowski, entering the elevator. Must be something big. The rapid ascent made him conscious of his body, of life. And of Relling's menacing face.

Wills opened the door. "Where the hell have you been?" he demanded. "You know not to leave without posting a destination!"

Porkowski removed his hat and topcoat. "I said I was going for a stroll." He rubbed his hands. "Brisk weather, eh? Excellent for an outing."

He nodded to Madderly, smiled cordially at Mrs. Week. "What's up—something remarkable, I hope?"

Sylvia said, "Katya has disappeared.

Sometime during early morning she and Stephan left London."

"We checked the airlines," said Wills. "They caught a flight to Helsinki." He paused, replaced the spent cigar clamped between his teeth with a fresh one, and lit it. "Looks like the KGB boys roughed them up."

"Katya left a note," Sylvia said. "She is very worried about her sister Natasha, and I shouldn't wonder."

Porkowski dropped his bulk on a leather sofa by the window. As the conversation continued, the others were not so much bringing him up to date as they were examining possibilities.

"Why would KGB get tough with them?" asked Madderly.

"They're Russians," Wills answered. "It could have something to do with Natasha, but then—" He tossed his hands in the air. "What's critical is we've lost our contact with Leningrad."

"I should hope you'd show concern for Katya and Stephan!" Mrs. Week exclaimed.

"I am—but I've also got a whole Goddamn country to think about!"

"Look," said Madderly, "this is getting us nowhere. The problem is what to do now, right?"

"Got any suggestions?"

Madderly went to the window and glanced down at the snow, the street, the park beyond. The monument to Franklin D. Roosevelt went unnoticed by the passing pedestrians. How quickly the dead are forgotten—so long as they stay dead.

"When in doubt, punt," he said.

"*Punt*?" said Porkowski.

"And hope the other team fumbles."

"My dear fellow, what does this mean?"

"Football," said Wills.

"Right," said Madderly. "If we can't go to

the Russians, then we'll make them come to us."

Wills raised an eyebrow. "Yeah, how?"

"This may sound simple-minded to old pros. Issue a news release that I'm going to Helsinki to attend a conference on ESP. Give all the details about me—background, bibliography, so forth."

Porkowski said, "That would be letting the cat *and* her kittens out of the bag."

"No, wait a minute," said Wills. "I like it."

"You *do*?"

"Yeah, it might work. Helsinki, because Katya and Stephan are there, and the KGB knows it."

"But I don't know anyone in Helsinki," said Madderly.

Wills smiled. "You do, yes, indeed, Professor. Leave the details to me."

"And how do I fit into this plan?" asked Mrs. Week.

Wills said, "For now, you don't."

"I don't?"

"No. Not in Helsinki. The Russians know you too well. We'll send you on a trip, all expenses paid. You'll fly to Rome, Istanbul, Athens, Vienna—a regular tour. And then you'll show up in Helsinki."

"Fine, so long as you pay the bills," Sylvia said.

Porkowski looked puzzled. "And where does that leave the two of us, old boy?" he asked Wills.

"Back where we started, in Washington. From there we'll come to Helsinki."

Madderly said, "This is interesting, but I can't hold a conference by myself."

"You won't," said Wills. "Leave the details to me."

Madderly frowned. "There are a lot of them."

"Trust me. After all, what else *can* you do?"

THREE

Tamara arrived at Sheremetjevo airport forty-five minutes before departure. She presented her diplomatic ticket to a guard by an information window, and he directed her to a waiting room marked "Private—Authorized Only." The door was locked. She knocked, and it was opened by another guard who checked her ticket and passport. He took her luggage and allowed her to enter.

As she returned her papers to her shoulder bag, Tamara surveyed the room. It was furnished in pseudo-modern style. The floor was covered in soft carpet. At the far end was a bar, at which several stylishly dressed men and women stood drinking and chatting. A double door to the right led to the boarding ramps.

There was no one in the waiting room that she recognized. Or so it seemed until she seated herself and happened to glance toward the bar again. A man standing so she could see only a hint of his profile seemed vaguely familiar. He was about five feet seven inches tall and rather portly. His bushy hair was unkempt. When he turned to comment about a remark made by the man beside him, Tamara saw his full face.

There could be no doubt. She had seen him in the newspaper and on television. He was Professor Pavel Ivanovich Golchov. That same morning he had given a lecture at the University which was broadcast. He said there were men and women in the Soviet Union who possessed tremendous powers—he called them "gifts"—which would revolutionize the art and science of mental telepathy. He introduced a boy who could look into people's minds and see their thoughts.

Should she go up to the professor and tell him she enjoyed his lecture? She was just a small fry in the vast bureaucratic sea. And her mission was not to congratulate dignitaries. It was to keep an eye on Comrade Gouzenko.

He was late for everything. Would he miss the flight? If he failed to come, she would try to put one of her grandmother's bugs in his ear!

She concentrated upon a mental image of his face; she peered into his almond eyes; she whispered his name.

Professor Golchov turned his back to the bar and looked across the waiting room.

A diplomat to his left asked, "Eh, Pavel, what goes?"

Another standing down the bar said, "Has he seen a ghost?"

Golchov ignored them. What did they know? The latest Moscow-Leningrad gossip? Bah! There was something of the infinite loose in this room. If only he could put his finger on it.

He examined face after face, sensing each for vibrations much as a hound tracked wind-tossed scent. His powers were very weak. He did not have the gift—worse fate! But through the years of study and fanatic dedication he had sharpened the little ESP he possessed to razor keenness.

Consciously or unconsciously, someone was using the power, but who?

Was it that stocky guard in the stiff uniform standing vacant-eyed by the entrace? Or the stout lady in purple? Perhaps it was the attractive young woman sitting in the corner, the same young woman who even now looked at him, then turned away, eyes averted.

The door opened and a young man was admitted by the guard. He was a small chap with faintly Oriental features. His hair was quite long and he wore a beard. After the guard returned his papers, he looked about as though bewildered, and ducked into the nearest chair.

Golchov examined him. A blank. Most decidedly this individual dressed in an ill-fitting suit and a shirt with collar much too big was not the source of the power he felt. It was gone now, anyhow. Like the dissipating concentric circles formed by a stone dropped into a quiet pond, the vibrations had ebbed and died.

It was a curious puzzle, Golchov thought. Someone within a radius of thirty feet had the gift; yet for all his expertise, he could not ferret him, or her, out. The experience reminded him of why he had left his work and come to Moscow. Podov, the Minister of Finance, and several other "leaders" were skeptical. They wanted "hard facts" to justify the expenditure of so many rubles. Hard facts to suit their hard heads! The young mind-readers gave them something to think about, the fools!

Shaking his head sadly, he turned back to the bar. How disappointing to fail again. Yet the incident supported his theory that psychic powers were widespread.

His assistant, Yuri Antonich, appeared beside him at the bar and whispered, "You seem agitated, Professor. Are you ill?"

"*Nyet*!" Golchov curtly replied. He started to tell Antonich of his experience, but thought better of it and instead ordered another drink.

Gouzenko cursed the worker who had constructed his suit. *Constructed* was the proper word! The crotch rode too high, the seat was too tight. His armpits were clutched by cruel talons. It was a suit designed to keep its wearer awake and raging. "Fit for an assassin!" Gouzenko muttered. His shoes were no better. They were so loose that each step was an adventure into unknown territory.

Gouzenko twisted and tried to find the position that caused the least agony. He felt certain his appearance was so absurd that everyone in the room was laughing. He spotted an attractive young woman several chairs away. She smiled, or seemed to. Then it was true—he did look grotesque! He was tempted to say—the devil take this assignment.

On the other hand, overseas missions were of no little importance in one's career. After years of watching a border few knew existed, he was given a chance to do something worth while. And the head wound was forgotten. If he handled the London job properly, rank and better assignments would surely follow.

All at once, the beastly suit seemed not quite so bad. Gouzenko thought of the future. What would he do in London? No one had yet bothered to say. He would report to the KGB *residant* at the Embassy. For now, that was all he needed to know.

At the Lubianka building they issued him a passport, fifty pounds in currency, instructions on how to reach the Embassy should he get lost—plus the inevitable suicide pill, this time in the form of the middle cuff button on his left sleeve.

Gouzenko fingered the disk. All one need do was bite it, and whatever secrets he knew were lost forever. Death was instantaneous and—they claimed—painless. But who could know since all who used it had died?

He removed his fingers from the button and

rubbed them on his trousers. Should wash his hands. Soviet technology led the world, but machines were still mindless, uncaring masses of nuts and bolts. Accidents happened.

Where was the washroom? The young woman who smiled at his suit still looked his way. Very well.

Gouzenko strolled over to where Tamara sat. Has he recognized me? she wondered. If so, it would mean the end of this mission, and now she wanted so very much to see London.

Gouzenko stopped before her and said, "Good day, Comrade. Can you direct me to the nearest washroom?"

Tamara almost laughed out loud.

On the way to Heathrow the first announcement of the Helsinki meeting came over the radio. When he heard his name mentioned by the BBC reporter, Madderly asked the cabby to increase the volume. A crisp British voice said, "—to the Finnish capital for a conference of parapsychologists and psychics. Although the specific subject they shall consider has not been officially announced, usually reliable sources indicate it is of paramount importance to the international scientific community."

The diversionary plan was now enacted. Every car was suspicious. Which belonged to the KGB? Had the Chinese picked him up? What if they snatched him now?

The cabby said, "That's a strange mess they're cookin' up in 'elsinki, eh?"

Madderly said, "Which mess is that?"

"The psychic business. There's so much ruddy trouble in this world without lookin' for more beyond it, don't you think?"

"You may have a point," said Madderly,

looking more closely at the man. His hair was graying—small ears—shirt collar frayed. An agent? Impossible. Picked the first cab at random.

"Going abroad, sir?"

Just in case wouldn't hurt to give him a bone to gnaw on. "Yes, I'm flying to Ethiopia."

The driver nodded thoughtfully. "Not such a bad spot, I'll wager, what with this bloody London traffic."

And it might as well be Ethiopia, thought Madderly. Wills had told him nothing, except which flight to catch. "You'll be met at the airport," he said. "Car will pick you up in front."

When he asked if all the secrecy was necessary, Wills nodded and replied, "What you don't know willl make your story more believable. You'll have to improvise. But don't worry, I'll be in touch."

Madderly left the cab and went into the air terminimal. At an information kiosk he got directions to the Fminair station. As he passed down the concourse he saw a crowd coming from the Airoflot area ahead. A sign above the exitway read: Flight 976—Moscow—London.

So this was the enemy.

He studied them as they went by. They seemed surprisingly commonplace. The clothing was perhaps a bit stiff. But the faces and figures, male and female, were no different from those at the TWA counter.

Except for one face which caught his attention.

It belonged to a slender young man wearing a tight suit and a beard. His eyes were decidedly Oriental. He walked beside a petite young woman who faced the world with a faint smile and who had to hurry to keep up.

As they passed, Madderly wondered who they

were. KGB? Neither matched his idea of the secret agent. More than likely they worked at minor jobs in the Soviet Embassy or Trade Mission. Perhaps they were in transit to positions in a developing country.

"Ethiopia?" he asked himself with a grin.

Now that the thrill of entering a foreign land had passed, Gouzenko fretted again about his clothes. This young woman beside him, did she notice how he shuffled like a criminal in leg irons? The devil take these shoes—if he would have them—and her, if she thought such misfortune amusing!

Gouzenko focused his scorn on the airport architecture. Very functional. That was a plus for the British, but obviously at core the building was rotten. Just like the people. Damn them—their suits were too loose. Take that fellow ahead. Gawking. If he doesn't move aside, down he goes and all power to the Soviet! Who is the rascal smiling at anyhow? Has he never seen a Russian?

"If I had time I would give you a lesson in proper manners!" said Gouzenko under his breath as he passed Madderly.

"I beg your pardon, Comrade?" Tamara said.

"Nothing!"

That was a poor answer. What, after all, did he know about her? She said she was assigned to the Embassy clerical staff. But there was something familiar about her, as though they had met before. She was positive they were strangers. Was she too positive?

He would give that question a high priority.

Madderly obeyed the seat belt sign and braced himself for the takeoff and the fast, climbing turn before the jet reached its cruising altitude and leveled off. The Finnair stewardesses distracted his fear of a crash. They were leggy blondes with wide blue eyes, cute noses, and sensual lips. After the pilot announced the destination, weather conditions and estimated time of arrival, one of the girls asked Madderly if he wished a drink.

"A scotch and soda, with ice, please," he replied.

The seat beside him was unoccupied, so he moved over to look out the port.

England was droping rapidly behind. Below were patchy clouds, and below them was the cold gray sea. They were flying northeast, away from the sun. It would be almost dark when they reached Helsinki.

"Your scotch and soda with ice, sir."

"Thanks. I changed seats. All right?"

"Of course."

"Care to join me?"

"Thank you sir, but I must serve the other passengers."

As she moved down the aisle, Madderly concentrated upon the base of her skull. What sort of ideas filled her pretty head? An image of sore feet came into his mind, and a tight girdle, followed by a hazy picture of himself, which was quickly superimposed by the grinning face of a sturdy young man.

Madderly shook his head. What bad luck!

He closed his eyes for a moment and wiped away all vestiges of the impressions he had gotten from her.

Then he sipped his scotch and looked out at the darkening sky. The world below had shrunk, vanished. For a moment he felt alien, strange, an intruder, one who dared too much.

The sun was touching the waves when the

jetliner went into a holding pattern above Helsinki. Madderly obeyed the warning lights and fastened his seat belt. As the plane banked into a turn, he saw the city spread out below like a display in a toy shop.

Sea broke the landscape into jagged pieces. Some ships lay at berth in the harbor, while others churned white wakes through purple water. There were no tall buildings. Dominating the apparent center of the city was the greenish dome of a church. The cars on the broad streets had already turned on their lights. Many roofs were glittering with snow.

The other stewardess took the seat beside him and said, "This is your first visit to Helsinki?"

"Yes."

"Then as we put down I will point out some landmarks." She leaned toward the port. "That dome is the Lutheran Cathedral. And do you see the tower there? It is the railroad station designed by our great architect, Saarinen. Helsinki is an old city—it was founded in 1550."

"It looks cold."

"Oh?" She smiled. "The people are warm. The winters are milder than your Minnesota. If you do not care for snow, you should visit in May, during the time of pitkia paivia."

"The time of what?"

"That is Finnish. It means 'the long days.' In May, daylight lasts twenty hours and in Lapland the sun does not set."

"Where the reindeer are."

"Yes. If you have no friends in Helsinki I will be happy to show you around."

Madderly looked at her pretty face, her blue eyes. Was she just being friendly? Was she attracted to him? Or—?

It would be interesting finding out the truth,

but his fate was already determined by the plan spun out by Wills.

He thanked her, saying, "I've already made arrangements, this time."

As he went through customs, the inspector scanned his passport and asked the purpose of his trip.

"Business and pleasure," Madderly replied.

"What business, sir?"

"I'm a psychologist. I'll be meeting with colleagues."

"Very good, sir. Do you have anything to declare?"

Oscar Wilde's deathless rejoinder came to mind: "Only my genius." But he said no, and the inspector waved him through.

He walked down the concourse through the crowd.

Suddenly, a light blinded him and a voice asked, "Professor Madderly? *The* Professor Madderly?"

Madderly rubbed vision back into his eyes. A blurred young man in a trenchcoat materialized.

"I'm Madderly," he finally said.

"And I am Birger Vakeri, reporter for *Helsingin Sanomat*."

A dark-haired girl with a flash camera stood beside him.

"We learned you were coming to Helsinki on a curious mission."

Were they really newspaper people, or had the KGB sent them to identify him? Maybe they were part of Wills' scheme? No matter. He had everything to gain by playing along. The more who knew, the better.

He managed an almost friendly smile and said, "What can I do for you?"

The newsman came to the point. While the girl shot pictures from several angles, he asked "Why do you really come to Helsinki, Professor?"

"For business and pleasure."

"What business?"

"I'll meet with associates."

"Why?"

"To discuss some matters."

"Is it true you are involved in psychic research?"

"I am."

"Do these meetings concern psychic research?"

"Well—yes."

"What aspect of psychic research?"

"Sorry—not at liberty to go into detail now. Perhaps later—"

"Is it also true, Professor, that you have extrasensory perception?"

"We all have ESP."

"One more question. Are flying saucers psychic phenomena?"

Madderly laughed. "I can't say. I've never seen one."

"Are the Soviets deeply involved in psychic studies?"

"Yes, but it's no secret."

"Is your trip to Finland in any way related to the Soviet research?"

"That's a broad question. I imagine some topics we discuss will be known by Soviet scientists, but—"

"Does this mean you chose Finland for your meeting because of its proximity to the Soviet Union?"

"Not at all. Helsinki is a beautiful city and quite historical. It was founded in 1550."

"Yes," said Vakeri. "Shall we return to the

subject?''

''You sound like a policeman.''

''Oh, and you do not care for the police? Are these meetings such that you do not wish the police to have knowledge of them?''

''Whoa! You said that. Our meetings are closed because we want to get some work done. When we conclude we'll be happy to release all our findings. Now, if you'll excuse me—''

But Vakeri moved into his path. ''Where are these so-called meetings to be held?''

''Sorry.''

''Professor Madderly, we know you have no hotel reservations. Will the meetings be conducted in a private home?''

No reservations? He was right. And Madderly realized he didn't know a single hotel in Helsinki. If Wills' person didn't pick him up—

''In whose home will they be held?''

He brushed past the representative of the media and headed for an exit.

The sun was down. A chilling wind blew in from the Gulf of Finland. Madderly turned up the collar of his corduroy suit and wished for something warmer. He also needed a destination.

Perhaps he should hail a cab and have the driver take him to a good hotel.

No. He must wait to be contacted. But his teeth were beginning to respond to the cold. He slapped his hands together, stamped his feet. His ears ached.

A Mercedes limousine stopped in front of him. A rear window whirred down and a female voice said, ''Professor James Madderly?''

Madderly bent over and discovered a pair of frosty gray eyes set in a small face marked by good cheekbones and a lovely mouth.

"Yes, I'm Madderly," he said.

"Mr. Wills asked me to meet you."

Her long dark hair was worn loosely over her shoulders.

"We are blocking traffic, Professor."

It could be a trick. He hesitated, said, "Wills?"

The girl smiled. "He says you are an excellent skeet shooter."

Madderly got into the car and closed the door behind him. As they moved into the traffic flow leaving the airport, the girl extended her hand and said, "I am Elina Hintsanen. My father is Dr. Utho Hintsanen."

Madderly pressed her warm fingers. Hintsanen? The name meant nothing. Perhaps they'd met at an international conference? The one in Washington last year? Shouldn't forget a name like that.

"My father is interested in your work, Professor. When Mr. Wills contacted him, he was more than happy to offer his hospitality."

"That's very kind," said Madderly. He noticed the driver, a thick-set man in a gray uniform and cap. Bodyguard?

"Did you have a pleasant flight?"

"Yes, very pleasant."

"This is your first time in Helsinki?"

"Yes. Miss Hintsanen, pardon—"

"Please, Elina."

"Elina, pardon my curiosity, but where are we going?"

"I am taking you home. We live beyond the city, on an island. Our family has lived there hundreds of years."

An island? Madderly tried to relax and enjoy the ride. But the heavy tires humming over the wet pavement seemed to say, KGB, KGB, KGB.

Elina gave him a guided tour. "We are now on the main thoroughfare, Mannerheimintie. It is named for our greatest national hero, who in. . ."

Her lovely lips formed words. He listened and wondered what was really happening behind that beautiful face. He tried to focus on her consciousness, to open his mind to hers. Images swirled, formed. One was of the street they traveled. Another was of a man who seemed to be reaching in an imploring manner. Another was of Madderly himself. He appeared as he now sat in the speeding car, with one slight alteration—his clothes had vanished.

"—are now turning on to Kaisaniemenkatu. In the distance is the university and across the street is the President's palace. The small body of water on our left is Elaintarha Bay, and now we are on the road to Borga."

In the nude? Again their minds merged. Now her likeness appeared beside his and she was also—well, well, he said to himself.

"Professor Madderly?"

"What?"

"You made a strange sound, as though you were choking. Do you not feel well?"

He noticed the seriousness of her eyes. "It's my ears," he lied. "Flying—the pressure—equalization—"

"Yes, I know," she said. "I am studying medicine. Had you delayed your visit two years I would be able to help you."

"Time is always my worst enemy."

"Your problem is undoubtedly in the eustachian tube."

"Undoubtedly."

"Then again, there may be a malfunction in the drum. One of your fellow Americans has done work in corrective surgery for such cases."

The car sped through the winter night. They were silent for a time. The road narrowed and trees closed overhead, shutting out the sky. Darkness was upon them like a black animal. The bright beams burrowed ahead, turning back the edges of the dense forest on both sides. Madderly thought he smelled the sea. Before he could ask where they were, the road twisted sharply to the left, and the lights revealed an expanse of water.

"How are your sea-legs?" Elina asked.

"Better than my flying-ears, I hope."

The car stopped at a barrier. On the right was a low stone house, and beyond, a long wooden pier.

The driver got out and opened the back door. Elina said, "We have almost reached our destination. Please follow Timo."

They went through the house and out onto the pier. A launch waited in the cold glare of lights suspended above the dark water. Elina and Madderly boarded and sat in the stern. Timo cast off the lines. The helmsman started the engine. As the craft headed into the night, snow began falling.

Elina turned up the collar of her fur coat. "Your welcome to Finland is now complete," she said. "You are in a boat between snow and sea."

Madderly tasted a snowflake. "At least it's clean," he said. He trailed his hand in the wake. "An the water's not freezing cold."

"Ocean currents. Our winters are not as severe as one might think."

And how does she know what one might think? She was a shadowy figure wrapped in furs. Her nude image came into his mind. What sort of person was she? First his ears, now warming ocean currents. Never mind the subject; she had the "right" answer. Cool, rational, logical.

The snowfall thickened and the wind swirled it

about the launch. Madderly shivered. He needed a topcoat. Tomorrow he'd buy one.

Timo's heavy shoulders were visible ahead. If there were a tomorrow! He was taking a great deal for granted. Still, he was inclined to believe the girl.

"A little while and we will be there," she said. "Can you see the beacon?"

Madderly's gaze followed her pointing finger. A flash of light showed momentarily through the snow.

"It is our lighthouse," she said. "It was built a thousand years ago."

"Tonight it looks as though it's placed at the edge of the world," Madderly said.

Elina's eyes found his. "There are those who say ships from the past are still guided by its light."

Was she trying to whet his psychic appetite? All right, he'd go along. "Ghost ships?"

"If you wish to call them that. I think of them in terms of a universal time scheme. Perhaps they coexist in another time reference that frequently intersects with ours. Those who have seen them are always filled with alarm and dread. You will think me quite mad, but I wonder how they react to *us*."

The light was swallowed up again by snow. Shades of the *Flying Dutchman*—did something more ominous than the KGB await him?

"Have you seen these—ships?"

"Yes. When I was a little girl, I boarded one. The men were very polite. They spoke another language and we could not converse. But we understood each other."

"Tell me about it," Madderly suggested. As she spoke he attuned his thoughts to hers again.

"It was a dragon ship and they were Vikings. I was playing on the beach. I remember skipping stones from wave to wave, when a cresting wave suddenly materialized into a Viking ship and the stone struck one of the iron shields hung in a row above the oars. I could not believe my eyes—nor, do I think, could they believe theirs! My nurse had told me fairy tales of magical men in the sea. But these Vikings seemed quite real. I wanted very much to run away. But they exerted a fascination I could not deny. They called out to me and steered their boat toward the beach. I went to meet them and they. . ."

In the images of her mind Madderly saw the encounter between a child of the twentieth century and a band of men of the ninth. They wore shaggy tunics of bear hides and helmets ornamented with horns. Their short swords were hilted with dragons of gold and silver. Elina was not fabricating this tale to entice him. It was real to her, regardless of its validity or lack of it.

Perhaps, when Elina was a child, the same nurse who told her bedtime stories had recounted Viking adventures, too. Elina might have seen pictures in books. On the other hand, the experience could be—

"—sailed away and left me alone upon the beach. The sun was shining, and overhead in the blue sky the birds flew and sang."

She brushed a wisp of darkest hair from her pale brow. "There, am I a mad woman or a liar?"

"Shakespeare said it better than I can."

Elina nodded. "'There are more things in heaven and earth than are dreamt of in your philosophy.'"

Timo spoke in Finnish. Elina said, "The island. We are here at last."

The launch drifted into a snug boathouse lit by overhead lights. Madderly helped Elina to the landing and followed her. The damp stones under his feet shook like the sea for a moment. But he regained his earth-legs and passed through a door into a snow-filled courtyard illuminated by sputtering torches.

FOUR

Gouzenko cursed the wooden bench upon which he had been sitting for two hours at the very least. Why in the name of God had the government sent him to London if this were to be his fate? There were benches just as hard in Moscow! For the *n*th time he tried escaping his predicament through daydream. He saw himself having a few drinks in a Moscow bar.

But the door before him opened and a shapely young woman squinted in his direction through small round eyeglasses and said, "Comrade Gouzenko, Colonel Zharkov will see you now."

Gouzenko stretched a bit to free the bench from his bones and brushed past the secretary. She smelled of perfume, of limes. They know how to live in London, and without those glasses, not to mention—

"Captain Gouzenko?"

Gouzenko came to attention and saluted the square-faced man who confronted him from behind a bare desk. "Reporting as ordered, sir."

"Be at ease," said Zharkov. He removed a folder from a drawer, glanced at its contents, then at Gouzenko, and said, "Your appearance is extraordinary. You wear a hair piece?"

"No sir."

"You are authorized to go about so?"

"Yes sir. My appearance was necessary for my

last assignment in Moscow."

"This is not Moscow," Zharkov said. "Yet, all in all, it's quite appropriate for the London 'scene.'"

"Yes sir."

Now Zharkov frowned. "But you will not be making the scene. The man you are assigned to watch has left the country. You will follow him."

Another country? Gouzenko's flesh ached in protest.

"You will depart Heathrow Airport for Helsinki on the early morning flight. Now look at these photos." He slid the folder across the desk.

Gouzenko saw three color snapshots of a man in his thirties with a mustache and medium-length brown hair. He wore a light blue shirt and dark green tie, a green corduroy suit. His clothes seemed to fit comfortably. Wait! There was something familiar about the man. Yes—the idiot at the airport—the one who was laughing! It was he, or his double.

In one photo he stood beside a middle-aged woman in front of a hotel.

Zharkov said, "This is Professor James Madderly, an American specialist in psychic research. Do you know the term 'psychic'?"

"Yes, it deals with extrasensory perception."

"Correct, but that is none of your affair. You will find Professor Madderly and report his activities. We have reason to believe he is involved in matters of great importance to the Soviet Union. Questions?"

"Who is this woman?"

"Mrs. Sylvia Week, a famous psychic. Madderly came to London with her."

"And she is with him in Helsinki?"

"No, at last report Mrs. Week is still in London."

Zharkov showed Gouzenko two more photos. "This man," he said, "is Gordon Wills, a special assistant to the President of the United States. We believe Madderly works for him."

"His control?"

"Not exactly. We have no reason to suspect the professor is a spy. The other man is Stanislaus Porkowski. He works for Wills and is, therefore, also involved in whatever Madderly is doing."

Gouzenko went through the photos a last time. It was Madderly who compelled his attention. Was he the man at the airport?

Zharkov noticed his concentration. "What's the problem?"

"I can't be sure. I feel I have seen this Madderly before."

"Then you will not soon forget his face. More questions?"

Gouzenko assessed Zharkov before replying. The KGB Colonel trusts me, he decided, and this seems an important assignment. What the devil—be a man!

He cleared his throat and spoke politely but with determination. "Comrade Colonel, there is one matter which causes me much concern. Granted, it may seem small, still—"

"Come to the point, *captain*."

"Yes sir. It is this suit of clothes. They are too tight. And my shoes are large enough for a horse!"

Pure and simple, the flight from Moscow to Leningrad had been the flight from Moscow to Leningrad. By now the journey was routine. What did it matter if this time the plane had been one of the newest jets instead of a turbo-prop? A few minutes saved, perhaps, but for what?

"In the future we will not use planes," thought Golchov. "Matter will be transported at the speed of light from point to point."

Yes.

He stood at the open window of his study overlooking the frozen Neva River. It was one of those nights that Dostoyevsky had often described. The falling snow muted traffic sounds from the Mendeleyevskaya Liniya Boulevard and wrapped the world in white for a long, dreamless sleep.

But it was not the weather that made him pensive. Yes, the flight from Moscow had been uneventful, although Yuri Antonich drank too much vodka and had to be helped from the plane.

Golchov closed the window. That Yuri! A complete fool—but he had youth! To be young again and get falling-down drunk. "The trouble with life," he told the bust of Lenin gathering dust in the corner, "is the absence of romance. In the old days everyone got drunk to celebrate the smallest accomplishment. Now those who drink do so out of foolishness or desperation."

He shook his graying head and sat behind his desk. What strange pranks life played. "Here I am in a snug room at the Pavlov Institute, located on a bit of land called Strelka, which is part of an island in the Neva River, which flows through the great and beautiful city of Leningrad, and I am not—"

He knew the word he omitted but he would not utter it. Had he a right to be happy on top of all else? It was presumptuous—no, worse—prideful. That was the worst human frailty.

"But Golchov," he said to himself, "you have every right to be proud. Have you not succeeded in doing what men have attempted since the dawn of history? Have you not established contact with a realm of existence beyond the material, the temporal?"

Yes, and still—

Golchov frowned at the memory of the reception

given him in Moscow by Popov and the science minister, Anatole Nikoyan. Popov's reaction was to be expected. The bearish economist was hysterical with questions regarding future events. "We can beat the capitalists at their own game now!" he exclaimed. "Give me a list of stocks that will rise. We'll put them out of business!" he shouted, wringing his sweaty heands, panting with greed, and completely misconstruing the true nature of the breakthrough.

Nikoyan handled himself no better, perhaps worse. Golchov knew the science minister from student days at the university. He was a boot-licker who attained his degree by activities in the party rather than by hard work in the laboratory.

"I am a practical man," he was always saying when big shots were within earshot. "Theory is of course necessary, but show me the application. Do not speak of thermodynamics. Give me economical tractor motors instead."

On and on the ass went, filling the air with his foul breath and fouler platitudes!

"Ah well," Golchov sighed, "if you wish to dance you must pay the piper."

He had paid dearly. But God, what a delightful dance! Now he felt excitement rise again in his tired bones. They had bridged the abyss, had leaped the chasm—and landed on the other side!

He held his hands to the light, studied the wrinkled skin. This was transitory. Worms will gnaw my flesh, but they cannot destroy the real *me*.

This awareness made him sit straighter and question his melancholy. Why was he in such a state? What had happened? Now was the moment for laughter, for rejoicing, for Yuri's burning vodka, not sadness.

"It is the burden of this knowledge that

weighs me down," he announced to Lenin's bust. He was one of a handful who knew. What would happen if—when—everyone found out? The Party promised its faithful a paradise here on earth. There was nothing afterwards.

Only there was!

There was a consciousness that transcended time and space. It was elusive. He could not prove it scientifically, not yet. But he *felt* it.

For practical purposes there were the successful experiments on the White House itself in Washington. Tractor motors! thought Golchov, laughing inwardly. And now with a generous new appropriation it was his *duty*—Nikoyan used the term—to refine and develop the technique so more applications might be realized.

"In view of this goal," Nikoyan had said, "it is of first importance that strict security be maintained. We do not want such a valuable scientific discovery falling into bad hands, eh?"

Golchov slammed his fist on the desk and cursed himself. Like a worm he had answered that whining "eh?" with a "yes," in spite of his conviction that Nikoyan's hands were the worst of all.

Beyond the courtyard Madderly and Elina ascended a flight of steps leading to a massive iron-studded door that swung inward as they neared.

"Photo cells and electric motors," Elina said, entering a foyer lit with hanging brass lamps. "Our castle was built in the sixteenth century to deter Russian aggression, but it has been modernized."

Yes, thought Madderly, and as in a fairy tale you are perhaps the king's fair daughter whom he must sacrifice to save his lands.

Elina gave her coat to an elderly maid who appeared from the shadows behind the door. "Erika will take your suitcase. Come, my father is waiting in the library."

They moved through a reception hall and turned down a broad corridor. The stone walls were hung with portraits of unsmiling men in stiff collars and gentle-eyed women with gracefully accentuated necks and limbs. There were shields and spears and shining swords set against red and gold tapestries and bright panels of inlaid woods.

Elina halted before a carved door. A hollow, disembodied voice said, "Yes?"

"It is I, father. Professor Madderly is with me."

The door slid back to reveal a large windowless room. There were neither books nor bookcases. The walls were lined with gray metal cabinets. A long table and single chair stood in the center of the floor, which was polished to a mirror gloss.

Madderly heard a whirr to his right. A man in a wheelchair moved from the corner beside the door.

Elina kissed the man's cheek, then, to Madderly, said, "My father, Dr. Utho Hintsanen."

The face of the man in the wheelchair was a grim mask. But his eyes shone with a luster indicating that they missed nothing that passed before them.

Now the lips of the mask moved slightly and the same hollow voice spoke again. "Welcome, Dr. Madderly. So good to have you visit. We will do all in our power to make you *mukava*."

"That is our word for 'comfortable,'" Elina said.

Madderly nodded, "I appreciate your kindness."

Hintsanen said, "I know my appearance shocks you. No, do not be polite. I am honest. *I* find myself shocking. As you see, I am paralyzed.

My voice is amplified electronically. I have partial use of my left hand with which I manipulate these controls built into the arm of my chair. I was a normal man until an airplane crash two years ago. Specialists assure me my case is hopeless. Yet I am not such a fool as to believe them."

The voice was artificial, mechanical, but Madderly detected a note of irony. He smiled.

"Excellent," Hintsanen said. "You recognize my humor. Unfortunately, my daughter does not."

"Father!"

"Elina is a dutiful child, but inclined to sadness. Her mother died in the crash which injured me. She feels obligated to remain at my side."

"It is more than an obligation, father. And I am sure Professor Madderly is not interested in our problems."

"Perhaps not. Please have a seat, Professor, and we shall talk."

Madderly sat in the chair at the table. Hintsanen maneuvered his wheelchair to the other side and faced him.

"I know something more about you, Professor, than what little our mutual friend Wills divulged. For example, please look at the screen on the wall to your right."

A black and white projection of a microfilm copy of one of Madderly's recent articles appeared.

"My library is a data-processing center," Hintsanen said. "Pertinent materials are reduced to microfilm and cross-indexed for rapid retrieval."

Madderly read his article's title and his name in six-inch letters. "I'm flattered," he said, "but I'm afraid I don't understand. What's your connection with Wills? And why do you bother with my scholarship?"

"Wills knows many men around the world. I am one. In the past we have helped each other in various ways. You, Professor, are of great interest to me because of your research in psychic healing. My family is among the oldest and wealthiest in Finland, but neither ancestry nor money has straightened my crippled body."

"I'm a scientist, not a miracle worker."

"Perhaps, but you have contacts, and miracles happen every day. You have seen some. Your article is proof."

"My article is proof only that something happened, in this case to a subject suffering from a skin disease. I don't know how the apparent cure came about. Perhaps the disease was psychosomatic."

"In the mind?" said Hintsanen. "But the pain is just as real. At any rate, I am helping Wills and you. Perhaps you will be able to help me in some small way. We shall see."

"Have you heard from Wills?"

"Only the message concerning your arrival. Now, I insist on being hospitable. Elina will entertain you properly. Good evening, Dr. Madderly."

Elina led Madderly to the doorway. As they passed through, he paused and looked back at the motionless figure watching him with the fixed stare of a statue. Was he really paralyzed? Perhaps it was a trick—but for what purpose? Madderly was tempted to wave goodbye and see if the man would respond reflexively. But as he raised his hand the door shut.

Through Hammersmith and out the Great West Road Porkowski became aware they were being followed. Ch'en, in a bright red Triumph with the top down, almost hung on the embassy limousine's bumper.

How droll, these Chinese! First the meeting in a Chinese restaurant, and now the mod agent in a flashy sportscar. At least the color was fitting.

From the front seat Wills said, "What's up, Stan?"

"Nothing, nothing at all—if one calls a transoceanic flight nothing. Frankly, I find it bothersome."

"But necessary," said Wills, squinting at the side mirror. The red car had been on their tail too long. The driver's face was obscured by shadows, but he supposed him to be either KGB or Social Affairs. MI5 would never use a Triumph. Come to think of it, KGB was too stingy. Whoever he was, he drove like a damn fool.

Porkowski said, "Perhaps you place too much faith in the professor's 'plan'?"

"Maybe," said Wills. To Towers who was driving, he said, "Speed up. When I yell *now*, hit the brakes hard."

Towers gripped the wheel with both hands. Wills watched the Triumph in the mirror. If we're gonna give them something to think about, he reasoned, it might as well be good.

The speedometer climbed to fifty, fifty-five.

"We're going too fast!" said Porkowski.

Sixty, sixty-five, seventy.

"I protest! Stop! I have no intention of—"

"*Now*!"

The sudden deceleration raised the rear bumper of the limousine. The Triumph impacted. Its radiator burst with a white flash of steam.

"Let's go!" shouted Wills.

The big car sped away as the Triumph spun around and rammed a parked truck.

"Good work," said Wills. "Damn good. Right, Stan?"

A sob came from the rear seat. "I think I've been injured. I must have medical attention."

"Later. We've got a plane to catch."

They drove to a private airfield west of Heathrow. A light plane flew them down the coast to an air force base where they boarded a military jet for Washington.

The ringing phone called him back from a dream of childhood.

Three of them were sledding on the hills of snow that the wind had heaped against the north wall of the Kremlin. He saw himself in his fur coat, wearing that silly little hat with the long muffs he refused to tie beneath his chin. They flapped like the ears of a running hound. Yes, he was twelve again and in Novgorod. It was the early thirties, before the purges, and his father was still alive. They had not yet moved to Leningrad, which some still called Petrograd. He was sledding, only one of his companions was a stranger, a young woman he did not recall from those days. She tagged at his side, exerted a force which played upon his mind—Moscow—airport—yes, she—now the great bronze bells of St. Sophia's Cathedral tolled the glory of heaven, which was a lie, silly superstition, but the bells made a beautiful sound, yes—and—

His hand, searching unconsciously before he awoke, found the telephone and brought it obediently to his ear. Was it the girl? How strange to be sledding and using the phone at the same moment.

The voice was not from the halcyon days of his youth. "Dr. Golchov? Comrade Professor?"

"Eh—what?" He rubbed his eyes. "Yes—yes—this is Golchov."

"Minister Nikoyan will speak to you now."

Nikoyan? Had the dream changed into a

nightmare? He saw by the desk clock that he had dozed for several hours. His neck ached, his foot was numb. What the devil could Nikoyan want?

"Pavel? Anatole here. Were you sleeping?"

"At this early hour? I am working. Or was! What do you want?"

"We have received some disquieting information from the Center. Does the name 'Madderly' mean anything to you?"

"What? Spell it."

"Madderly. M-A-D-D-E-R-L-Y. Madderly."

"What is a 'madderly'?"

"Not what—who. Madderly is an American professor of psychology, of parapsychology, to be exact."

Yes, now he recalled that name. Yuri abstracted a recent article by him on—was it psychic healing?

"Pavel?" Nikoyan was getting impatient.

"So what about this Madderly?"

"You know him?"

"I know he has written an article in the last year." Was the ass trying to implicate him in some plot? "He is a respected scientist."

"Oh, that's not good."

"What's not good? Are you trying to drive me mad? Come to the point or say goodnight!"

"It's a complicated mess."

"So untangle it and send me a letter!"

In his mind's eye Golchov pictured Nikoyan lolling on the plush white divan in his fancy apartment. The furniture was flown in from Paris as part of a "cultural exchange."

"Our agents in London report Madderly has been seen in the company of a special assistant to the President of the United States."

This *was* news. Perhaps American leaders were not as stupid as Popov declared. Still, nothing was proved.

"And you conclude they have discovered the nature of our successful experiments?"

"I conclude nothing," Nikoyan said. "This Professor Madderly is now in Helsinki for the avowed purpose of attending a meeting of psychic researchers. In a press interview at the airport, he stated they will discuss a subject of interest to the Soviet Union. Finally he was last seen in a car registered to Dr. Utho-Hintsanen. I believe you know him?"

"Personally, no," said Golchov. "The Hintsanens are a powerful family. The doctor has expressed curiosity about psychic matters."

"So what do you make of this? Is our project in danger?"

Now it is *our* project, as though his greasy face should adorn a niche in the Hall of Soviet Academicians! Better I should die first! But death was as outmoded as the horse.

"Pavel?"

"I am thinking."

"Think quickly. KGB wants an opinion."

"For what purpose?"

"For dealing with this Madderly. If he presents a danger, then he must be eliminated."

Of course, KGB was practical too. "And Hintsanen and the presidential assistant?"

"This is no time for idealism. Your opinion?"

Idealism? Golchov frowned at both the word and Nikoyan's tone. Condemning men to death was no longer dreadful, was no longer the ultimate evil. But it would be interesting to find out what Madderly knew. We have discovered the new land, he told himself, but we have not explored it.

"My opinion is we need more information," he said. "Suppose Yuri makes contact and we see what develops?"

"It could be a trick. Perhaps the best plan is to take no chances."

Golchov groaned. "Do you know, your lack of curiosity is unscientific?"

"Yes," Nikoyan replied, "but did not curiosity kill the cat?"

Madderly loosened his tie and looked about the suite of rooms located in a wing on the third floor of Hintsanen's castle. One narrow window allowed a glimpse of the sea as the snowfall slackened and the moon shone through an opening in the clouds. A second window overlooked a snowy lawn bounded by high walls. Beyond loomed the dark forest.

He went into the bathroom and washed his face and hands, drying on a towel bearing a simple monogrammed H. There was a small bar in an alcove beside the bath. He was considering having a drink, when there was a knock at the door.

"It's open. Come in."

"It is I, Elina."

Her long hair was piled upon her head and secured with a green ribbon. She wore a white robe edged about the neck and hem with silver fur.

"I was going to have a drink," said Madderly. "Would you like a short snort with me?"

"Pardon. I do not understand."

"Perhaps you find my Southern accent difficult?"

"If what you have is a Southern accent, I like it very much, but I find your American idioms difficult."

"I asked if you would join me in a drink."

"No, thank you. Dinner will be served in one hour."

"That's plenty of time."

She shook her head. "We have

other—business. Pleae go to your closet and change into the robe and slippers. I will wait in the sitting room."

Madderly was puzzled. "Is that the accepted dinner wear in Finland?"

Elina smiled. "Of course not. I am inviting you to share our sauna."

"You mean—"

"The robe and slippers are in the bedroom closet."

When in Finland . . . There were several robes and pairs of slippers. He found those which fitted him and changed his clothes.

"How do you feel?"

"Hot!"

"Is it a bad feeling?"

"No."

"Then please do me again."

Madderly diverted a rivulet of perspiration from his eye and felt along the rough cedar bench for the bundle of branches. The heat was one thing—after your pores swelled open it was refreshing. And being confined in a small space with a young woman of exceptional beauty was fine, too, even if both of you were in the buff and the first several minutes were awkward. But flailing her was something else again.

"Do not be afraid," she said. "Strike me with force. The stimulation is good for one's system. It purges and unlocks energies."

If I did this at home, they'd lock me up and swallow the key, thought Madderly. He gave her shoulders several hard strokes and watched the pale skin turn pink.

"Thank you," she said, "Now please turn around."

"Around?"

She frowned. "You don't wish me to strike

you?"

Fair was fair. His first reaction was surprise. The rough limbs and leaves did not hurt. His skin was stimulated, invigorated.

"How do you feel now?"

"Fine, No, better than fine. Great!"

"I am happy. Please relax. That is good."

Yes, it was good. To hell with the Soviets and the other side. They might be on the brink of paradise, but this was close enough.

God!

The shock was so intense he blacked out momentarily.

She had doused him with ice water!

He tried to cry out, but his breath was gone and he could only gasp, "Why—why did you—do that?"

"For the circulation. Don't you feel your heart racing?"

"I'll give you something for circulation!"

He lunged. She dodged and scrambled over the benches. As he went after her, she exclaimed, "Stop! Would you like an authentic Finnish massage?"

Madderly calculated the distance separating their naked bodies. She'd be through the door and gone before he caught her. Massage might not be so bad. And when he got within reach, he'd teach her a lesson.

"All right, but no more ice water."

"I promise. Lie on the bench on your stomach and close your eyes. Do not look. Agreed?"

It was a little late for modesty. "Agreed."

Her fingers probed the muscles of his neck. For a woman, she was very strong. Tension seemed to flow out of him into her hands. He was secure, safe, and happy.

Still, she was unnaturally powerful. Ouch!

Was she sitting on his back? The family sauna was doubtless an ancient tradition, but this—he groaned—was absurd.

"Elina—I—" he grunted.

"She go," said a deep voice.

Madderly tried to roll over, but the hands grasping him were as strong as chains and he succeeded only in looking up into Timo's sweaty smiling face.

Yuri Antonich was coherent.

"My head aches, of course," he explained to Golchov. "But I am sober."

"You have discovered a cure for hangover? Your fortune would be assured—were this not a sober nation." He smiled at his own sense of irony.

Yuri nodded across the desk at his mentor. Old Golchov was crusty. He had worked with him for three years and the professor still did not quite accept him. But so what? The research was exciting and, besides, he was a good KGB agent as well as an aspiring young man of science.

"In my day, the remedy was raw egg." Golchov made a sour expression. "But to get it down I had first to take a drink to numb the throat. All too often, one drink called for another, and so. . ." He winked at Yuri.

Should I return this wink? Antonich wondered. It was improbable but not impossible that the old fellow was KGB and their relationship was a setup to test him. Yes, the wink was a bit conspiratorial. No—to be serious. "You indicated this matter was urgent?"

"Quite. At least comrade donkey in Moscow thinks so."

Yuri flashed his practiced Mona Lisa expression which might be taken as a smile or not according to the observer, and said, "Does Comrade

Nikoyan's interest concern our project? The funds have not been . . ."

"Terminated? Certainly not! Without us, that simpleton would be experimenting with organic fertilizer—at the end of a shovel. This relates to a possible development by the Americans. You recall a Professor Madderly?"

"The author of a study dealing with psychic cures?"

"The same. KGB reports he is in Helsinki for a meeting with other psychic researchers. Nikoyan believes they are on to something relating to us. To thicken this plot, he assures me Madderly has been seen in London with one of the American President's special assistants."

Yuri suddenly realized his mouth was agape. If what Golchov said was only half true, then the Americans might know of their discovery—or perhaps they had made the same breakthrough independently.

Golchov said, "Well, what is your opinion?"

What indeed? The old boy was the genius—why ask him? Perhaps he should remain silent, but the great professor always required a sounding board. Best to be forever scientific. "Data is insufficient."

"My thought, exactly. I suggested we make contact with this fellow and see what he knows. You will go to Helsinki."

"I? But tomorrow I begin work with the new subject, the one called Natasha. Could not the KGB handle this?"

"Those killers? Yes, they will be more than happy to 'handle' Professor Madderly—by assassination. He may be a goose who lays golden eggs."

Yuri nodded. Golchov made sense. And Helsinki was not a boring city.

"You will find him with Dr. Utho Hintsanen. You recall the crippled Finn?"

Hintsanen had plagued Golchov with requests for information about psychic healing. It fell to Yuri to draft the replies. Once, his daughter came in person to the Institute. A pretty girl with a mind of her own. Seeing her again would not be unpleasant.

"Well?"

"I will go."

"We must make a contribution to the meeting. What do you think of the film of Anna Letovskaya demonstrating her psychokinesthetic powers?"

"They should find it interesting."

"Take a print. Promise this Madderly what you wish. Tell him nothing. Good luck."

It is not a question of luck, comrade genius professor, thought Yuri as he braved the wind-driven snow and crossed the Mendeleyevskaya on his way to his office at the university.

Nor is it a matter of friendship. Duty—it is that and nothing more—save, perhaps, curiosity and the perfectly human instinct to advance one's position. Time marched on, and the old must give way to the new.

He entered a gray brick building and climbed two flights of stairs to the psychology section. "First I must clear this with Moscow," he told himself. The operator gave him a line to the Center and he asked for his control, Colonel Bazarov.

"Bazarov here." The voice was gruff.

"This is Yuri Antonich, in Leningrad. Something has come up."

"Concerning Golchov?"

"Yes, Comrade Colonel. He was told by Minister Nikoyan that a Dr. Madderly, now in

Helsinki, may have information—dangerous information—regarding the project."

"Yes, I have heard. And?"

"He wishes me to go to Helsinki and determine what this Madderly knows. Shall I?"

"Of course, but with one stipulation. Report to me before Golchov. Understood?"

"Yes."

"You will not be alone in observing Professor Madderly. A Captain Gouzenko is assigned to him. Should you need help, contact Major Tushin at the Embassy."

The line went dead and Antonich was left alone with his thoughts. Perhaps in Helsinki opportunities would arise? Golchov would not last forever, no one did in these times. And then—

Such plotting was dangerous, even in thoughts! Yuri cautioned himself to exert self-control.

But it was difficult to sit in a drab office on a snowy night and force oneself *not* to think. It required a new approach to thinking, one which he was developing in connection with the project. Yes, this discovery was a two-edged sword. Golchov had found it possible to snoop psychically. Even now at this moment in the seemingly empty air of this office . . . one never knew. The only defense was to create interference by the production of certain brain waves. Thus far, however, very few subjects could do so at will.

Tomorrow he would fly to Helsinki and see what Madderly had to offer. Most probably it was a trick. Yet the American had impressive credentials.

Yuri locked the office and went out through the snow to his comfortable apartment on the University Embankment. After a glass of cognac, he fell into a fitful sleep.

FIVE

It was a—a cavern.

The walls were pitted, cracked, dark with moisture.

Madderly tried to concentrate, to open his eyes wider, but it did no good, yet soon the shadows parted—he did not know why—and he knew it was not a cavern.

A room. Where, he had no idea. Walls, damp. A hanging lamp cast long dusty beams across uneven block of stone. The first object he saw plainly was a length of iron chain set in one wall close to the floor. The links were rusty. A dungeon? There were no prisoners, no bones, no rats.

Now he saw a pile of—skins, furs? Yes, and something else—a body—a man, sprawled upon the furs, sleeping.

Madderly searched for his face. But there were too many shadows, and he would have stopped and let his mind drift to less perplexing images had he not seen a door. It opened and the light beyond outlined the form of a woman.

She was young—a girl just entering womanhood. She carried a tray covered with a scarlet cloth and wore a thin red gown through which light shone like blood, and Madderly knew her body.

It was strange—yes, he felt his mind breaking free and gliding into her thoughts. It was like watching himself breathe a cloud of incense, the way he went into her, and now he was no longer a professor of psychology—no—he was—her name was Sonya, and she was afraid.

Of what is she afraid? Madderly wondered. As he felt her body move inside the strange room, he knew. The man on the bed of furs. Yet it was not terror, not horror, that made her heart pound. There was awe in her fear of him.

Madderly veered away from her consciousness. Her emotion was one he had not experienced, and he sensed an inadequacy. But the fascination she exerted was great, and he could not separate himself.

She was a sweet young girl who, even as she stepped toward the bed of furs, thought of her home, her family, of her mother and father, how far away they were, and how alone she was.

But I am not alone, she told herself. *I have him to serve and he will cherish and protect me, and I may have no fear, for he is with me even to the end of time.*

She knelt at the bed of furs and held forth the covered tray. Her head was bowed, as though she offered a gift to a divinity. She uttered a name, but Madderly heard only the first syllable—*Ra*.

He felt the keen, chaotic mingling of emotions in her heart. He did not like being part of her consciousness. The sleeping man was dangerous to her, and he wanted nothing more than to cry out *Beware*! before the figure opened his eyes and led her through the valley of shadows to the place of ultimate despair and final destruction.

The recumbent figure stirred, propped itself up on one elbow. The great yellow eyes blinked, narrowed, found Madderly hidden within the innocent girl. They knew him but they did not summon him to battle for her soul. No, a mockery lurked in those depths, a cunning which said *I know you and I am stronger*!

Madderly recognized a terrible strength. This—*thing*—that had been sleeping on a bed of furs in the guise of a man was an undeniable presence which slipped into one and took without asking that which it required to maintain, to expand, its power.

Now, the yellow eyes burned into Sonya's. She saw him not. To her mind the chamber was bare. Yet she sensed he was there, and so she spoke to him—to the awful emptiness—in a small girl's voice and said, gently, sweetly, *I have come to serve you*.

He made himself visible to her, though Madderly saw he did not move from the bed. He appeared as a fair young man, crowned with gold.

Now his voice spoke, saying, *I am here, across the room. Look upon me*!

Madderly knew terror as her eyes sought and found this apparition. No man, nothing human, stood against the sweating walls. A shaggy, fanged beast hulked there, reaching out its ragged claws for her flesh.

And I am here as well, he said.

Music, the sweet strains of a harp. Madderly saw him plainly—a dwarf with a kindly face who strummed the golden instrument as though it were his own heart and sang of what was and would be. He promised wealth, a handsome young man with eyes only for her, eternal beauty, love—and she accepted his gifts and let fall the crimson gown and entered the bed of furs, crying happily, *Yes, yes, I am yours*!

The yellow eyes mocked Madderly. There was a warning of lightning, a growl of thunder.

He must help her, but he could not move, and

now the images dimmed and faded and he passed over into the sleep that denies existence.

"You slept well?"

Hintsanen once more faced him across the bare table in the library.

"And was breakfast satisfactory? I wish I might join you, but my affliction makes me liable to weight increase, so I eat little. Daily massages by Timo are necessary for continued muscle tone. I shall not wither away. When I am healed, I will take up life where I left it. I am boring you. Still, I shall not apologize, for it seems you are the cause of a certain difficulty I face."

"What might that be?" asked Madderly. Now was the time to try Hintsanen's thoughts. He looked into the fixed gray eyes and made his mind receptive.

"This morning I learned that a person who might have helped me refuses because you are here."

Madderly perceived an image forming.

"Are you not curious? This person has healed cases said to be more hopeless than mine. I begged her to help me, and at long last she agreed, but, alas, now she will not."

A face appeared—Katya.

"I now find it necessary to come to the point. What do you intend to accomplish in Helsinki?"

Katya's dark features vanished and were replaced by a construct Madderly recognized as himself.

"I know I am rude," Hintsanen continued, "but under the circumstances . . ."

He asked a straight question, thought Madderly, and he deserves a straight answer, but answers were Wills' department.

"Wills told you nothing?" Madderly replied.

"Mr. Wills informed me that you would supply details in good time."

Madderly hesitated. Wills was an ass for not developing a more comprehensive plan!

But perhaps Hintsanen was feigning ignorance so as to compare Wills' revelation with whatever he told him? In any case, truth was the best strategy now, Madderly decided.

"The person you mention is named Katya," Madderly said. "I know she is in Helsinki with a man called Stephan."

Hintsanen's voice made a clicking sound, like a machine resetting after a power surge. "But how did you know? Elina? Or—?"

Madderly was cautious. "I knew Katya was in Helsinki. But I had no idea, till now, that she worked for you."

"She works for herself. From time to time she uses her powers to help others, though not for purely altruistic reasons."

"Even psychics have to eat."

"I will remember that. But to the point. What are you after?"

"Wills has a theory," said Madderly. "He believes the Soviets have made a major breakthrough in psychic research. My job is to discover its exact nature."

"Then the conference is a trick?"

"We hope it will draw the Russians out into the open."

"And you will read their thoughts like you did mine?"

"An extremely unreliable technique," said Madderly. "Scientists are human, and are usually more cooperative than politicians. Who knows what might develop if we can mingle with them. But we don't yet have a meeting place."

There was a moment of silence. Then Hintsanen said, "I know the Soviets too well. They are not generous with information. Still, yours is a good plan. By nature the Russian is both superstitious and curious. I suggest we announce the conference will be held here."

"I don't want to endanger you and Elina."

"This island is a safe location, for we can exert some control over the situation. Also, I am known by the Soviet scientists. I have been in contact with Pavel Golchov."

Golchov? Was Hintsanen trying to feel him out? Hintsanen's information gathering facility could process much data. Given time he could learn much. But for what purpose? A cure for his paralysis?

Hintsanen said, "I see by your reaction that Golchov is involved. Have you dealt with him?"

"I know his work."

"I do not know the man personally. Elina is acquainted with his assistant. What part does Golchov play?"

"We're not sure."

"No matter. I shall put our plan into operation immediately. By noon, radio and television will give it wide coverage. If we were co-sponsors. . ."

Cooperation reminded Madderly of Katya's reluctance to help Hintsanen.

"Professor?"

"Yes, of course," he answered. Then, "Did Katya explain her distrust of me?"

"No."

"I would like to talk to her."

"In good time. She and Stephan are staying in the lighthouse. You received a message from Wills a short while ago."

"He's on his way?"

"That I do not know. He requests you to pick

up two delegates to the conference, a Dr. Chambers and a Mr. Relling. They will arrive on the noon flight from London. Shall I send Timo?"

Two of Wills' operatives? Or were they for real? Madderly shook his head. "I have to do some shopping anyway. I need a warm coat—came unprepared for snow."

"A student of the psychic who is unprepared?" The mechanical voice came close to registering laughter. "As you wish, but since you do not know Helsinki, Elina will be your guide. Rest easy, Professor, I am not spying on you."

In the cafe at the Helsinki airport, Gouzenko sipped tomato juice and forced two aspirins down his throat. He drank the rest of the juice and scowled at Tamara. Both had taken the 6 A.M. flight from London. She was a victim of some administrative foul-up too, she had told him, and was also being shifted to the Helsinki Embassy. They were rushed to Heathrow at midnight and passed the long wait in a bar where Gouzenko, wearing the new mod clothes Zharkov had authorized, had thoroughly enjoyed himself. By lift-off time he was as dashing as his costume, but now he felt more dashed than dashing.

"It is late," Tamara said. "We are expected at the Embassy."

"I cannot understand," said Gouzenko. "I had only two drinks, as did you. Yet I have the headache for both. Is this Socialist justice?"

Tamara grinned at his error in counting. "I enjoyed the nightclub. Are such places allowed in

Moscow?"

"Shhh! Would you get us in trouble?" He winked. "We Soviets are sober, serious people, not given to drink and dance."

"Then there are such places? You have visited them?"

"Frequently. It was my—" He almost said "assignment," but caught himself and whispered, "great sin."

"Oh?" Obviously he was aware of how close he had come to compromising himself—but even so, what would I do? Tamara wondered. "You do not seem sinful to me."

"I am a great villain. Millions tremble at my name, and what is more . . ."

"Yes?"

"I am modest, not to say humble."

Tamara laughed and shook her head.

He rose and stepped around the table to help her. "It is time to report. Perhaps if we arrive at a run and breathlessly cry out *work*, *work*, *work*, they will overlook our tardiness."

"Very good," said Tamara. "But may I get some hose on the way? These are in shreds."

Elina steered the Jaguar sedan through the heavy traffic. "There is the Cathedral," she said. "We shall leave the car near the railroad station and walk. The exercise will do us good."

She found a parking space. They crossed the trolley tracks and went down the block, looking into shop windows. In one bright yellow building were hundred of animals fashioned from steel strands and metal beads. The bird shapes caught Madderly's eye. They reminded him of childhood dreams.

Elina said, "Do you like them? They are by Kaipiainen, one of our most gifted artists."

Viewed superficially, the birds were charming, like cartoon characters depicting the simple two-step of life. But looked at from another perspective, charm metamorphosed into terror of the sort every child feels when bare branches scrape windowpanes on lonely winter nights.

They continued down the street. At the corner Elina paused before a fabric display. "These are by Armi Ratia," she said. "I often buy her work to be made into dresses, but," she tossed her head and smiled, "they are so lovely I cannot bear to cut them, so I have perhaps the world's best collection of her art."

"You can't have your cake and eat it too."

"Oh? What does cake have to do with textiles?"

"Everything—and nothing. That's an old American saying."

He took her arm and they crossed the intersection and went into Stockmann's department store. A woman told Elina that men's coats were on the third floor. They rode an elevator in the company of a mother and father and six children, all pink-faced from the cold and excited at the wonders of the store.

When they stepped off, they found themselves in the ladies' wear department. Madderly felt a premonition, a warning. He sensed that somewhere in the crowd circulating through the aisles was a person he knew.

He hesitated, studied the faces.

Elina took his hand, saying, "Coats are to the rear in men's wear. You are not shopping for a slip, are you?"

He allowed her to lead him. The feeling of a fated rendezvous increased. They turned a corner into women's lingerie, and Madderly stopped so suddenly his hand pulled free from Elina's.

The man and woman at the hosiery counter looked up. The feeling was so overpowering that it must be them. But who—where—?

Yes, he recognized them! The man's beard—he had changed his clothes though—was wearing a tight suit—now a sportcoat and turtleneck sweater. Heathrow—deplaning from the Moscow flight. Last night. Why were they in Helsinki?

He focused on the man's thoughts. Their eyes met and Madderly read a shock of recognition. Whoever he is, regardless of his reason for being here, *he knows me*.

Elina said, "Madderly, what is it? I almost fell. Are you—"

He glanced away from the couple. "I tripped. Caught my foot on the rug."

She looked down at his feet. "There is no rug."

"Then I slipped."

Now she searched the faces near them. "Who is it? Did you see someone you know?"

"Later—after I get the coat."

He insisted, so she took him to the men's department. As he passed the couple from the airport, he noticed that only the man knew him. The young woman was unconcerned. In fact—Madderly frowned in disbelief—she was sneaking several pairs of hose into her purse. By her feet stood a pair of small suitcases, both tagged with Heathrow baggage checks.

Elina said, "The coat is handsome. Camel looks well on you. Now will you please tell me?"

They were having coffee in a cafe facing Kaivopuisto Park. The lawns shimmered with snow, and the stands of birches with their black and white bark created a melancholy setting, lacking only wolves or a band of Tolstoy's cossacks. Beyond the trees a sea sparkled, but there were heavy clouds on the horizon.

"Tell you what?" he replied.

"You know. In Stockmann's."

"I saw a man and he saw me, that's all."

"I beg your pardon but I feel that is not *all.*"

Madderly tried the coffee. "I didn't expect to see him, so I was surprised."

"Who is he?"

"I don't know. I saw him at the airport in London. He arrived from Moscow as I was leaving. Probably a coincidence."

"Was he following us?"

Oh, so now it's us? He sipped his coffee. "I don't think so."

"But if he is, then the Soviets are interested in the conference, correct?"

Madderly nodded, thinking, *Or in me*. Damn, why had he let Wills be so vague?

"Well, that is what we want," said Elina. She checked the time. "We must hurry or we will keep the delegates waiting at the airport."

The communiqué from Rome arrived moments before Tamara's report. Colonel Bazarov noted with curiosity the terse message that Sylvia Week was now en route to Istanbul. Her profile revealed she was a "practicing psychic." How fitting. Byzantium was built upon superstition as well as mosaics. She should have used her broom, though. Much cheaper than BOAC.

He alerted Istanbul to keep him posted on her movements and turned his attention to Tamara. His initial reaction to her personal contact with Gouzenko was negative. But perhaps this was, after all, the best way. She was a lovely little thing, and Gouzenko—well, for all the metal in his head he was a man.

Aside from the new relationship with Gouzenlo, her report was vague. One statement, however, caused an eyebrow to rise: "Subject became agitated in department store upon seeing man and woman. Apparently he knew them, but gave no explanation."

Finland's nearness to the Soviet Union made possible chance encounters with old acquaintances. But—no, never mind. His record was clean. He was a safe risk.

The phone rang. "Andrei? Ilya here."

The duty officer, Colonel Kuragin.

"Yes, Ilya?"

"Communiqué may be of interest."

"Go ahead."

"'London: Contact at LeMay AFB reports three Americans—Wills, Porkowski, and embassy marine guard identified as Towers—arrived here late last P. M. and departed immediately via stand-by jet Washington."

Washington?

Bazarov thanked Kuragin and hung up. The situation was now passing from the comic to the absurd. He went to the world map on the wall facing his desk. A professor in Helsinki; a witch in Istanbul; a special assistant to the President in Washington. What did it mean?

He studied the map. Look for a common denominator. All are traveling, but where will they stop?

He shut his eyes and moved his fingers across the chart paper. Perhaps a supernatural force would lead him to the truth.

He opened his eyes.

One thing in common was Madderly.

He fixed Helsinki beneath his fingertip.

Chambers and Relling were unknown factors, so far as Madderly was concerned. As he heard them paged over the airport loudspeaker system, he tried with no success to relate them to parapsychological research. Of course, there were many at work who had yet to publish, so it was possible they were professionals.

He was not surprised to learn that Chambers was a woman. She had a nice smile and a pleasing, open manner which contrasted dramatically with Relling's cool composure.

As they made the trip through the city to Hintsanen's island, Chambers carried on a running conversation with Elina and seemed determined to learn everything there was to know about the country before they reached their destination.

Relling said nothing. He smoked one cigaret after another, being careful to keep the ashes off his suit.

Madderly was puzzled by him and tried to enter his consciousness, but no images appeared. Either he was one of those who were immune to sharing their thoughts or, like a machine, he had thrown a switch and stopped thinking altogether.

After a time, Madderly smiled at him and said, "Nice you could make it to the conference. What's your specialty?"

"What?" Relling replied.

"What's the subject of your paper?"

Chambers replied for him, breaking off in mid-sentence a remark directed at Elina. "Statistical analysis is buddy-boy's territory," she said. "He's a parameter—or is it perimeter?—man."

"Take your pick," said Relling.

"At what odds?" Chambers countered, adding quickly, "He's got a cute little paper dealing with measuring results in ESP testing. It'll never be a best seller."

"But it's a living," said Relling.

"And what is your subject?" Elina asked.

"I've got two, actually, both exciting. One's sense deprivation and ESP. The other's hypnosis and ESP. I won't do both, of course, though they're more fun than graphs and numbers."

Relling lit another cigaret.

Madderly zeroed in on Chambers' smile. Yes, she was a fraud, but a delightful one. He detected a scientific background, but not in psychology. Considering the short notice, Wills had come up with two passable "experts."

"And what's your specialty?" Chambers asked Elina.

Elina blushed. "I have none, at present. The conference is being held in my father's house."

Chambers turned to Madderly. "You don't need any introduction. Your article on psychic healing is clever. Thought you'd be older though."

Relling coughed. His thin lips fashioned a quick smile that sliced through all deception. He said, "Let's turn off the static. We'll need as much as we can muster for the bad guys."

Hintsanen cordially received Chambers and Relling in his library and informed them that Golchov's assistant, Yuri Antonich, had arrived in Helsinki and made contact.

"He's eager to know the subjects to be discussed at the conference," said Hintsanen.

"What did you tell him?" Madderly asked.

"Nothing specific, except that we wished to establish a flexible agenda to allow all ideas of interest. I said I would confer with you to determine general boundaries."

Madderly thought for a moment, then, "Why

isn't Wills here? This is his show!"

"He'll be along," said Chambers. "Have faith."

"And look into your crystal ball," said Relling.

Madderly would have given a great deal for a crystal ball. He analyzed his position and understood that his lashing out at Wills was a symptom of the inadequacy he felt in this situation. A perfectly normal reaction, actually.

He calmed himself and considered the possibilities. The day was half-gone already, so no official meetings could be held before tomorrow. Would be best to get together with this Yuri Antonich, to size him up, see what his interests were.

"Why don't I see the Russian?" he finally said.

"He is eager to meet you," said Hintsanen. "I shall invite him here this evening."

"How long have you been a psychic?" Golchov asked.

The tall, strong-boned woman, who wore a tailored blue woolen suit, ignored him.

"Come, come, Comrade Natasha, I know you feel resentment at being brought here against your will. I assure you it is for the interest of science and the building of an even greater Soviet Union."

The plea had no effect upon her impassive face. But Golchov was not surprised. Those phrases were concocted by hacks to excite idiots. One thing she was not was an idiot.

As she was escorted into his office by two lab assistants, Golchov was aware of her great power. No doubt at the present she is reading my mind. Very well, listen to this, Natasha: *I am a man like any other. After a reasonably good night's sleep, I rose, shaved, dressed, and took my morning con-*

stitutional down Nevsky Prospect. I breakfasted upon a roll, orange juice, and coffee at the Aurora Cafe, next door to the Foreign Language Bookshop. After a second cup, every bit as bad as the first, I returned to my quarters, cleaned my teeth, and came here, where I waited impatiently for a psychic named Natasha of whom I have heard remarkable tales. I say again, I am an ordinary man. Politically, I am a scientist. I could work anywhere, provided I had the necessary facilities. My interest in you is genuine. Trust me.

As an afterthought Golchov focused his energy on the First Minister, crowning his round dull face with a splendid pair of donkey's ears.

The woman smiled.

"Ah," said Golchov, also smiling, "I think that now we understand each other. Take a seat. Be comfortable."

Her expression changed, but the ice between the two was broken. Natasha sat down and said, "You have a reputation for sensitivity which is deserved, Professor."

"Sensitive? Yes. But I do not have the gift. All my life I have tried to acquire it. Nothing! I am a hopeless case!"

"A gift is a gift. It is given, not taken. But perhaps you have not used your sensitivity correctly? It is our experience that sensitives are often successful with telepathy."

The idea was not new to Golchov. In experiments he had sent "thoughts" telepathically, but the results were so random he compared their coherence to an infant's attempts at speech. If the powers of the sender and receiver were of greater magnitude, however, he suspected the technique could he almost as dependable as radio.

"And you have done this?" he asked her.

"Perhaps. I do not say unless I am sure."

"Sure of what?"

She pointed to him, "Of you, of this place. Of why so many are held prisoner." Her green eyes narrowed. "Some say the KGB will kill us for our knowledge."

Her eyes held his attention. They gleamed as though her power moved within them. He felt his lips part, heard his voice say, "It would be absurd to kill those who possess wisdom. What would be gained by destroying them?"

"You would no longer fear us."

"I did not know you were feared."

"You lie! Your thoughts are as obvious as fish in a mountain pool. We are greatly feared, and rightly so."

The harsh tone of her words diverted his attention from her eyes. A dizziness passed through him and was gone in an instant.

"Yes, you were in my power," she said. "Do you believe you can control us? We remain thus far under your 'protection' because we do not wish to destroy. But should you refuse to set us free, then upon this nation will come a wrath so horrible you will pray for death!"

Images of the plagues visited upon Egypt in the time of Moses, put into his childhood mind by priests, flashed in his memory. He knew intuitively this woman was not making empty threats. He stood and walked around the desk to regain his composure. He must reassure her they meant no harm.

"I swear to you, Comrade, not only in Socialism but also in truth, we are scientists here. Upon my heart," he touched his left lapel, "there are no politics for those dedicated, as are you and I, to universal good. Come now, have faith, trust me. Let us be more than observed and observer. Let us dare to be friends."

He offered his hand. She pushed it away. With a knowing laugh she said, "Who wears the donkey ears now, Professor, eh? And who is the observer? I run through your mind like one of your laboratory mice through a maze. You cannot hide your thoughts from me. I am curious. What are you investigating? What is your big secret?"

"We are—" he began, and stopped, for he realized he had thought the truth and now she knew without his saying.

"You are what?"

He shook his head and sat again behind the desk. "You know all things. Tell me."

"Not all. They must be thought before I see them, and even then not all minds reveal themselves. You are working on a form of telepathic communication. You have had some success, though you do not understand the principles involved—as if anyone does."

She paused. As she spoke, her cheeks took on color. Now, perspiration appeared on her brow.

"And?" said Golchov.

"You are moving into things best left alone. There are aspects of which you can have no knowledge. Your science—what is it? Nothing! It can give you no protection."

"Why do we need protection? You make it sound as though we experiment with hydrogen bombs. Come now, let us end this raving of doom and begin our business."

Natasha's eyes fixed his again. Her voice was sharp, powerful; it penetrated his consciousness like a scalpel probing for malignant tissue.

"You are in league with evil! We know you have raised the dark powers of the other side. You make deals with blackness rather than light. Now you go as a child in a gaily painted boat drifting down a peaceful stream. Lost in the wonder of his own daydreams, he does not hear the whirlpool waiting to suck him down. We know you have used blood! Do you know why you meet with failures? It is our magic working against you!"

Her words were absurd. But tangled in the web of her gaze Golchov knew they were true. Many experiments were unsuccessful. But could scientific criteria be used to judge non-science? And yes—yes—they broke through at last with "black" magic which could not be explained scientifically, at least not yet. But they were working.

"I know your mind," said Natasha. "I know what is true, no matter what you say."

"Then know this also. We have won! In spite of your interference!"

His outcry was foreign, even to his own ears. What makes me act so? he wondered.

He avoided her stare and, calmer now, said, "I mean we have conducted successful experiments and have, thus, made a significant contribution to mankind. We believe—"

She raised her hand. "You recite press releases. Listen, while there is still time. In ancient days lived wise men who knew truth not by your science but in their hearts and souls. They urged nations to heed the word, and when they ignored them, they were destroyed. It is the same with you and me, Comrade Professor. A true adherent of the Old Religion works for goodness, not for evil. It is written in the secret books which have been handed down since the beginning of time that no man shall know the dead. That which is done is done. Death is a part of life. The powers on the other side are great *because* they are of the other side, and not of this world! To draw that power into this world is to twist the very nature of things; it is to violate the most sacred law!"

"But we did it!" Golchov cried out. "Cannot

you get that through your skull! That power is ours!"

"Ah, is it? Evil is a mirror made of many pieces of glass and all give back the face of him who looks into it. I do not doubt you have touched the power. We know *he* is here in Leningrad, and we acknowledge his great psychic gift. But we cannot understand why you, a rational man who, unlike his fellows, loves humanity, should choose the wrong path."

"It is not wrong! In science there is no good, no evil. We experiment and we report our results."

"In science, yes. But science does not exist outside of time. You have a marvelous facility here at your Pavlov Institute. But did you know that so-called witches were burned here in times gone? Their ashes are in the soil. You cannot escape the burden of the past."

"The past is history! I deal with the now, with you, Comrade Witch, with me."

"Then leave this madness. Turn from darkness."

Golchov pressed the buzzer on his desk to summon the lab assistants. "It is obvious we cannot work together at present."

"Unless you heed my words, I can never work with you."

"Perhaps, perhaps not," he replied as the door opened. "I recommend meditation, soul-searching, if you like. Time heals all wounds and makes all things clear, eh?" He nodded to the KGB men. "We are stocked with an assortment of hours, weeks, days, months, years. Choose what you will."

The nerve!

Golchov paced the floor and tugged at his hair. Yes, she had peered into him into his very heart, his core, and she knew the nature of the work that had been done.

And she knew the questionable means by which it had been done, and that *he* was here, although she did not name him.

Golchov scowled. She knew too much!

What would be the consequence if the world learned that a Soviet scientist, a Lenin Prize winner, was doing business with—

Golchov stopped in his tracks, stroked his jaw. Was it possible—Natasha—Madderly—the Americans—?

He asked his secretary to check the information on Natasha, and nodded impatiently as she gave him the usual details—height, weight, and so on. When she came to the personal data, his pulse quickened. Something was there. He felt it.

"Subject's family consists of a husband, Stephan, and a sister, Katya. Both left the Soviet Union last year for work at the Psychic Institute in London. Present whereabouts unknown; KGB investigating. Subject's—"

"That's enough, thank you."

A husband and a sister in London. Madderly. He saw it clearly now. Natasha was with the Americans. Her hysterical warning was an attempt to stop his research. It would not work!

He moved to the window and looked down at the frozen river. The ice was dotted with skating children, watched over by an adult or two and a cloudy sky.

The Neva ice reminded him of the life and death of another "Holy One," Rasputin, the monk who cast a spell over the Czarina. After poison, bullets, and knives had failed, it was the freezing water beneath the ice that had finally made his power harmless. Or? There were reports, drunken sailors' tales, of a hermit who looked like

Rasputin, who lived on a remote island in the north Pacific.

"But no, I must remain objective," Golchov told himself.

The KGB worked quickly and Natasha's power could not protect her from their crude but efficient weapons. On the other hand, would not *he* wish to use her in his rituals?

"What am I thinking?" he moaned.

No longer might he blame the power in her eyes. He was at fault. Could it be that what she said was true, that he was drifting nearer and nearer the fatal whirlpool?

SIX

Yuri Antonich was dumbfounded. What a mansion! As the maid showed him through the rooms, he appraised the paintings hung upon the richly paneled walls. Not Old Masters, perhaps, but still of great value. The limousine that picked him up at the Marski Hotel was a Mercedes. The launch which transported him across the bay was modern and very expensive. There could be no doubt that Hintsanen's castle was as magnificent as most of those constructed by Peter in Leningrad and now preserved by the government to attract tourist dollars.

Yes, and decadent, rotten to the core!

Only . . .

A stubborn question in the back of his practical mind would not go away. How is it to be so wealthy?

The answer sprang from his lips: "Wonderful!"

The maid glanced back at him.

He smiled to show her he was all right. And I am, he told himself. There were things of greater importance than wealth. Capital in private hands was exploitation.

He saw his own hands swinging at his sides, made fists, recalled the old slogans: Workers of the World—Man the Barricades—Power to the Constituent Assembly!

That was reality. Hintsanen's castle was fantasy. He felt his iron resolve return. He turned away from the paintings, shifted his weight to his heels, and walked heavily upon the fine carpet.

The maid opened a pair of exquisite inlaid doors. Elina Hintsanen came forward to greet him.

"Professor Antonich, welcome."

Antonich's heart skipped a beat. She was the same girl he had spoken with a year before, but she had changed. She was attractive then, but now she was beautiful.

For a moment his voice failed him.

"Professor?"

There was a hint of laughter in her tone, a tinkle of gold coins.

"I'm" he began. "Yes—hello—and it is good to see—to see you again."

"You remember our meeting? I am flattered."

"We spoke at some length."

"Yes, but I was such a child then."

Yuri wished to utter a gallant phrase, but all that came into his mouth was, "You have a splendid place here."

"It goes back to the old days. Our ancestors built it to defend their land against the Russians—your ancestors."

"Thankfully, those days are gone forever."

"Let us hope so. But forgive me. Please be comfortable. May I get you a drink?"

Yuri eyed the bar equipped with all sorts of interesting bottles. "Would it be appropriate?"

"Certainly. And I will join you."

"A Scotch, in that case. With ice, no water, please."

They left the bar and sat facing each other on blue velvet sofas before a fireplace in which a cozy blaze crackled. Through a tall window were visible a snowy lawn and the dark trees beyond.

What a snug existence! It was so far removed from his tiny, inadequate office . . . perhaps even from his tiny, inadequate existence? The Soviet Union was a just provider, but it did not supply castles and beautiful creatures of wealth and breeding, such as this one sitting in front of him now, smiling as though she had not a care in the world—and perhaps she did not.

"I hardly belong in the company of scientists such as yourself," Elina said. "I am only a medical student."

He wanted to ask why, why with all her money and beauty she wished to throw her life away on dull lectures and duller books. But instead, he replied, "How interesting. You must tell me your experiences. Are they still playing jokes in the dissection room?"

He immersed himself in her presence and drew great satisfaction from the whiskey, the fire, the room, the snow and the trees.

But he did not lower his guard. As she recounted the day-to-day routine, another level of Yuri's consciousness bore upon the coming meeting with Hintsanen and Madderly. Did the girl's manner indicate all was aboveboard? If she were acting, then her medical training was a waste, for with such talent there were fortunes to be made in motion pictures.

In moments like these, Antonich wished for the elusive "gift" that Golchov would sell his soul to get. But he knew his own limitations—he had not one iota of "power." And so he placed his faith in realities. Major Tushin at the embassy made available this Captain Gouzenko. When the meetings began, he and a young woman who was a secretary would attend as his aides.

Elina said, "I am talking too much. Another

drink?"

Yuri considered his empty glass. It was fine Scotch. He would have said yes, but Golchov's image rose in his mind's eye like a bad omen.

"One is enough for now, thank you. I must keep a clear head so as to miss no word of wisdom."

"No doubt there is much wisdom to be received," Elina said. She turned toward the door. "Here are Father and Professor Madderly now."

Madderly warmed his hands at the fire. The meeting with Antonich had gone well. The Russian's chief characteristic so far was reticence, and his few questions seemed designed to force the answerer to divulge his knowledge without getting any in return.

Initially, Madderly suspected Antonich's silence was an indication of psychic power, so while Hintsanen spoke, he opened his consciousness to the Russian's. There was little interference. He received indistinct images involving two figures. One, an older man in a white jacket, was probably Golchov. The other, a voluptuous girl in nothing at all, had certain mannerisms reminiscent of Elina.

Once, during the long meeting, the images changed drastically. Madderly apprehended a dark room inhabited by shadowy forms. He could not be sure what the scene meant. One figure caught his attention. Its eyes . . . He felt he had seen them before, or they had watched him, but he did not know where or when.

"Well," said Dr. Chambers, who now sat on the sofa sipping a Scotch where Yuri had sat before, "what's the story? Is our brother in science up to something or not?"

Madderly said, "I think he and Golchov are

involved in a project they believe is very important."

"Upon what do you base this assumption?" asked Hintsanen.

"I have a . . . feeling about him."

"I know the nature of your 'feelings,'" Hintsanen said. "You looked into this fellow's mind and read his secrets."

Elina laughed. "Another empty-headed Russian."

"Almost—but not totally empty," said Madderly.

"So where does that leave us?" asked Relling, who stood by the window watching the snow and smoking a cigaret.

"Wishing Wills would show up," said Madderly.

"'Wishing Wills' sounds like 'wishing wells,'" Chambers said. "Be careful. Your wish might come true."

"What does that mean?"

"Nothing, except I know how you feel. Helpless, right? Look, Wills is no dummy. His not being here is part of his plan. For now, Professor, you're the decision-maker, like it or not. So decide."

Relling said, "Give her two more drinks and she'll recite the Scout oath."

"The what?" asked Elina.

Relling grunted and readdressed himself to a careful scrutiny of the landscape.

"Well, one thing is sure," said Madderly. "Antonich's strongest reaction came when I alluded to experimentation dealing with drug-induced long distance telepathy. I'd like to give him a demonstration that will raise eyebrows in Leningrad."

"You have been working in that field?" asked

Hintsanen.

"Not exactly, but I've got an idea. We'll have to persuade Katya to help, though. Could I talk to her?"

"That is easily arranged. Elina will guide you to the lighthouse."

Yuri Antonich stood by his window at the Marski Hotel and surveyed the city.

From the tenth floor all was childishly simple. A traffic jam might be cleared away by the careful touch of a gentle giant, and those steamers entering the harbor could easily be unloaded if they were turned keel-up and their cargoes dumped into waiting vans.

So, too, regarding his own situation.

Three giant steps would take him across the harbor. Another fifty to the castle. He recalled that delightful vacation on the Black Sea, when he'd built a sand castle and, for no reason, destroyed it with a stamp of his foot. Had there been people within . . .

An attack, carnage. A mad rush up the beach and through the forest, then over the wall, across the lawn. One satchel charge here, another there. The doors were breached, and now it was room-to-room. The old man in the wheelchair died without a sound. Madderly resisted, as did the chauffeur, but they were two against fifteen.

Bodies, the castle in flames. Elina? He was carrying her kicking and screaming to the beach. Capture was her fate. It was of the tradition from which she derived. Was it not possible that a male of his line had sacked a fortress and carried off her female kin?

And then?

Ah, yes, then . . .

The phone rang.

The city swam back into view. Major Tushin had a message from Leningrad.

"'Have encountered a difficult subject in N. All else goes well. Advise subjects to be discussed. G.'"

"Acknowledge thusly," Yuri said. "Possible long distance TC demonstration. Sorry N troublesome. Unruly, often requires strong measures."

"Signed 'A'?" asked Tushin.

"Yes, and when is the best time to speak to mother?"

"She is always at home."

Yuri hung up. So the direct-voice communication operated twenty-four hours a day. After supper he would drop by the embassy and have a few words with Bazarov. At this point he had nothing specific to report, except that he had nothing to report. But Bazarov would want to know even that.

And for now, a shower, a shave, clean clothes, a drink or two, followed by an excellent meal. He rubbed his hands together. Later? Who knows?

At sunset new snow was falling. The last light painted the winter landscape a pink that faded to lavender, then blue.

Elina led Madderly through the forest on a path that grew less distinct as clouds of flakes danced down green branches. Once he glanced back and saw that their footprints were already covered. It was as though all evidence of their prior existence were being purposely obscured by nature.

Madderly kept his eyes on Elina. She moved gracefully and quickly, while he stumbled and slipped on stones lurking underneath the snow.

Once he fell down. She turned around and saw him and laughed, her eyes bright, her cheeks pink from the cold.

He made a crude snowball and tossed it in her direction. She dodged behind a tree. He tried to sneak up on her. She greeted his attack with a snowball of her own, perfectly aimed.

He wiped the powder from his face and pretended she had hurt him. When she came within reach, he grabbed her and washed her face in the snow.

She kicked and squirmed, and he held her close till she stopped struggling and put her arms around him.

Their cheeks touched.

Madderly looked up at the falling snow, at the bright trees above his head. There was a perfection here. He did not want to ruin it, to cause it to cease.

Her hand found his. She squeezed his fingers and said, "We must hurry. The lighthouse is still a long way."

Katya did not trust him.

In halting English she said, "You are the one from London. Why do you follow me? I do nothing to you."

Madderly explained he meant no harm. But she refused to hear him and stood shaking her head as she stood behind the plain wooden table set for supper.

Elina said, "You must not be afraid. We are friends. My father has given you protection."

"Your father wants something from me so he protects. This one," she pointed at Madderly, "he wants something also. But I know from London what he is."

"Yes, I met you at Mrs. Week's," Madderly said. "You made telepathic contact with Leningrad, with a psychic named Natasha—"

"Natasha!" cried Katya.

Stephan, who sat at the table, tried to comfort her. To Madderly he said, "You do not know everything. Natasha is Katya's sister and my wife."

"She is gone, gone!" Katya sobbed.

"And yesterday we learned that Natasha is captured by KGB," said Stephan.

"How did you learn?"

"We have ways."

"And you are certain the KGB has her?"

"Proof, it is always proof you want!" said Katya. "You come with money to buy our power and when we see . . . still it is not enough. Give us proof, you say. The power *is* proof!"

"Yes," said Madderly. "But did she contact you when it happened?"

Katya nodded and dried her eyes on a corner of her apron.

"Has she contacted you again?"

"Before the sun came today."

"For what reason?"

"Questions! It is painful to speak of my sister in the filthy hands of the secret police. Even now as she is being held!"

"Where?"

"Strelka!"

Stephan explained. "It is part of an island, in the Neva River. The school is there."

"Yes," said Katya, "the Institute. That is the place. And she is not alone. Many are with her. There are others, evil ones!"

"I am sorry to learn of her misfortune," said Madderly. "But this is all the more reason for us to help. May we talk?"

Wearily, it seemed, Katya gestured that they should join her and Stephan at the table. From the pantry, Stephan brought a dusty bottle of brandy and four unmatched china cups. He pulled the cork and poured the amber liquid, saying, "The date upon the label is 1896. We are consuming years as well as wine."

And sun and moon and rain, the touch of human hands. Madderly sniffed the brandy. 1896. Another century. Who was President then? Who was Czar?

Stephan raised his cup for a toast. "To Natasha!"

As they drank there was the shrill lonely cry of wind swirling round the lighthouse and, in lulls, as the wind drew its breath, the murmur of the winter sea roving back and forth over gray rocks.

Stephan moved to refill Madderly's cup, but Madderly indicated no with his hand. To Katya he said, gently, "We need your help. It concerns a plan which, if successful, may help your sister."

"Excuse me if I doubt," she said. "You want my power so you speak what I wish to hear."

"If you don't believe my words, look into my thoughts."

"There are many ways to deceive if one is determined."

"Then look into mine," Elina said. "I have no gift. I can show you the truth."

"Ha!" said Katya. "Your heart is his; his mind is yours."

Elina averted her eyes.

Madderly said, "You mistrust me because you think I'm responsible for Natasha's arrest. You believe Sylvia and I called attention to her and then the KGB acted. Maybe you're right. I can only say we did not intend for this to happen."

"I know what you intend. America!" She laughed bitterly. "America is what you protect! And now my sister will suffer! I see it clearly now. She will die!"

"My Natasha?" said Stephan.

"Yes, she will not leave Strelka among the living!"

"No! Natasha has power! Who can destroy her?"

"Others have power also. I see them. They are not with us. Darkness, darkness! Only darkness."

Madderly felt a shock of recognition. A room . . . eyes. But the image would not focus.

"No, I will not believe this!' Stephan declared. "I will not believe unless Natasha speaks it to me!"

"Have it as you will, but she is my flesh, and I know."

Madderly considered this precognitive experience. Was it authentic? Perhaps, like a child, she sought to make sure an event would not happen by insisting that it must?

"But she is not dead, not yet," said Elina.

"The time is coming," Katya replied.

"Then there's still a chance we can save her," said Madderly.

"No."

Listen to him," said Stephan. "She lives. There is hope!"

"A false hope."

"But hope!" Now Stephan spoke to Madderly. "What can we do?"

Madderly told them of Yuri Antonich, of his connection with Golchov, of the conference. Then he said, "We've got to make Antonich so curious that he'll take me to Leningrad."

"And then?" said Katya. "What can you, one man, do in that place?"

"More than I'm doing here," he replied. "At least we would have someone there."

"Another one to be killed!"

"Perhaps, perhaps not. It's a chance I'm willing to take."

Katya shook her head.

"What sort of man is this Russian?" asked Stephan. "How can he be dealt with?"

"He's on the make, ambitious," said Madderly. "He's part of an operation which rewards scientific achievement. Our best bet is to appeal to his interest in the psychic."

"Katya?"

"Yes, if she will help."

"And what am I to do?" she asked skeptically.

"Only what you already do so well," said Madderly. "Use your telepathic gift."

"That is easier said than done," she replied. "With Natasha it is as though our minds were one. Since childhood it has been this way. But with strangers it is not so certain. Sometimes their minds are shut."

"Let's try," he suggested. "Give your mind to me. Put your thoughts into mine."

She closed her eyes. Her skin colored slightly. Madderly willed his consciousness open as one would part a curtain to reveal the vast night sky.

The images were clear.

He saw himself holding Elina. Above them rode the moon through ghostly clouds, like a haunted vessel. And now a third figure came into view, a faceless form wearing a long fur coat and hat. Antonich?

"Yes, the Russian," said Katya.

She opened her eyes. "Well?"

"You have a vivid imagination," said Madderly, "but I think it'll work. My gift functions best in a receptive capacity. You're a strong projector. For a demonstration you'll project images from here to me at the castle."

"But they will check," she said. "And then they will know I am here!"

Madderly smiled. "No, that's where the trick comes in. We'll allow Antonich to prepare several messages and seal them in envelopes. Then we'll permit him to select someone at the conference to serve as a transmitter. This person will be brought to the lighthouse. There's a basement, isn't there, or a room above?"

Elina said, "There is a cellar."

"Good. You and Stephan will be out of sight in the cellar. As the subject opens and scans each message, you will absorb his impressions and project them to me. They will think the subject is transmitting the messages directly to me, not through you to me."

Katya shook her head. "That will be very difficult, perhaps impossible."

"Yes, but there is ten times more chance of success if you do the transmitting and not the subject. As for absorbing the subject's thoughts, that part should not be too difficult for you. Will you try?"

"If I agree, what of my sister?"

"First get me to Leningrad."

Colonel Bazarov leaned an elbow on the desk and absently tugged the lobe of his right ear while Yuri Antonich phoned in the latest developments.

"And you have not spoken with Golchov?" Bazarov asked.

"No."

"You sent him no message?"

The message! Yuri cursed himself for forgetting. "I merely replied to his communiqué."

"And is this not a message? I ask because you are the Doctor of Philosophy. I am a simple colonel, educated only by life."

"In the rush, I . . . "

"Forgot? Perhaps you should be replaced

with a more reliable Doctor of Philosophy?"

"No, Comrade Colonel, I am able to handle this assignment."

"What causes this 'rush' you speak of?"

Now Yuri was into it. The "rush" was an excellent dinner and four cocktails, or five? The Colonel wanted a "rush." Very well.

"The conference begins tomorrow. Madderly may be on to something of importance. I am making a thousand arrangements. We cannot ignore his discoveries."

"What arrangements?"

"I have this Gouzenko with me and a secretary, Tamara Rostov. They will be my aides. I am taking all necessary precautions."

"Be explicit."

"Should we require Madderly at the Institute, don't you know?"

"No, and I wonder—do you?"

"If he proves reluctant, then we shall have no alternative."

"Are my ears trustworthy?" Bazarov exclaimed. "Are you plotting assassination?"

"Only if necessary. I was trained to prepare for any contingency."

"Contingency? Do you carry a death capsule in the event of your own contingency?"

Yuri placed his hand over the receiver and swallowed. But the lump that had suddenly formed in his throat did not go away.

Bazarov said, "Comrade Antonich, in your specialty you are an expert, as I am in mine. We are now in *my* specialty. Your mission is to evaluate Professor Madderly. If he becomes esential to our interests, measures will be taken. *But not by you.* Put Gouzenko on."

Yuri gave the phone to Gouzenko and stepped from the communications center into the hall. He lit a cigaret and leaned against the wall.

Bazarov was a pig! He inhaled and blew a cloud of smoke. Leaning against a wall and enjoying a cigaret—good God! Was his unconscious warning him?

He ground the cigaret beneath his heel and reentered the communications room.

Gouzenko said, "Colonel wants you now, Comrade."

"Antonich? Gouzenko will handle the contingencies. I leave Madderly's evaluation to you. We wish no embarrassing incidents, but we will permit nothing to hinder this program. Understood?"

"Yes, Comrade Colonel."

Bazarov broke the connection. Yuri went into the hall where Gouzenko was waiting. "Shall we meet now, Comrade?" he asked.

Yuri gnashed his teeth. The idea that this bearded hireling should tell him what to do! But, alas, orders were orders.

"I need fresh air and a drink," he replied. "We'll talk at my hotel." A sad waste of free time. But the girl—Rostov. . ."Bring the secretary also. She is part of our operation."

Sweat rolled down Golchov's cheeks and found his lips. The saltiness reminded him of the sea, of blood. It oozed from his flesh and soaked his trousers and shirt. He felt it collecting like rain in his shoes.

The door to his study was locked. Now he moved across the rug slowly, undecided if it would be least uncomfortable to sit or to stand.

"What heat!" he exclaimed.

And why was it necessary?

He saw his reflection in a frosted window. Absurd! Professor Pavel I. Golchov, unkempt and sweaty as any schoolboy.

He pulled off his shirt. Ah, that was better, but he must be careful not to catch his death. He removed his shoes, his sticky trousers, and arranged the clothes to dry on a chair before the fireplace.

"Tonight I have shed ten pounds, and for what? Nothing!"

The connection had not been made. They went through the ritual seven times—*seven*—and there was not the faintest indication of a link.

Golchov slipped into a blue woolen robe and dropped with a sigh into the chair behind his desk.

He scribbled random impressions on a yellow pad.

Why did something happen sometimes and other times not at all?

He printed the word "science" and followed the letters with "ha-ha!"

Duplication of results was the basis of scientific experimentation. Yet, though they tried the process—the ritual—exactly the same way each time, tonight it would not work!

Witchcraft, sorcery, shamanism, or voodoo—whatever it was called by whichever culture—was not science, no matter how many "scientists" observed and recorded it. There was an irrational element which ran contrary to logic. It was like a river suddenly reversing its course and flowing up a cliff in defiance of gravity!

Golchov glanced at the yellow pad. While he thought, his fingers were moving. They had formed the letter R.

The subconscious knew more than the conscious?

Could the failures be due to Ragusa? Was he holding back his power?

No, he was in too deep. He wouldn't, unless. . .

He was a hoax, a fraud?

But there was absolutely *no* way Ragusa could deceive him! True, Ragusa was a skilled hypnotist, and the setting for the ritual was extremely suggestive; yet—

"What am I thinking?" Golchov exclaimed. "I know him too well, I understand him!"

Or was even that part of a hoax? The brain was another continent, another world. Its charts were yet to be drawn. Those fellows in Moscow, Leskovitch and the others, were making some progress working with brain-damaged soldiers. But they had only scratched the surface.

Could Ragusa be exerting his influence to make me think I know him?

Golchov stared at the yellow notepad.

Or perhaps my distrust is merely human. Who, after all, can presume to comprehend the infinitude of parts making up another individual?

You knew the skin—its moles, the facial features—and you might x-ray the vital organs. But could you see into the soul? The purest science could not do that!

And this Ragusa was no ordinary mortal. A second Rasputin, he was called by the fanatics who hailed him as the next savior of Russia.

"Savior—bah! A dream, a wish. Freud was right!"

Ragusa made no pretense of being the next "deliverer." He was what he was—a cruelly handsome, larger-than-normal young man who claimed to have been born of a girl-mother in the same eastern wilderness as Genghis Khan.

Golchov saw he had made a few uncertain lines on the notepad: a crude picture of this warlock, standing on the obsidian floor constructed in the sub-basement of the Institute. To secure the black stone they had desecrated the

Church of St. Basil—one of its most holy places. Terrible! but what was one church more or less?

So Ragusa got the black floor, and all else he required. Golchov lost count of how many psychics were taken by the KGB so that Ragusa could use their psychic energies to power his work. Once when Golchov questioned such practices, Ragusa merely replied, "It is necessary," and the yellow eyes stared at him so intensely that he had to flee to avoid being trapped in them, like an insect in amber.

"Amber," whispered Golchov. "The perfect description."

He remembered the bits of crystalized resin he found during his childhood while playing on the shores of Lake Il'men. They were palpable links with the "old times" when men were hunters who followed grazing herds. Amber was strong magic to them. Rub it on fur and it drew bits of straw unto itself. Peer into it deeply and the future might appear. Before the time of Homer, Greeks traded red gold for Russian amber.

Golchov frowned at recalling the childhood wishes he made upon the amber he found. They did not come true—or did they? He sought fame, fortune. Now he was a scientist of international reputation, and while he was no milliionaire, he was highly placed.

"And likely to fall!"

Yes, like the proverbial man holding a tiger by the tail.

The one called Ragusa had come to him in a routine manner. Golchov was operating under government authority to investigate all psychic phenomena to determine if it in fact existed, and if it did, to put it to practical uses of benefit to the nation.

Ragusa did not stage demonstrations as did

other great figures, such as Wolf Messing and Lupanta. He operated on the fringe, among the poor, the inherently superstitious. Legends arose that he possessed powers unseen since Christ walked the earth.

"Christ!" Golchov exclaimed. "The strength of the eternally ignorant!"

Though skeptical, Golchov made contact. They met in a backwater of Leningrad, a suitable scene for *Crime and Punishment*. Lovely girls clad in diaphanous gowns moved about the darkened rooms. Physically, Ragusa was overwhelming. He stood almost seven feet and his body was as muscled and well-proportioned as a carefully bred animal's. His voice was deep, soft and dreamy—it lulled the listener into a receptive state of mind.

But his eyes—they held the secret of his power!

In that first encounter Golchov knew that anyone those yellow eyes gazed upon came under Ragusa's control. Was it a super-hypnotic gift, or something beyond hypnosis? He did not know then, nor now. That Ragusa posssessed genuine psychic power was a proven fact. Under rigorous experimental conditions he willed objects to move. He read one's thoughts with amazing accuracy. And he healed medical cases written off as hopeless by Soviet specialists.

He cooperated with—no, he *led*—the research. And thus far he had sought no payment. Whenever Golchov asked what he wanted, Ragusa replied in that beguiling voice, "When the time for settlement comes, you will know. Until that moment, the work itself is all I desire."

"If he does no better than tonight," Golchov muttered, "the moment will never come."

He touched his brow. The dampness was gone. He was cool. Must be careful not to fall ill.

But wait, with Ragusa in his employ, what disease need he fear?

Such irony made him smile.

And shudder.

He opened the desk drawer and removed a revolver placed there on some papers. He brought the icy muzzle to his head. Could Ragusa cure even that? He swung open the cylinder and shook six bullets into his palm. The slugs were a lustrous gray-white. He had ordered them made when Ragusa came to the Institute. Superstition, perhaps, though he was a man of science and this was an age of reason.

Still, he felt safer with silver bullets at the ready.

SEVEN

By the time they arrived at Helsinki airport, Wills was as out of sorts with the world as Porkowski. There was a limit to human endurance, and flying thousands of miles in a brief span was the best way to realize it. All I want, he told himself, is a shower and a bed. But he knew he could have neither yet, so he relit his dead cigar.

"What time is it?" Porkowski asked.

Wills looked at his watch. Damn thing said—but that couldn't be right. How many time zones had they passed through?

He checked the dash clock of the embassy car. Four-thirty.

"That the correct time?" he asked the driver.

"Yes sir, four-thirty hours."

Wills moaned. The driver was a young fellow in plain clothes, but the cut of his hair announced he was an embassy marine. Towers sat beside him. Something about their postures, too. Erect. Rode like they were marching on parade. Was the whole world gung-ho?

"Well, what is the time?" asked Porkowski.

"Am I your nursemaid?"

"If you were, I would discharge you."

"Shut up."

"I asked only for the time."

"All right, it's four-thirty, *ante meridiem*."

"Thank you."

Wills sighed. If he ever saw another plane! And what the hell was Madderly up to? He told Relling to stick like glue, and so far there were no reports.

He squinted at the snowy night. Blacks and whites everywhere. Damn little gray. By now Madderly might be dead. Joke to—ha-ha—end all jokes. At least they'd have a man—no, a spirit—on the other side.

He considered Porkowski from the corner of his eye. Madderly was too valuable. Send good ol' Stan on the longest trip of his miserable life. From one world to another. Of course, the S. O. B. would sell out on arrival.

"Don't do that," Porkowski said.

"Me? Do what?"

"Stare. I get the feeling you see me the way a butcher sees an animal ready for the knife."

Was the bastard reading his mind? Be damned if he'd go easy on him! "We all have to die sometime. It's in the contract."

"True. However, that is not what bothers me. I simply do not like being looked at as an object."

"Well, what the hell are you?"

"Frankly, Wills, I resent it."

"You do? You can take your—"

"Beg pardon, sir," said Towers. "We're at the Embassy."

Wills abruptly stepped from the car. As he mounted the icy steps, he realized that treating Porkowski this way was foolish. Might have use for him in the near future. Still, Relling would like nothing more than a few minutes alone with him.

The night officer met him at the door and took him into the Ambassador's office. On the desk were several urgent messages. One from Washington advised that operatives in Rome reported much Soviet interest in Sylvia Week.

Another from Istanbul said the same and reported her en route Athens. The third was from Relling. Wills sat in the Ambassador's chair and scanned the typescript.

"Chambers and I at estate of Hintsanen who agrees to hold meetings on his island. Madderly has seen Yuri Antonich, assistant to Golchov. Antonich and Madderly to meet tomorrow afternoon."

Tomorrow? Wills checked the message date. The meeting had already taken place.

The message continued: "Madderly edgy. But plan developing as calculated."

Which meant what?

No more, no less than what it said: Madderly could land on his feet, so long as he wasn't dropped from too great a height.

He tossed the communiqué in the destroy basket. The duty officer asked, "Any orders, sir?"

"Got a room with a bed?"

"Yes sir, the Ambassador's. He's gone up to Rovaniemi with President Kokkonen."

"President of what?"

"The country—Finland, sir."

"Nice," said Wills, rising slowly.

"May I get you something to eat, sir?"

"Later."

"Any messages?"

"No."

He started for the door, then stopped. Fatigue clouded his reasoning. The meeting was yesterday. Had to find out what happened. Of course, if it were earthshaking, Relling would've sent another message. And he *had* to get some rest, if only for an hour or two.

"Sir?"

"Wake me at seven. Got that? Seven."

As he went into the Ambassador's suite he

heard a roar like a sawmill. Porkowski had beaten him to sleep.

Major Tushin placed the photograph on the desk in front of Gouzenko. "On the left is Wills," he said. "And that is Porkowski. They are now here in Helsinki, at the American Embassy."

"And the black man?"

"Sergeant Towers, a marine assigned to the London embassy. A bodyguard, we suppose."

Gouzenko studied the dark face, the heavy build. "How is he to be handled?"

"Cautiously. He is an excellent shot. A plus for our side is that, according to Bazarov, the Americans have no knowledge of you or comrade Rostov."

"Shall I carry a weapon?"

"No, only your good sense. We want you doubly on guard, both with the Americans and Antonich."

Gouzenko smiled. "The KGB is—"

"No humor, Captain. This is deadly business, so take care. I passed one winter in Ust'Kuyga. I have no desire to pass another."

Ust'Kuyga? thought Gouzenko, departing the Embassy elevator for the garage. Wartime assignment? Perhaps Tushin guarded the infamous labor camp? A breath of icy wind found his cheek. It was best to read books about Siberian geography. Yes, and leave trips there to fools.

Tamara waited in the car. After the meeting with Antonich the night before, Gouzenko felt inclined to consider her as more than a secretary. Antonich had drunk too much, had gone so far as to make—*suggestions*, which Gouzenko questioned. The meeting ended with Antonich in a rage brought on by his embarrassment when Gouzenko backed him down.

Gouzenko got into the car, closed the door, and the driver went up the ramp to the street. He placed his arm on the seat behind Tamara's head and asked, "Are you prepared?"

"I have my notepad and pencil."

"Let us hope comrade scientist is himself today."

"Yes, he is an unhappy man."

"Oh? I had not thought of him that way. How do you know?"

"Is a happy person always angry?"

"Aie! You should know my father and mother! One unending fight and they are the happiest people in the world."

Tamara smiled. "Perhaps, but you are biased."

He touched her hair, pretended a frown. "Do you dare question me? I am a happy man also."

Tamara went along with the fun and feigned a scowl. "In all my life I have never been so happy."

Gouzenko thought about trying for a kiss. Why not? He bent toward her face, but then the driver turned to the back seat and said, "Marski Hotel."

The right door opened and Yuri Antonich got in, pressing Tamara against Gouzenko, who suddenly understood that from the worst misfortune good may come.

Antonich punched the driver's shoulder and said, "Go!"

As the car moved through traffic, Antonich said, "About last night, comrades, I trust you did not mistake my concern with the mission for something else?"

"Of course not," Gouzenko replied.

"Good. You have the film and the projector?"

"Yes, in the trunk, with extension cords and voltage adaptor, should they be necessary."

"I have been in touch with Madderly again," said Yuri. "He thinks it best to begin the conference with more academic matters, such as papers by two other delegates. If all goes on schedule, the American will give us a demonstration of his so-called long-distance telepathy this afternoon.'

"And our film?"

"If not today, then tomorrow."

Gouzenko nodded. "It is always best to be prepared for any contingency, is it not, comrade?"

Antonich gritted his teeth and looked out the window at the snow.

The duty officer—a new one, fresh from a good night's sleep—roused him precisely at seven. For a moment Wills didn't know where he was. When at last he did know, he wondered why he was there. In the shower he almost fell asleep again. It took an effort of pure willpower to get dressed and go into the next room and, literally, roll Porkowski out onto the floor.

Stan's anger made the getting up too early almost worth it.

The military attache had no difficulty borrowing a chopper from a NATO group. Actually Uncle Sam was paying most of the NATO bill anyway.

They stowed their bags in the craft and took off in the other direction from Hintsanen's island, just in case the Center boys were up that early. Wills had no doubt they were. He also figured they were smart enough to know that the island was his destination. But evasive tactics served to make the blood flow a little faster, on both sides. And an aerial reconnaissance never hurt.

The chopper came in low over the snowy forest, slowed, and settled gently on a clear space between the house and the wall.

Wills unfastened his safety-belt. His stomach wasn't exactly queasy, but there was a familiar bitter taste in his mouth and throat, signaling exhaustion, hunger, and general malaise.

The rotors slowed to a lazy, whining turn. Wills jumped from the door onto a patch of grass exposed by the blades' whirl. Towers followed, and then Porkowski, who stumbled and almost fell into a low drift of snow.

Then the pilot made a thumbs-up signal and lifted off. Wills got a faceful of flakes, but they were cool, refreshing. As he watched the chopper disappear behind the trees, he was struck by the beauty of this isolated place.

Beauty was one thing he had no time for now, though. First, get into the house. Second, see if Chambers had any of her magic pills for banishing fatigue. Then, maybe a cup of coffee and some toast, after which he'd see what Madderly had to offer.

The pill did its work before Wills finished his first cup of coffee. It was as though a mist were blown away from before his eyes and things once more appeared in sharp focus.

Madderly sat across from him at the table. Relling and Chambers stood by a window. Porkowski was in a corner of the room, as far from Relling as he could get. Hintsanen's wheelchair was pulled up near the table between Wills and Madderly. Elina stood behind her father.

"Thanks for the breakfast," said Wills. "I needed it."

Elina smiled.

Chambers said, "I'll be happy to prescribe

your lunch, too."

Wills ignored the doctor's comment and fixed his gaze on Madderly. "So you've met the enemy?" he asked. "And you've made plans. You don't waste time."

"He had no choice," said Elina.

Wills let this comment pass, also. He said, "So, what do you think?"

"About what?" asked Madderly.

"The situation."

"I don't know what to think. Antonich was here. We talked. He seemed interested in long distance telepathy."

"And you cooked up a demonstration?"

Madderly nodded. "With Katya's help."

"What's the angle?"

"Main problem with all ESP phenomena is unpredictability. If you don't know when a subject is going to be telepathic then you can't make planned use of his power."

"Go on."

"Katya and I appear to have sympathetic powers."

"You mean you and she can communicate anytime, like dropping a dime in a pay phone?"

Madderly smiled. "Not really. But we can do pretty well, if the wires aren't down. But look, I intimated to Antonich that we've been working with a drug which 'turns on' telepathic power, even in those who supposedly have none at all."

"And that turned *him* on."

"Yes. I spoke to him late last night and said I'd attempt a demonstration today. If it's all right with you."

"Sure. Sounds great. At least, it will be great, if it works."

Madderly frowned. "Is that all you can say? I mean I don't know from nothing, and here I'm running the show."

Wills grinned. "You only think you are. It's my show, from beginning to end."

"Then why . . ."

"The games? Throws the other side off balance. See, they know I'm boss, but when they see you, an amateur, giving orders, they get confused. They begin to doubt, even though they are positive I'm in charge. The end result is they take the show more seriously; they become more committed and more determined."

"But what if I hadn't come up with this ideas?"

"You'd have come up with something, or I would've, or Elina, or somebody."

Madderly whistled softly. "That's one hell of a way—"

"Not really," Wills said. "Give me the details. You got pills?"

"A couple of aspirins will do."

Chambers said, "Capsules would be better. People tend to be more awed by capsules."

"You have some empties, doctor?" asked Wills.

"I'm always prepared. I'll load a few with sugar."

"Make sure that's all you load them with," said Wills. To Madderly, he said, "Who'll be the subject for transmitting the message?"

"That'll be up to Antonich."

"You'd let *him* choose?"

"How else can we prove we're on the up and up? Anyway, Katya will be the real transmitter."

"But you told me that not everyone has ESP."

Madderly nodded. "I'm counting on Katya's great sensitivity to pick up even a feeble message. But if Antonich selects a real dud, then the demonstration fails and we try again the next day with a new subject, whom he'll also choose. In this business you don't expect to hit a home run every turn at bat."

"That's nice," said Wills. "But we don't have a lot of time. I hope to hell he picks a real radio." He lit a cigar. "Anything else I should know?"

"Well, if it works with the first subject, then we say we have no more capsules left. If it doesn't, then we try again."

"How will you begin the meeting?"

"I think we'll lead off with Relling's paper."

"Professor Relling, of the Institute of Human Potential," said Relling.

"All those numbers and formulae—it's too boring," Chambers said.

"Exactly," Madderly said. "That paper will put Antonich in a receptive state for the demonstration."

"And what does the Russian offer in return?" Wills asked.

"It seems he has an amazing film—living color, sound—of Anna Letovskaya, their expert on psychokinesis."

"Important stuff?"

"A film of hers is available in the United States," said Madderly. "Antonich says this is a new one. She's wired to various instruments to show body functions—brain waves, respiration, blood pressure—while she performs. Could be interesting."

"Could be faked, too, right?"

"Sure, just like our demonstration."

Wills laughed. "It takes one to catch one."

"Actually," said Madderly, "there's no reason for *them* to fake it. They've got loads of authentic, amazing stuff at their Pavlov Institute. By the way, it might be best if you and Porkowski drop out of sight while the Russians are here."

Wills thought about it, then, "You're right. We'll stay behind the scenes." To Hintsanen he said, "Are the meetings being held in a place where we can watch without being seen?"

"We are using the old Mead Hall. Timo will set up video cameras and sound system. You gentlemen may oberve in my library."

"Can we make a video tape?" asked Wills.

"Certainly."

Wills smiled inwardly. He was all at once very confident, very happy. Perhaps this was another effect of the pill Chambers gave him. But he liked to believe his pleasant state of mind was caused by a premonition that this scheme would be successful.

Antonich, Gouzenko, and Tamara arrived on schedule at half-past ten. Timo brought them over from the mainland in the launch and saw to their projection equipment. He led them into the castle where Madderly and the others waited.

Madderly did the introductions, presenting Chambers as a researcher associated with the West Coast Psychic Group. Relling was on the staff of the Denver-based Institute for Human Potential.

After a polite cup of coffee and twenty minutes of small talk, Hintsanen suggested they move along to the meeting room and open the conference.

Timo led the way, bearing for effect a sputtering torch. They crossed a snow filled courtyard and entered a large stone building attached on one side to the castle proper. It was dark inside. Cobwebs floated like trapped clouds from the great oak beams supporting the roof.

Hintsanen said, "This is our Mead Hall. Archeologists from the University tell me it is the oldest part of my estate. Some assert it was under construction as early as the ninth century."

Timo laid the torch to a stack of logs in the giant fireplace at the far end of the hall. In a moment the fire caught and the room danced with shadows and became comfortably warm.

"The lighting is poor," said Antonich. "We have a film to show. Is there no electricity?"

"But of course," replied Hintsanen. "Timo, give us light."

Timo tripped a switch and fixtures recessed in the walls illuminated the chamber.

"What you see is a compromise," said Hintsanen. "The archeologists wished me to leave things as they were. But I convinced them it would be possible to do some modernizing without damaging the feeling of centuries which this structure evokes."

"Yes," said Antonich, "I know the feeling."

"Very good," said Hintsanen. "Shall we take our places?"

They sat around a huge circular table. Madderly was flanked by Elina and Chambers. Hintsanen sat between his daughter and Relling. Antonich faced Elina across the table, while Gouzenko and Tamara sat on either side of him.

In the library, Porkowski adjusted the focus of the video cameras positioned overhead and to left and right. Reception was clear, audio excellent. Wills engaged the tape machine, sat back and lit a cigar, and watched as Madderly addressed the group.

"Ladies and gentlemen, fellow delegates," he began. "Shall we dispense with formalities and get down to business? We know why we are here. We share a common interest in parapsychology, and, as scientists, we must therefore share our discoveries so that we may progress in our research."

"Yes, yes," said Antonich. "We must cooperate."

Madderly saw that the young woman with Antonich, the one called Rostov, whom he had seen in Stockmann's stealing hose, was taking down on her notepad every word said. He also observed that the bearded fellow with Antonich, who was introduced as Professor Gouzenko of Moscow University, was the same man he had seen first at Healthrow and later, with Rostov, in the department store. Madderly was not shocked by their presence. In fact, the situation struck him as being so ludicrous that it was all he could do to keep from smiling.

Madderly said, "Let us begin with Professor Relling's views concerning the analysis of experimental results. Professor Relling."

Relling opened the folder on the desk before him, glanced at the first page, then the second, then took a cigaret from a crumpled pack and lit it. He blew a cloud of smoke and looked around the table.

"Actually," he said, his voice sharp with a tone of superiority, "Dr. Madderly's introduction missed the point. Actually I should like to discuss problems inherent in determining trustworthy results from paranormal psychological experiments."

Having made this point clear, Relling began his paper, which introduced the listeners to the subject by reminding them of Coover's laborious work at Stanford University during the spring and summer months of 1917, the results of which were erroneous due to Coover's gross miscalculation of standard deviation.

Relling next touched upon Dr. Rhine's work with Zener cards at Duke, calling special attention to the controversy which erupted when Rhine's experiments proved ESP. His detractors howled that the results were due to a manipulation of probability formulae, in particular his avoidance of binomial expansion to compensate for depletion in card stock during each run. However, disinterested statisticians were able to show that Rhine's calculations were correct.

Now that his audience was attuned to his subject, Relling plunged into the world of numbers and models, spewing forth formula after formula, each fleshed out with one positive and one negative example.

Fifty minutes later he concluded with his first completely clear statement of the day. Lighting a fresh cigaret, he said, "And that is how the matter currently stands."

Porkowski's head was nodding. Wills knew that he himself must have dozed off at least once. He rubbed the back of his neck, squinted at the television set.

In the Mead Hall, Madderly said, "Thank you, Professor, for an extremely informative paper."

Dr. Hintsanen said, "It is noon. Shall we adjourn for lunch?"

Antonich stiffled a yawn and nodded in agreement, saying, "And afterwards we shall give the floor to Professor Madderly."

"But I don't understand," said Chambers. "I thought I was next."

"There is time for everyone to be heard," said Hintsanen. "For the moment let us return to the main building."

Luncheon was served by the maid, Erika, assisted by a young woman from the kitchen. The meal was light yet tasteful and satisfying. A dry wine was served. Madderly noticed that at first Antonich appeared suspicious of the clear liquid. Did he suppose it was drugged? If so, did that indicate that such action was typical of life in Leningrad?

At last, however, Antonich took a sip, found it good, and downed the whole glass. He did not resist when Erika offered a refill. Two glasses later his eyes twinkled and he was smiling at Elina and trying to be witty.

After a fruit plate was passed the group returned to the Mead Hall and took their places at the circular table.

Chambers said, "Before we begin, I've changed my mind." She smiled. "Lunch was so good! I'd rather sit back and be entertained than do the entertaining."

Antonich laughed.

"So," she said, "please let me go on tomorrow, with Yuri?"

"Certainly," said Madderly.

"I shall be pleased to appear on the same day with you," said Antonich.

"This means, then, that Professor Madderly's demonstration is next in our order of business," Hintsanen said. "If he is prepared."

All eyes fell on Madderly.

He managed a careless smile and, having fumbled in his coat pocket, held up a clenched hand and said, "So long as I have these I'm always ready."

He opened his hand. Two capsules nestled like small white eggs in his palm. Grasping one between thumb and forefinger, he showed it around the table.

"And what is this?" asked Antonich.

"A certain drug which, we have found, induces a telepathic state."

The Russian frowned. "This drug and this

alone creates ESP?"

"I didn't say that," Madderly replied. "In fact, I make no claims. We've discovered, experimentally, that the drug stimulates telepathic power in subjects for a period up to twenty-four hours."

"And you will show us how it works?" asked Yuri.

"I hope so."

"Hope?"

"Professor, does every experiment conducted at the Pavlov Institute go according to plan?"

"Then you are not certain. What percentage of success have you had?"

Madderly shook his head. "Sorry, but you'll have to wait till my article comes out for facts and figures. Let's say we haven't been disappointed."

Hintsanen said, "And what sort of demonstration have you planned?"

"A very simple one." He showed them the second pill again. And now he swallowed the first. The capsule lingered a moment in his throat, then slid free.

"Since Professor Antonich is interested in telepathy," said Madderly, "he may choose a person to take this second capsule. That person will be escorted to a lighthouse approximately three miles from this room where he, or she, will be given messages known only to Professor Antonich to be telepathically communicated to me."

There was an excited murmur around the table. Chambers whispered to Gouzenko, then across the table to Relling. In Hintsanen's library, Wills leaned closer to the video sets.

All eyes swung round to focus on Antonich. "Well," he said, slowly, "I am always ready for a good show. You say I may pick anyone in this room?"

"That is correct."

Yuri looked around the table. He smiled. "Beauty and mystery go well together, don't you think?" he said, and, not waiting for an answer, nodded at Elina, saying, "I choose you, Miss Hintsanen."

The capsule in Madderly's palm suddenly took on an enormous weight. What if—? But no, no time for doubt, not now. This was just a demonstration, nothing more, and he had already told Antonich they might have to try a second time.

He gave her the capsule. Timo brought a glass of water. She swallowed the sugar-filled capsule and looked at Madderly.

After a moment she said, "I feel no different."

"Nor has your appearance changed," said Antonich. "Fortunately." He chuckled at his own witticism.

Hintsanen said, "And what is the next step, Professor?"

"The subject and the messages will be taken to the lighthouse. Perhaps your man, Timo, will escort her?"

"One moment, please," said Yuri. "You will have no objections if Gouzenko accompanies her? I wish to observe both the sending and the receiving."

"I was going to suggest that. He may also inspect the premises."

"And one more point. I will prepare my messages after Miss Hintsanen leaves this room. Agreed?"

"Certainly."

Relling said, "I'd like to go along with Professor Gouzenko."

Antonich laughed. "A double double-check? I have no objection."

Timo and Elina left the Mead Hall. Antonich tore several sheets from Tamara's pad. He looked up at Madderly before writing and said, "Do you speak Russian, Professor?"

Madderly shook his head.

"Then I will make it easier by using English."

Elina sat on the edge of the chair and concentrated upon the words printed on the paper Gouzenko handed her. She shut her eyes and formed mental images of them one by one.

"Boy—dog—cat—fish."

Now she focused upon each word in turn, then upon the words in series. Did Katya read her mind? She opened her eyes and stared at each letter of each word. Was Katya relaying her thoughts? Was—?

No, she warned herself, *don't think of anything except these words*!

The Russian said, "This is the second message."

She exchanged another squre of paper for the first, at the same time noting the man's beard, the cut of his clothes. She had seen him before, but where?

"The message, miss."

She unfolded the paper and looked at geometrical figures. A square, a circle, a triangle, another circle, a third circle. Code? Perhaps the figures were not as significant as their arrangement?

"Square, circle, triangle, circle, circle."

Five symbols as in my name, she thought.

Don't think!

Drops of perspiration trickled down her back. Was Katya receiving?

"Square, circle, triangle, circle, circle."

"The third message," said the Russian.

The paper was blank.

A mistake? How did one communicate nothing?

Relling detected her agitation. He said, "Something wrong?"

"See for yourself. There is no message."

Gouzenko intercepted the paper. "This is the communiqué Antonich wishes to be sent. Can you do it or not?"

It was too late to retreat. "I will try," Elina said.

She stared at the whiteness until her eyes watered, saying again and again, *Blank. It is blank*!

Madderly sat erect, eyes shut, palms flat upon the smooth cool surface of the table. He opened his mind. He waited. For a time sea sounds held his attention and an image of Elina's Viking ship materialized, then it sailed away and the sea turned to night.

The first intimation of Katya's power was a point of light. It burned like a star in cosmic darkness, then grew larger and larger still. Madderly's flesh tingled. An image came into being—a child—no—it wore short pants—he—yes, a boy—and the season was summer—

The image vanished.

Madderly said, "Boy."

Antonich leaned toward him, his eyes intent upon his face.

In Hintsanen's library, Porkowski said, "Do you think he got it correct?"

Wills replied, "Did he! Look at the Russian's expression!"

The second image came quicker than the first. A tail—wagging in darkness—legs—a cat? A brown head marked with floppy ears. A white spot between brown eyes.

"Dog."

The third image sprang into his mind like a creature leaping into a circle of blinding light. White—fluffy—whiskers—pink nose—

"Cat."

The next image attacked the cat and chased it away. Its teeth were rows of knives, its skin gray sandpaper. There was water, blue, waves, and a tropical sun. The boy momentarily appeared, then slipped from view, and a shark rolled and snapped at the crest where he had stood.

Madderly said, "Sha—" and checked himself. The shark rolled again and now it was a goldfish, which transformed into a—sardine?

Now he said, "Fish."

"Astounding!" cried Antonich. "Incredible!"

"There are two more messages," Chambers said.

"Of course, but I have never seen—such—"

"Please," said Hintsanen. "Professor Madderly must have silence."

Antonich's words drew Madderly from his trance, but with the new quiet he found himself sinking into a dark sea. Were there more sharks in those depths? He relaxed, sought the warm currents. The water was ink, but it was cozy, and before his face rose a creature of glowing red and yellow light. Jellyfish? Madderly moved after it, took it in his hand, smiled at the joke. It was an incandescent configuration of lines. He turned it over—a shape, nothing more—a rectangle whose four sides were of equal length.

"Square," he said.

His voice propelled him from the sea into a snowbank and he wondered why he did not shiver. Things rushed at him, struck him. He caught one in his bare hand. The snow was warm—no, not warm, but rather without a discernible temperature. The object glittered and dissolved into its own outline. A ring? The square and the—

"Circle."

The reasoning portion of his brain intruded to make the obvious—the Soviets were setting a series of geometrical figures. Laughable! Antonich had chosen some of the structures used on standard intelligence tests!

Now he drifted like a cloud through the winter sky. He saw his shadow below, and an island, the castle, the lighthouse, the sea. Sails dotted the gulf. Vikings? He was too high, but they ran before the wind faster than the cresting waves. There was the glint of sunlight from disks of metal. Circles? No, he broke through a wall of cloud a saw a flight of geese so close he peered into their wild eyes.

They veered up and away from him—or did he stop?—no matter—they were at a distance flying in a three-sided formation—in a—

"Triangle."

He fell.

A snowbank caught him. It was soft as cotton, and when he worked his way into the sunlight a ring of ice looped about his neck. He pulled it off, would have tossed it aside, but it was sticky, it—

"Circle."

A second ring fell around his neck.

"Circle."

Now the rings, the snow, and he himself vanished into a silent darkness. End of message?

But it wasn't the end. There was a greater darkness. And within it another still greater.

Madderly strained but he could not penetrate, could not see anything, could see only—

"Nothing," he said. "The message is blank."

Antonich slammed his hands on the table and exclaimed, "Fantastic! Never in all my experience have I seen such results!"

Madderly blinked and rubbed his eyes. "How accurate was I?" he asked.

"You made no errors!" said the Russian. "None! A perfect score!"

Chambers said, "I'm impressed, really. But can you transmit messages, sentences, I mean?"

Yuri turned toward her, his voice trembling, "He has sent a great message, but you have not yet received it. He has told you of a new sort of communications which requires no mechanical devices and no external power supply! Only a simple capsule!"

"Yes, but—" said Chambers.

Antonich ignored her. To Madderly he said, "You have more of this drug?"

"With me? I'm afraid not. It's precious and at this stage very difficult to produce."

Yuri frowned. "Yes, I supposed not." He thought, then, "And what did you say is the duration of the drug's effect on the subject?"

"It depends on the subject," Madderly answered. "On the average, twenty-four hours is a safe figure."

"Are there harmful effects if one uses the drug repeatedly?"

"None that we know of. We haven't completed our work, but indications are that the drug breaks down into amino acids readily absorbed by the body."

Antonich took this in and smiled. He stood and reached across the table and offered his hand, saying, "I congratulate you again!"

"We must have him, Colonel, at all costs!"

"Calm down. Be coherent. Explain," said Bazarov.

"Madderly. We must have him at the Institute. He—"

"Operator, put Gouzenko on!"

The operator plugged in an extension and Gouzenko said, "Here, Comrade Colonel."

"But Colonel—"

"Silence! Now, Captain, you and I are simple fellows who know reality when we step on it. Please, calmly, what does the Doctor of Philosophy mean?"

"It is a matter of—" Antonich began.

"*Professor*!"

Gouzenko spoke to the point. "The demonstration of long-distance telepathy was successful. I admit at first I suspected trickery. But I watched closely, and in my opinion the American did what he claimed."

"Antonich?"

"What Gouzenko says is true. I believe he has made a discovery that will revolutionize communications. In space exploration alone, think of the weight per payload we could save if—"

"Yes, yes," said Bazarov. "What do you suggest?"

Ah, this is more like it! thought Antonich. "We must move quickly. Time is now a factor."

"How so?"

"The drug must be analyzed. Madderly revealed that its potency has a duration of twenty-four hours."

"And to do this analysis?"

"We must 'persuade' Madderly and Miss Hintsanen to allow us to examine them."

Bazarov whistled under his breath. "You are requesting an abduction?"

"I hardly suppose they will come by invitation," Antonich replied. "And there is no time for such niceties. Madderly indicated the drug decomposes into animo acids. This suggests it is based on DNA, which has been proved to affect brain functions. We must obtain a trace of the drug before it breaks down."

Bazarov thought for a long moment, then, "Captain, what is the overall situation? We must avoid a dispute with the Finns."

"There seems to be no security. I estimate no more than five men on Hintsanen's staff. Major Tushin briefed me that Wills, Porkowski, and Towers arrived via helicopter, but I have not seen them."

"Manpower?"

"With support from the sea, the Professor and I can bring it off. Surprise is worth one assault squad."

"You have another ally. Rostov is also KGB. You may depend upon her."

Tamara an agent? She seemed so different from the women he had encountered at the Center. She was less hard, more—human.

"Captain, a word of caution—do not act hastily. But when you do act, remember the only sin is failure."

"Comrade Colonel," said Antonich, "I will need equipment on the scene when you pick us up."

"Such as?"

"Two facilities for thorough physical examination—blood, urine, total basic workup. Also stomach pumps and a centrifuge for fractionals. Understand?"

"Professor, I cannot sneak a hospital ship into Finn waters."

"You would rather I rang up Minister Nikoyan?"

Bazarov sighed. "I will do what I can. Gouzenko, Tushin's supply room should be adequate to meet your needs."

"Yes, Comrade Colonel."

"And you will inform me of details as soon as your plan is complete."

Antonich said, "I will have something to say about that plan."

"No doubt you will, Professor," said Bazarov. "I will sign off now. Good luck."

EIGHT

Wills stopped the video tape machine. He hit the rewind switch and said, "That was a very convincing performance, Professor. If I didn't know better, I'd trade my mother for one of those capsules."

"If you hadn't already traded her for something else," said Dr. Chambers.

Relling chuckled.

Wills lit a fresh cigar and tossed the spent match in the fireplace. He glanced out the drawing room window at the snow and said, "Knowing the nature of the Soviet beast, we can assume Antonich is in touch with someone higher up."

"Golchov?" asked Madderly.

"Maybe, or maybe someone in KGB. Got any names, Stan?"

Porkowski thought a moment, then replied, "There's Katov and Letts. The old hand is a Colonel Bazarov. Very neat fellow."

Madderly frowned. Wills noticed and said, "It's really simple, Professor. The other side has counterparts to what we have. You're their Golchov, I'm Bazarov, Gouzenko's Relling, and so on. We're not all that different from the Soviets, really."

"So where does that leave us?"

"In a comfortable position. We've put on our part of the show. It's up to them now. Antonich is going to roll a flick, right?"

"Yes."

"And then you may get a nice little invitation to attend an after-the-performance party in Leningrad."

Hintsanen said, "Do you discount the possibility of violence?"

Wills shook his head. "I don't discount anything. In this case, however, I don't see what they can gain by busting in and shooting up the place. They want Madderly alive, not dead. Why take chances when a few nice words will do?"

"Antonich is a vain, ambitious man," said Hintsanen.

"The world is full of them," Wills replied. "What do you say to a few hands of poker after supper? Excluding the Professor, of course—unless he can be my partner."

Gouzenko paid the cab driver, gave him a generous tip, and sent him on his way. Then he left the road and joined Tamara and Antonich who stood out of the swirling snow in the hut at the foot of the pier.

"I don't like it," Antonich said. "That driver can identify us."

"You would rather I killed him?" said Gouzenko. "A waste of bullets as well as life. By the time he is asked, if he is, we will be in Leningrad. Rostov, did you signal the launch?"

"The one called Timo is bringing it over."

Not even the stress of action had changed the gentle quality of her voice. When Gouzenko told her that Bazarov had revealed she was KGB, the girl made no reply beyond a simple nod, though in her eyes Gouzenko fancied the hope that they might meet another time, another place—but they had no right to such dreams.

He pulled down his glove and checked his

watch. "In ninety minutes the ship from Kronstadt will be at the lighthouse. It will land a party which will move inland toward the castle to intercept and support us. Are your weapons ready?"

"You call this—this *toy* a weapon?" exclaimed Antonich.

"Do not wave it about. Should one of us be incapacitated now, the mission must be aborted."

"But a dart gun, and drugs!"

"A proven technique, Professor, designed by other professors and tested by men like me in the field under real conditions. It is gas-operated. The clip holds ten darts. The drug is akin to thorazine."

"Yes, they use it to stun animals," said Antonich. "But will it take effect quickly enough? Suppose—"

"This drug reacts instantaneously," said Gouzenko. "The subject, though conscious, is paralyzed for up to thirty minutes."

"But bullets—"

"Comrade, the Colonel has ordered us to avoid an incident. Murdering a dozen people is an incident."

Antonich tucked the bulky dart gun under his coat. "Very well," he said, "but do not under any circumstances shoot Madderly and Miss Hintsanen, understand? At least do not shoot them with this drug of yours. It will ruin my tests. A slug in the arm or leg would have no adverse effect."

Tamara said, "I hear the launch."

"Let us go! No mistakes!"

Gouzenko advanced toward the pier as the boat materialized in the wind-driven snow. Timo steered to the loading stage. The three Russians came aboard without mishap and Timo brought the wheel over hard and turned the bow against the cold wind into the channel.

Ch'en saw the maneuver and first watched, then heard the boat vanish into the clouds of snow. He put the rented car into low and crawled from the wooded ravine near the water's edge back to the road, shifted to second gear, and went slowly through the blinding whiteness to the road's end at the stone house.

His head hurt, his feet were freezing. Damn Finn weather! Damn American tricks! The bastards had almost rammed his skull through the windshield. For the hundredth time he muttered, "When I get my hands on that Porkowski!"

Ch'en rolled down the window and tried to see beyond the house. Snow, nothing but snow. Couldn't tell where air ended and water began. His head! Twelve stitches from the right brow to the hairline. He slipped a tin of aspirin from his pocket and swallowed three dry. The bitterness made him forget his pain for the moment.

He fastened the top button of his greatcoat, pulled the fur hat over his ears, and stepped into the snow. The wind slammed the car door. He stumbled into the stone house and went out on the pier.

Ch'en had done his homework. The Americans' cute trick with the auto slowed him down but didn't stop him. At the London Embassy the communications center kept him advised of Porkowski's movements. By then, Chinese agents assigned to watch KGB reported the Soviet interest in Dr. Madderly, who was involved in the meeting with the Secretary of State at the airport. It was simple to discover Madderly's destination was Helsinki. And when Porkowski showed up again in London and immediately embarked for Finland, Ch'en was cleared to follow. The local media informed him of the meetings on Hintsanen's island.

The next step was routine detective work. He picked up a Finn operative and staked out the pier. The telephotos were sent to London and several faces were identified, the most significant being that of Dr. Yuri Antonich, assistant to Professor Golchov of the Pavlov Institute.

An urgent communiqué came back with Antonich's I.D. "Peking assigns top priority to Golchov. Imperative you discover link between Madderly and Antonich. Repeat—imperative."

Ch'en ducked away from the icy wind. What now? First things first. Had to cross the bay to the island. No more boats at the pier. He felt for the automatic that was holstered underneath his left arm. All right. Get in the car and drive until he raised another boathouse.

Timo brought the craft through the blinding snow with unwavering accuracy. The illuminated boathouse appeared before them like a yellow eye. A boatman guided the launch in and made it fast fore and aft. Timo shut down the engines and signaled them to follow.

As Timo stepped from the deck to the dock, Gouzenko shot a dart into his broad back, then put one into the boatman's chest. Both men staggered and fell without making a sound.

The Russians crossed the courtyard and entered the castle. Tamara shot the maid who stood ready to take their coats and, a moment later, a housekeeper who happened to walk in from the foyer. Then Tamara went to the kitchen and took care of the cook and his staff.

"Fast!" whispered Gouzenko, his gun ready.

Antonich followed him down the hall to the drawing room. Elina and Madderly were there, along with Dr. Chambers and Relling.

"What's all this?" shouted Relling.

Gouzenko shot him.

Dr. Chambers sprang to her feet and tried to run past the two Russians. Gouzenko shot her in the thigh.

Madderly put himself between Elina and them. "Are you crazy?" he exclaimed. "What—"

Antonich aimed the gun at his face. "No madness here, Professor," he said. His hand trembled. "We do not plan to shoot you and Miss Hintsanen, provided you do not give us reason to. Please sit on the sofa."

"They are your responsibility," Gouzenko said. "I will see to the others."

Gouzenko moved out of the room and down the hall. He knew Wills, Porkowski and Towers were in the castle. But where?

He tried one door after another.

The rooms were empty.

Then he heard voices and slowed his pace. A door at the end of the hall opened. Gouzenko flattened himself against the wall and waited for it to close.

Hintsanen, in his wheelchair.

Did the paralyzed man show any shock of recognition at what was happening? Gouzenko could not tell. He aimed and put a dart in his shoulder. Hintsanen slumped forward in the chair, one pale hand touching the carpet.

Now Gouzenko flung open the door.

A strange room, lined with cabinets, void of furniture save for a table and several plain chairs. Television equipment on the table and the floor around it.

The one called Wills looked up, a cigar clenched between his teeth. Gouzenko aimed for his heart and pulled the trigger. The cigar dropped from his lips.

Porkowski screamed. Gouzenko shot him in

the back as he tried to escape. The fat man rolled over once and was still.

Towers?

No one else in the room.

Gouzenko stepped over Porkowski's body.

A shadow brushed by the door.

The Russian crouched, waited, the gun held in both hands now, and aimed at the opening.

A blur, a figure hurtling through the door.

Gouzenko fired, blindly, quickly.

One dart missed. Another caught Towers in the stomach.

Gouzenko saw him struggle against the numbing drug. It was as though the scene were on film and the projectionist had switched abruptly to slow motion. Towers clawed at the dart, plucked it free, and fell to the floor. His eyes followed Gouzenko's movement, but his hand could not reach out for the pistol that fell from his fingers.

Gouzenko went cautiously down the hall, checking the rooms once more.

Empty.

Tamara was with Antonich. "All is well in the kitchen," she said. "I turned off the oven. No need to spoil lunch."

"How thoughtful," said Madderly.

"Your coats," said Gouzenko. "Get them."

"Suppose we refuse to go with you?" asked Madderly.

"Then I will shoot the girl," said Gouzenko, pulling a small automatic from his waistband. "With real bullets, not these darts."

"I am not afraid!" said Elina.

"No. But then you are still alive at the moment," the Russian said.

"The others are not dead?" said Madderly.

"Incapacitated," Antonich replied.

Gouzenko checked his watch. "Let us go.

Now, quickly!"

Wills tried to move. He concentrated on the fingers of his right hand. He focused on the little finger.

Sweat popped out on his forehead. But the finger did not move.

God, what a mess! he thought, trying to speak the words. But his voice was gone too. Whatever it was the Soviets used, it was mighty powerful.

He would have smiled, but his lips—it was as though they weren't there; it was as though every part of him except his mind had been turned to stone.

Death, is this what it's like? he wondered.

And the Russians, what the hell were they up to? How could he have miscalculated? Or had they miscalculated? Yes, he was playing the game according to the rules, such as they were. But the other side broke the rules—not that breaking them wasn't allowed. But there were certain ways of breaking them. And this action just wasn't called for. It didn't make sense.

Unless—unless they knew something that he didn't.

Wills gave off thinking and tried his little finger again. There seemed to be a slight movement. Yes, he detected the texture of the rug on which he lay. And now he smelled something burning. His cigar? The carpet? His own coat?

Porkowski groaned.

Wills lay with his head propped against one leg of the table. From this angle he saw the door and Towers and Porkowski. Stan's foot moved. He was big, heavy; perhaps the drug dosage in the dart was measured for a certain average weight?

The foot moved again and now Porkowski moaned, "Oh, help me."

A shadow moved in the doorway. A form took shape. An automatic pistol held in a gloved hand attached to a bulky sleeve that was part of a bulkier coat wet with snow.

An Oriental face. A bandage above one eye going up and across the forehead, burrowing underneath a fur hat.

The eyes were slits. The mouth was a slit that moved, that formed words:

"What the hell?" it said.

"Help me," Porkowski moaned again.

"I'll help you, you fat bastard!" said the Chinese. He drew back a wet boot and kicked Stan in the ribs.

"No, Ch'en, don't—help me," said Porkowski.

Ch'en—Chinese, thought Wills. Social Affairs? Sure. Everyone including the referee was in on the action.

"Talk! Fast!" said Ch'en.

"You—you got my message?" said Porkowski.

Ch'en kicked him again. "Message my ass! I got you, Sweets, in the groove." He pressed the automatic to Porkowski's cheek.

"No—wait—a mistake."

"Killing you is no mistake. I'll get a Nobel for it."

"It wasn't—my—doing—Wills caused your—accident."

"So maybe he gets it too."

"But—but I have—information—Madderly—"

"All I hear is pig squeals. Talk sense while you got breath."

"Madderly—and the girl—the Russians—abducted them—to Leningrad—Golchov."

Wills studied those strange eyes. It was as though, for the moment, he too was psychic. He knew what was going on in Ch'en's mind. Stan was a known liar. But this shameful demonstration was proof that for once he was telling the truth.

Wills felt his own hand make a fist. The drug was wearing off. Question was, would the Chinaman give him a dose of something more substantial, like lead? In his shoes, Wills knew exactly what he would do.

"The truth—it's the truth—I swear."

Ch'en laughed. "So the Bears pulled a little job, yeah? Only to avoid bad press they used drugged darts, right? Like to say, No hard feelings, folks, just fun and games!"

He laughed again and aimed the automatic at Porkowski's stomach.

"Maybe I should ruin their press, yeah? Do the real thing with you nice people. They get the blame. Cool!"

"But—the truth—I told—"

Wills was confused. Stan had not sold out completely. Of course, that was shrewd, actually. Always keep a little something out of sight for an even worse time.

"And I'm going to enjoy plugging you!"

Plugging? A B movie.

"You first, Sweetie, then, him, and afterwards the rest."

"But—Madderly—Antonich—they're escaping. You must—catch them—you—"

Ch'en frowned. "Yeah, but first things first."

Ch'en aimed and fired twice.

The big automatic rocked back. The room shook with the reports. But in spite of the noise, Wills heard the two slugs tear through Porkowski's flesh. It was the same *thump! thump!* he had heard as a boy when a cop had put an injured dog out of its misery.

Stan's body shook, then shook no more.

The gun now aimed at him.

Wills tried to move, but succeeded only in raising his hand.

"Batter up!" said the Chinese.

Another shot, but a different sound to it.

Wills winced but felt nothing, saw nothing, realized his eyes were shut, opened them, and saw the Chinese backing through the door.

Another shot from down the corridor. Then two more shots sounded as Ch'en returned fire at whoever it was. Towers, it must be Towers, thought Wills.

Then the sound of running.

God, thought Wills, what now?

As he passed through the courtyard, Ch'en reconstructed the island in his mind's eye. Snow made air escape impossible. Had to be a boat. Where would it land? At the far end was a lighthouse and a cove opening to the Gulf of Finland.

He paused, the snow whirling into his face, his head injury throbbing anew. Which way? Boathouse was to the north. Right, turn right. Yes, a door. It opened and he felt a hard surface under his feet. He staggered against the wind and tucked the automatic in his coat pocket to prevent the mechanism from freezing.

A wall loomed before him, then a gate that opened automatically as he passed. Electric eye? Never mind — move! Now he was going uphill into the forest. Among the trees he could see perhaps five yards. Footprints were barely visible. They had come this way.

Ch'en increased his speed. What would he do when he caught them? Porkowski said Madderly was involved with Golchov. That's why KGB nabbed him. The girl, who was she?

He pulled himself through the snow, searching for tracks, damning the terrible ache in his wounded head. Twice he slipped into depressions hidden underneath drifts. As he topped a hill overlooking a clearing, he saw dark figures blurred against white.

He slipped the automatic from his pocket, checked the clip and slide, and started down after them.

His foot caught on an outcrop of rock and he stumbled, waved his arms in a vain attempt to regain his balance, and fell. He rolled, then skidded to the bottom of the hill.

When he got back on his feet, they were once more in among the trees. He heard them shouting. They had seen him, and now it was a race. Perhaps to the death.

He plunged after them, throwing caution to the freezing wind. He had nothing to lose. His orders were clear. Get Madderly, or stop the Soviets from getting him. If they got away with the American professor, there'd be hell to pay.

He saw them again, through the trees, moving. All right, time to let them know he meant business. He dropped to one knee, braced the pistol with both hands, fired.

The report flushed a flock of birds from the limbs overhead, dislodging a shower of powdered snow. The bullet zinged off a branch, kicked up a plume of white. He fired again through the haze and heard a cry of pain.

He went slower now, more carefully. He must have hit one of them. There were five bunched together. Odds were when you fired into a group you'd hit something. But no good to rush in like a damn fool.

Ch'en moved to the left to make a circle and approach from the flank.

"Go, go on!" Gouzenko said.

Tamara knelt beside him. "Where are you wounded?"

Antonich said, "In the chest—look at the blood."

"Nothing—it's nothing," Gouzenko said. "Go. We must link with the other force."

"I cannot leave you."

"We must," said Antonich. "The mission!"

"Yes, the mission," Gouzenko said. "And I will not die. Take them—go."

Tamara glanced at Madderly and Elina crouched nearby. Antonich guarded them. Gouzenko was bleeding terribly. Blood seeped through his heavy coat and made an ugly red stain in the snow. She touched his cheek, tried to speak what she felt.

But he turned his face away from her fingers and said, "I order you! Deliver them to the ship. Send back for me. I will—will be all right—I—"

"Hurry!" urged Antonich.

Tamara searched Gouzenko's eyes. She knew that whoever was out there would kill him. Orders or not, she could not leave him.

"I'm going," said Antonich.

He opened the front of Gouzenko's coat and found his pistol. He tossed the dart gun into the snow and covered Madderly and Elina with this new and lethal weapon.

"Let us go," he said to Tamara.

Tamara shook her head. "I will stay. Send aid."

"Yes, aid," said Antonich. He waved the pistol at Madderly and Elina. "On your feet now, move!"

Gouzenko stared at Tamara. "You are wrong—crazy—obey me."

Tamara refastened his coat, then took off her

own and placed it over him. "I cannot leave you," she said. "You are right. I am crazy."

She sat in the snow beside him, the cold seeping through her clothing like ice water, and waited for the one who would kill them both.

I must be crazy, indeed, she decided. But so be it.

Ch'en worked his way down an icy slope into a ravine. He stopped to listen. The birds raised by his shots had resettled. The only sound was wind moaning through the firs. And blood pounding in his temples. The pain! His head was splitting!

He leaned against a rock and fought back a feeling of nausea. He tried to forget the pain by formulating a plan. He would wait, yes, give the wounded time to weaken from loss of blood. He had seen what looked like blood. And someone cried out. A man—or woman—hit by a nine-mm slug would not get far in this terrain under these conditions.

He waited three minutes by his wrist watch.

It was all the time he could allow.

By now the ones in the castle must be pursuing. And what about the Soviets at the ship?

Three minutes.

He manipulated the slide again to make sure the automatic was functioning, then picked his way up the reverse slope of the ravine. Exposed roots made the going easier, though they were coated with slippery ice. At the crest he paused and listened. Wind—a flutter of birds—a cough!

They were just beyond!

His first impulse was to turn back, to try another way. But time was running out. His foot slipped. Did they hear him?

He rested for a moment and pressed his hand against the bandage to squeeze away the pain.

He had the advantage of surprise. He had to act—now.

Ch'en felt for a step in the rocks, found one, grasped a stunted fir above with his left hand. The gun was ready. One—two—three!

He came over the crest clumsily, hit the snow and rolled for cover behind a tree. There was a small valley, hardly more than a depression, and a clearing ringed with firs. They were in the clearing facing the direction from which he fired at them.

How many?

It looked like two—one sprawled on the snow, the other crouched beside.

And the others?

A faint trail went into the trees beyond.

Ch'en moved farther to his left and worked into the firs. He was now close enough to hear labored breathing and to see a red splash across the snow.

Tamara sensed he was there behind them, watching, waiting. She wiped moisture from Gouzenko's lips and tried again to stop the flow of blood. No use. Everything that touched him came away crimson.

The enemy was closer now. Any moment he would come through the trees and shoot them. Unless. . .Where was her dart pistol? She dropped it when Gouzenko was hit. The snow hid it. His was missing too. They were unarmed, helpless.

She heard the crunch of boots breaking through crusty snow, then a voice:

"Don't move! Yell and you're dead!"

She turned slowly and saw Ch'en coming towards her.

A Chinese.

They were dead now, unless she could reason with him, convince him they had information.

His head—a bandage—and blood. Yes, a spot of red against the white. She stared at the bandage. He weaved as he walked. He seemed tired. And now his hand touched the bandage and his thin lips clenched as though he felt great pain.

"The others," he said, "where are they? Where's the ship?"

His voice was sharp with pain. She focused all her attention on the bandage and said, "You are wounded, also, Comrade."

He laughed weakly. "Comrade? The others? Tell me!"

The automatic became a deadly third eye gazing down on them. It was a black hole into which they would tumble, unless. . .

Tamara remembered her grandmother, the tricks she had played on others by making them think they had bugs in their ears. She recalled Golchov's demonstration on Moscow television. If only she had that power.

"You are weak, lightheaded, Comrade," she said, her eyes staring at the wound. "You feel faint! The world is spinning round like a top inside your head. Your brain is on fire. You are falling, falling."

Ch'en blinked.

He lowered the automatic.

He raised his left hand to the bandage, then looked at the fresh blood on his glove.

"It is too late for the others now," Tamara said, her voice a firm monotone, her eyes never leaving his face. "You must think of yourself, Comrade. Do not struggle against the pain. Give it freedom to act and you will feel it no longer."

Ch'en dropped to his knees. Something within him seemed to swell and burst. It was as though his skull had split and all the pain ran out, and now he felt only a terrible need for sleep.

He sprawled, face first, into the snow.

Tamara sprang to his side and pried the pistol from his fingers.

She aimed down at him and turned her face away as she pulled the trigger.

How long she stood between the two fallen men she did not know. Perhaps seconds, perhaps long minutes. Then she was aware of a voice shouting from a hill in the direction of the sea. A man was there among the black trees yelling in Russian for her to hurry. The party from the ship. They would help! She ran toward the hill.

Gouzenko saw her moving away from him. He thought of her pleasantly, as he might have considered a summer sky or a field of sunflowers or a moonlit lake. He no longer knew pain. In the snow it was warm. Overhead, the clouds were soft, comforting.

But he was not dead yet, and if the Americans captured, him, he would not be able to resist their interrogation. They would find a way to make him tell all he knew about the Center, about the mission.

He struggled to lift his arm and bring his hand close to his face. The heavy coat did not wish to fall away, but he gathered all his strength and shook his forearm, freeing the cuff. The buttons glistened like jewels. Zharkov's secretary, the one with the round eyeglasses, had been kind enough to make the switch. He pressed the middle one to his lips, took it between his teeth, and forced his jaws shut.

There was a faint crunch, as of candy breaking.

Death was quick, death was merciful, they said.

But it did not come. The pieces of button did not dissolve into poison. Someone had made a mistake. He would die when it was time, no sooner, no later.

The irony of his situation made him shake his head in wonder. The slug moved deep within his chest like a knife blade. He felt a warmth on his lips. New blood.

He would die like a warrior on the field of battle, yes, and if no one claimed his body, birds would dine upon his flesh, and it was all one because. . .because. . .

At the sound of the gunshot Madderly halted and looked back. Antonich pushed him roughly, saying, "No tricks—move!"

"Who is shooting?" asked Elina.

"It does not matter," Antonich replied. "Perhaps she has ended his pain."

"She would not do that. We are being followed."

"All the more reason to hurry."

They did as Antonich ordered, and soon men in white camouflage suits appeared on either side of the path. One spoke Antonich's name. The two conversed rapidly.

Elina touched Madderly's arm, whispered, "They found Katya and Stephan in the lighthouse."

Madderly frowned and watched the two pairs of lips spouting Russian.

"But they don't know who they are," said Elina. "The marine captain wants instructions regarding them."

"And Antonich is a bloodthirsty—" Madderly began.

"No. Antonich says lock them in the cellar." She smiled at this joke. Madderly squeezed her hand.

Now Antonich commanded them to follow him and his three armed men to the beach. They boarded inflatable dinghies. The marines slung their automatic rifles and manned the paddles.

A shot sounded, distant but audible, followed by an echo.

The Russian marines on the beach crouched behind boulders and trees and took aim.

The dinghies moved across two hundred yards of smooth black water to a sleek gray craft, a hydrofoil, whose turbo engines whined like those of a jet plane. They floated past one of the insect-like arms which would drop down at a certain speed and raise the ship up on pontoons. A seaman secured the dinghies and they were helped aboard and taken immediately through a large cabin down a companionway into another cabin below deck.

Two men and two women dressed in hospital whites were waiting. Still pointing the pistol at Madderly and Elina, Antonich said, "You will cooperate with the doctors or you will be forced to cooperate. Have it as you will."

Madderly eyed the two hospital beds, the various pieces of equipment laid out wrapped in sterile plastic. The situation reminded him of something once viewed in a long-forgotten high school play, something juvenile, absurd.

Antonich noted his smile. "This is not a humorous moment, Professor," he declared. "Blood has been shed to bring you here. You will submit, or else!"

The pistol trembled underneath Madderly's nose.

Antonich's nerves weren't to be taken lightly. Madderly said, "All right, what do you want of us?"

For openers, they gave him and Elina rubber tubes to swallow. As they gagged them down, the nurses took blood samples. What Antonich was up to became clear to Madderly. He was after the magic drug.

The tube was bitter, rough. Elina was choking and so was he. Would it be easier to tell the truth, to explain the drug was sugar, nothing more?

But that revelation would create more problems than it would solve. Katya and Stephan, for one.

Madderly felt the suctioning tickle the pit of his stomach. He thought of the augurs of old, disemboweling animals and tossing their entrails into the dust in vain attempts to foretell the future.

The future?

NINE

From the drawing room window Wills watched a detail of marines from the embassy muscle the stiff bodies of Porkowski and Relling to the far side of the lawn, where, the next morning, a NATO chopper would pick them up.

Relling. Porkowski.

Those were not the names their loving mothers bestowed on them. He did not know their real names. It was better that way. The game itself was so unreal to a thinking man that—

He shook his head. Still dizzy from that damned drug. Cigar tasted bitter. He tossed it in the fireplace and lit another.

Porkowski and Relling.

Men from nowhere, headed nowhere.

To avoid embarrassing questions, their corpses would be hauled to an American naval vessel in the Baltic. Maybe they would be shipped stateside for burial; more than likely they'd be sewn in bags, weighted, and slipped over the side.

Wills returned to the window and again observed the marines. Towers was leading them. He recognized—or thought he recognized—the young fellow who drove them in from the airport.

Three more bodies were laid across the lawn by the wall.

Gouzenko. The girl, Rostov. The Chinese, Ch'en, or whoever he was.

After Relling crawled into the hall and fired the shot that drew the Chinese away and saved Wills' life, Towers was the first to shake off enough of the effects of the drug to move around.

Relling was dead. The Chinese had shot him through the heart.

And Porkowski was dead.

Towers took off in pursuit of Madderly and Elina.

It was tough going in the snow, and he would have gotten lost had it not been for the sound of Ch'en's pistol. Towers arrived on the scene as Rostov was moving away. He saw the two bodies in the snow. They might have been Madderly and Elina—he couldn't be sure—so he fired and hit Rostov as she reached the crest of the hill.

By the time Towers made it to the lighthouse, the Russians were gone. He released Katya and Stephan from the cellar and brought them back to the castle. Now, Wills was able to function almost normally. He immediately called the embassy and requested help to straighten out the mess.

The bodies could be disposed of easily enough. Even now the marines were digging a common grave for the three communist operatives. Blood could be mopped up. But there were other aspects of this mess which Wills was powerless to tend to.

Where the hell had he gone wrong? He still had no idea why the damn Russians did this. God, it was so stupid! But maybe it was he who was stupid, not the Russians.

He studied the neat white ash on his cigar.

Looking on the bright side, if it could be called that, no one could prove a government connection. Yes, Washington was in the clear—as usual. It was one thing for Madderly and Elina to go to the Soviet Union at invitation; it was quite another for them to be hauled off at gunpoint.

There was absolutely nothing he or the government could do now except play the waiting game. There would be no inquiries; couldn't be, without blowing the whole thing to the world.

No, they were out on a limb, alone.

Dr. Chambers came into the room. "How's the patient?" she asked. "Ready for another shock?"

"What now?"

"Our host has vanished, along with the launch and Timo."

Wills said nothing.

"My guess is he's bound for the city of Lenin. What's yours?"

Wills was exhausted. It was out of his hands now. "How in hell do I know?" he said.

Chambers shrugged. "Maybe Hintsanen thinks he can persuade the Russians to release Elina. And let's not forget that he wants to be healed more than anything else. Of the two theories, I'd bet on the second."

"But she's his daughter."

Dr. Chambers laughed. "Sentiment? From you? Son-of-a-bitch! That Finn's a tough case."

Wills rubbed his eyes. Maybe what she said was true. If so, Madderly was in even deeper water, if that were possible.

He had to think about himself now, had to get his mind and body back together, had to reestablish his objectivity. He needed rest, sleep.

Chambers had pills for every occasion.

But he knew that this time she'd turn him down.

He wouldn't give her the opportunity.

"One happy note," said Chambers. "Katya and Stephan are safe. Maybe we can use her 'gift' to help the lost children?"

Anything was worth a try. Wills nodded. "Have a talk with them. I'm going to take a nap."

"Sure. Sweet dreams. Don't have a nightmare."

"If I do, it can't be worse than what's been happening while I'm awake."

The Neva ice groaned and tossed its massive weight against the Strelka bulkheads like a colossal amphibian of a bygone era when the world was new and primitive monsters ruled the planet.

Golchov poured a brandy from a crystal decanter set upon the mahogany side table. Both decanter and table had come from the president of the University in recognition of some achievement of which Golchov was no longer certain. The pieces once graced one of the Czar's pleasure nests. Forward-thinking workers had liberated them during the victorious revolution.

The brandy was aromatic, heady. He swirled the snifter, sipped, and relaxed in a wing chair before a window overlooking the river. The fire crackled cozily. How good to be surrounded by the amenities of life. The uncooperative "guests," the imprisoned Russian sensitives, shivered in the basement. Let them—the damn fools! They had their chance to serve the cause, as did Pavel Golchov.

Ragusa would whip them into line, the brute. Or genius?

Golchov circled the snifter beneath his nose and inhaled the vapor.

He had drunk stronger stuff, stuff more potent by far. At mid-morning Ragusa slipped into a trance state and was able to see a great distance. The words he uttered were recorded and sent to the proper authorities for verification.

Golchov smiled.

This time the subject was none other than the

donkey himself, Nikoyan. Perhaps he would be impressed to hear the sweet private names he called his newest "secretary?" Perhaps this little reminder would serve as a cordial warning that he should attend to official matters and leave science to scientists.

Golchov laughed out loud and enjoyed his prank.

Then he frowned.

Where would this work lead, finally? What were the implications?

And how, exactly, did Ragusa do whatever it was he did? That was the big question.

Natasha was trying to block his power. It was possible that at times she succeeded, for Ragusa's misses now far outnumbered his hits.

But he still got results in spite of her foolishness. A bitch and a witch!

Now she sulked in her cold cell, muttering nonsense about *white* magic and *black* magic. Since there was no such thing as magic, he cared not what color she painted it so long as the power, whatever it was, worked.

That was the problem. If he could isolate the power itself and learn to produce it in the clean, well-lighted labs of the Institute, then he'd have no further need of Ragusa and his sinister machinations.

Until then, well, it was good to keep an ace in the hole to use against this man, or beast, or devil—or whatever he was.

A silver bullet and a white witch. He was ready for any contingency.

Even this Madderly.

Golchov checked the time. How far to Helsinki by sea? Antonich's message was taut with excitement: "Have Madderly. Repeat: Have Madderly. Arrive Kronstadt ealry A.M. and proceed to Institute."

"And what does one have, exactly, when one has a Madderly?" Golchov asked the distorted reflection eyeing him from the bright surface of the brandy snifter.

At Kronstadt searchlights guided the icebreakers as they forged ahead, opening a path. The KGB hydrofoil found clear water and crossed the harbor to the restricted landing zone.

Bazarov left the bridge and went below deck. He found Antonich in the dispensary. His face was quite green and his round eyes shone like puddles of oil. The silly fool was seasick. A corpsman had dosed him with several remedies, but only stiff drinks of vodka had any effect, and they did not solve his problem. The alcohol gave him a nonchalant attitude and he seemed to be considering his plight from a distance of several feet.

"How goes it?" asked Bazarov.

"It comes, it goes," Antonich replied, his tone remindful of the steady rhythm of the sea.

"And our guests—your examinations are completed?"

"The specimens are ready for analysis. There will be other tests at the Institute. For now they are drugged."

"Then they will present no difficulty during the trip to the Institute. I have arranged for an ambulance. Can you handle this responsiblity?"

"Yes, I shall be my old self once we land."

"We are tying up now. End your—medication, and prepare the two for transport."

"Yes, Comrade Colonel." Antonich wiped his brow with a damp cloth. "And may I inquire your estimation of the manner in which I discharged my duties?"

"A first-rate job. I imagine there will be a commendation. At the proper time, of course."

Antonich smiled weakly and extended his hand. Bazarov had no choice but to congratulate him again. Antonich grasped his fingers, as though he would never release them and said, "I will accept it, of course, as a matter of duty. But I confess I had my doubts about this mission. That Gouzenko—and Rostov. Had they followed my suggestion and used lethal weapons they would be alive today!"

Bazarov succeeded in disengaging his hand. His palm felt greasy. He nodded, mumbled a few meaningless words that someone like Antonich would take for agreement, and said, "I must return to Moscow. You are responsible for Madderly and Miss Hintsanen. Understood?"

"Certainly. Have no fear. All is under my personal control."

The new confidence of the ass is dangerous, thought Bazarov, coming on deck. How ironic that he, who seemed most inept, should survive, while two good agents like Rostov and Gouzenko did not. Soon Antonich would be impossible to deal with.

The gangway was secure. Bazarov wrapped his greatcoat about him and hurried across the dock into the security check, where he found a samovar of tea and a moment's reprieve from the numbing wind.

The trail ran fast and narrow through the dark trees, a ribbon of snow sparkling under a fat yellow moon. Madderly crouched on the skis, the poles held ready in his gloved hands, listening to the runners' hum, feeling a knife thrust of cold slicing between his goggles and skin.

The path dipped, then rose. Madderly's weight shifted forward to take whatever lay just over the ridge. But there was nothing—no trees, no snow—only the smiling yellow moon, and, as he soared over it, stars, forming serpentine designs upon the night.

He flew, the skis becoming leather wings, hollow bat-like things, stinking of smoke and sweat.

He fell. . .

The bed caught him.

At first he did not know it was a bed. It was a certain tangible softness which held him suspended above the rocks below.

Then the rocks were gone and he rolled over on his side and opened his eyes.

A window presented itself.

Through the streaked glass lay a city of gray buildings and a river of grayer ice bordered by dirty drifts of snow.

Children scrambled about on the frozen river. The sky was a still deeper gray, patched by a few spots of bright blue through which shafts of pearly sunlight shone.

Madderly's throat hurt. The pain made him remember. A rubber tube, and afterwards a quantity of blood drawn from the vein in his right arm. He felt a bit of adhesive tape there now. Later they wanted a urine sample. At first he balked, but when they waved a catheter under his nose, he said what the hell and gave them what they wanted.

He blew up a red balloon. He supplied them with saliva. He watched as they checked his pulse, blood pressure, respiration rate and reflexes.

And in way of payment for his cooperation, they jabbed a needle in his left arm.

Madderly sat up in the bed and rubbed the bump that the needle had made as it pumped in a drug that brought sweet dreams. The room was square, the bare walls done in oak paneling. A single light hung from the ceiling, which was traced with a crazy-quilt of fine cracks. Madderly wondered how many before him had lain in this same bed, studying that overhead map of unknown territory.

The bed was the type used in hospital wards—high, equipped with wheels and gears for adjustments. The sheets smelled of starch. A small table by the head of the bed supported a water bottle capped with an inverted glass. On the wall by the door hung a framed picture of Lenin; his cool eyes seemed to be peering out the window at the city bearing his name.

The door was painted a bright yellow. No knob or lock, so it must be opened from the outside. Three-quarters of the way up its surface was a small blemish. Madderly slipped from the bed and discovered a wide-angle viewing device which permitted persons on the other side to observe the interior.

And what would they see?

Madderly looked at himself. They had taken his clothes and dressed him in green cotton pajamas and a green robe reaching to his ankles. A pair of slippers were under the bed.

What time was it?

His watch was gone.

How long had he been out?

He went to the window and tried to get his bearings. Children at play meant no school, but what were holidays in the Soviet Union?

He was thirsty, dizzy. Elina, was she safe? And what happened to Wills and the others?

He tried to reason out answers to these questions, but the more he thought, the more confused he became.

He drank a glass of water and climbed back into bed.

What would happen when Antonich learned he had been tricked? That was the big question.

Before he could imagine an answer, there was a quick knock, and almost simultaneously the door opened.

Yuri Antonich strolled in, followed by two women in white laboratory smocks.

"Good morning, Professor Madderly," he said, smiling broadly. "Welcome to Leningrad. Are you rested?"

"I've got a hangover—know what that is?"

"Of course. Perhaps a raw egg would help?"

"Two aspirin would be easier to swallow."

Antonich spoke in Russian to one of the women. She left the room and returned in a moment and handed Madderly a paper cup with two white tablets inside. He shook them into his palm. Aspirin looked the same the world over. He popped them into his mouth. Tasted the same too.

Antonich filled the cup. As Madderly drank, the thought crossed his mind that Antonich must not have gotten the results of the tests. Time to gain all the advantage he could—before the Russian's cordiality went as sour as the aspirin.

Madderly crushed the paper cup and tossed it on the floor. "Some dirty thief stole my clothes," he said.

Antonich laughed. "They were filthy with the capitalist grime of Finland, so I took the liberty of having them cleaned. Anna!"

One of the women pushed a small cart through the door. His things were neatly laid out upon it, even his watch. His shoes had been shined.

"Dress," said Antonich. "Then we will eat. You have an appetite?"

"Sure. Got any horses lying around?"

"Horses? This is the Soviet Union. We have modern automobiles."

Then I'll have one Ford, over light, thought Madderly, after the Russians left him alone.

The dining room was dominated by a large window hung with slightly faded purple drapes. Elina sat at the table, her back to the window, facing the door. Antonich directed Madderly to a chair beside hers and said, "And so we are all together again."

To Elina, Madderly said, "Are you all right?"

"Yes. They gave me an injection and I am a little dizzy, but otherwise I am fine. And you?"

Antonich said, "Dr. Madderly is in excellent health. Notice the bloom on his cheeks."

"Yes, I feel well enough to travel."

"Not away from us?"

"Suppose I said 'escape'?"

"From me? From the Institute? My dear comrade in science, you are not a prisoner."

"Oh?" said Madderly. "And you didn't kidnap us.?"

"Kidnap is such a crude word. The truth is we borrowed you for a time."

"Does that mean you will return us, like perhaps a book to a library?" asked Elina.

Antonich's smile became a trifle strained. "Let us face facts—clear the air, so to speak—so we may enjoy our food. At this moment our analysts are determing the makeup of the drug you used to induce telepathy. Once we have an approximation of it, we will have no further use for either of you."

"So you shoot us."

Antonich shook his head. "I will admit the thought crossed my mind. But I dismissed it as being an unnecessary action, and hardly in the spirit of détente. When we are satisfied, you may leave. We will buy you plane tickets—first class, of course. Or, if you choose, you may stay in the Soviet Union and join in the great task of bringing lasting peace to the world."

"Very pretty words," said Madderly. "But haven't you overlooked one point?"

The worry lines that sprang upon the Russian's brow told Madderly that he had made his share of errors before.

"What point is that?" he asked.

"Both sides will have the telepathic drug."

The worry lines went away as Antonich replied, "But you have the drug already, correct? Killing you and the lovely Miss Hintsanen would not change that fact. No, this time you have made the mistake."

"Perhaps," said Madderly, "but I imagine that at this moment my government is protesting to yours. You've created an international incident."

"The disappearance of two persons is not an incident on the international level," said Antonich. "Washington and Helsinki have said not a word. More than likely they will remain mute."

He smiled again. "And so, you must accept my hospitality, like it or not. And I think you will like breakfast, at least. Try the coffee, please. It is excellent Colombian."

"And afterwards Golchov will join us?"

"Perhaps sooner. At present he is in his laboratory."

Dish after dish was served. Madderly found the eggs and fluffy potato cakes to his liking. The herring was tasty too. He sampled a cinnamon and sugar pastry, and could not resist a small cheese omelette garnished with green onion.

The condemned man ate a hearty meal, he thought.

Elina picked at her food. Madderly said, "Eat, we'll be on bread and water tomorrow."

Antonich smirked. "Or champagne and caviar, not to mention—"

The door opened and a middle-aged man wearing a long white laboratory coat entered.

Antonich jumped to his feet. "Professor, will you join us now?"

"Certainly. Why else should I be here?"

"Yes, yes. This is Miss Hintsanen and here is—"

"Yuri, sit. Your food grows cold. I looked in on our guests when they arrived. Miss Hintsanen. Professor." He bowed slightly, then took a seat. One serving woman filled his cup, while the other prepared a plate.

Golchov undid his napkin with a magician's flourish and tucked one corner into the collar of his shirt. He tried a bite of the herring, smacked his lips, and said to Madderly, "You are not eating. Is it our menu or our manners that are at fault?"

"We're not here by choice."

Golchov nodded as he chewed. "But the food is good."

"We wish to contact our people, to let them know that for the moment we are all right."

"Your people—yes, that reminds me," said Golchov. He took a folded piece of paper from his lab coat and carefully placed it beside his plate.

He had another forkful of herring, chewed slowly, thoughtfully, swallowed, and said, "I am a busy man. You would not believe how busy."

"Yes, we are indeed busy," said Antonich. "The work, the thousand details—busy."

Golchov shut his eyes, then opened them and looked at Madderly. "However, my crowded schedule does not diminish my interest in stories. Yours is most exciting. It has a sort of Tolstoyian expansiveness which is fascinating, although, frankly, I prefer to plumb the depths with Dostoyevsky."

Antonich said, "I told him every detail."

"Yes, Yuri, you did that. Yuri has a great capacity for detail. He is a goldmine—of misinformation."

Antonich beamed. But as he realized that Golchov's remark was unflattering, his smile faded and he balanced on the edge of his chair, pale, at a loss for a single word to utter.

Golchov finished the herring and tossed down a cup of tea.

This is where it hits the fan, thought Madderly. Was the old fox fishing or, more likely, did he know the truth by now? Madderly attempted to open his mind to the Russian's thoughts, but a slight dizziness from the sedative disrupted the process.

"More time is wasted," said Golchov.

"They—they have deceived us?" asked Antonich. "But the tests, the—"

"Not us. *You*!" said Golchov. He handed him the folded paper. "Your test results. Read them aloud, please."

Yuri opened the paper, then turned it over and over. His face pinched with confusion, with fear. "But this is blank. There is nothing. Do you mean. . ."

"Nothing. The same as your results."

"But that is not possible!"

"Perhaps not possible, but true nonetheless."

"I do not see—"

"There is much you do not see, Yuri. Perhaps you look too hard? Yes, you have strained yourself. A long vacation during which you rest your eyes is in order."

"Vacation? They are giving me a commendation!" He shook the piece of paper at Golchov. "You are tricking me!"

Golchov slowly shook his head. "The substance which you claim induced a telepathic state in our guests does not exist. I suppose the capsules were loaded with something harmless, like powdered milk or plain sugar."

"No!" cried Antonich. "If you are not tricking me then it is Bazarov!"

"First 'they,' then 'Bazarov'? Tell me, Professor Madderly, who can he mean?"

"I don't know, unless it's the KGB."

Antonich's face was crimson. He stammered, "I do not know why you ridicule me! Did I not carry out my assignment?"

Golchov patted his assistant's hand. "You have done a wonderful job, even if it was stupid. And if you are KGB, what does it matter? We are all Soviets, eh? Now that I think about it, the name Bazarov is not unfamiliar. Did he not lend a hand in rounding up our psychics?"

Watching the exchange between the two Russians, Madderly was aware of an unfolding drama. One did not call a KGB man an ass unless one held a pat hand. Golchov was bringing Antonich to his knees and at the same time announcing his power. The KGB might be the secret police—but Golchov was Golchov. They made mistakes; he did not.

"And one other point," said Golchov, "minor, granted, but still a point. In your report you do not account for the film of Anna Letovskaya. Did you lose it?"

Antonich's lips trembled. "I left it behind when we evacuated the Hintsanen estate."

"Then I suppose it cannot be recovered. Very well, you will have to pay for it."

Madderly said, "He left the projector too."

Golchov laughed. "Oh? Well, that is part of

the Helsinki embassy's inventory."

Yuri stood up and pounded his fist on the table. "I do not understand this!" he exclaimed. "I was there. I saw with my own two eyes. Gouzenko and Rostov saw also. Madderly and Miss Hintsanen did communicate telepathically! They did!"

"Yes," said Golchov, "that they did."

"Then what—"

"The drug was a clever ruse designed to whet your appetite to know more," said Golchov. "In actuality what you observed was an authentic telepathic exchange."

"You mean they can communicate at will?"

"No. There was another party involved, a woman named Katya, who is, in fact, the sister of one of our guest psychics, Natasha. She was hiding in the cellar of the lighthouse. As Miss Hintsanen concentrated on your messages, Yuri, Katya was able to use her gift to read her thoughts and send them to the professor."

Antonich sat down and buried his face in his hands.

Golchov touched his shoulder and said, "There is one thing more. In your report you mention a man and a woman found in the lighthouse by the soldiers. The woman was Katya. You had her in your grasp for a moment, Yuri, and you let her go. But how were you to know? You have no gift."

Antonich took his hands away. His eyes were red, his lips drawn in a tight, bitter line. "Someone will pay for this! I will—"

Golchov squeezed his arm. "Control yourself. They shall pay, but according to my terms. For now we must be courteous to our visitors."

Out of the pan into the fire, thought Madderly. But who sold them out? Porkowski, or Wills, for some convoluted governmental reason?

Elina said, "Assuming for the moment this is true, tell us please how you know so much."

Madderly said, "Drug interrogation. Crude, but effective."

Golchov said, "Professor, I would have employed certain substances had it been necessary. In this situation, however, the information came to me as a wonderful gift. My source stands even this moment in the hallway just beyond that door. Miss Hintsanen, to answer your question, you have only to turn the knob."

Elina crossed the room. Madderly's mind momentarily cleared. He recognized the informant, and he wanted to prepare Elina, but the door was opening.

In the hall stood Hintsanen.

Elina cried out "Father!" and threw herself into his outstretched arms.

"Yes," said Golchov to Madderly, "Utho Hintsanen, in the flesh and looking good as new."

Hintsanen came into the room. His walk was unsteady; his legs trembled. But he was undaunted. "Don't be shocked, Professor," he said. "I am no apparition. I am real. Watch!"

He held Elina in his arms and moved around the room in a halting and awkward parody of a waltz, then stopped by the window and laughed for the sheer joy of it.

"Well?" said Golchov to Madderly.

"Remarkable."

"By no means. Dr. Hintsanen's will was not paralyzed. All he lacked was a focus for his own healing power. We gave him that focus and—behold—he is a complete man once more."

"I am, truly I am," said Hintsanen. "My body is not atrophied. I have my strength and now my life may resume."

Elina kissed him, her eyes bright with tears of

happiness.

Madderly said, "And what price did you pay for this so-called miracle?"

"He cooperated with us," Golchov replied. "Therefore, we cooperated with him."

"Let him speak for himself," said Madderly.

"Yes," said Hintsanen. "Please recall I made a pilgrimage to Russia once before and they refused to treat me. Now, in exchange for information, they have healed me. Was that not a fair exchange?"

"Even at the cost of sentencing your daughter to death?"

"There is no question of death for her or you. Dr. Golchov gives me his word of honor the Soviet Union has no wish to harm anyone."

"And you believe him?"

Elina said, "My father is an honorable man! Do not speak to him as though he were a criminal!"

"But that's exactly what he is!"

Elina sprang at him. Hintsanen caught her arm and pulled her away.

"I hope you appreciate her," said Madderly, "while there's still time."

"But there is as much time as he needs," said Golchov. "We wish no harm."

"When I'm safe and sound back in the States I'll believe that."

"I would never let them go!" said Antonich.

"Oh, and why?" asked Golchov.

"They know too much."

"But not as much as we. Correct? And that is why they are here. They would have come by invitation. But you had to resort to tactics from *Taras Bulba*."

"But—"

"Silence!"

"No, I will not be silent! Where have you been all your life? This is the Soviet Union. We never make errors. The KGB lost two operatives in bringing them from Finland. This matter is larger than the vanity of one old man!"

Golchov's cheeks colored, but his voice remained calm. "Today, Yuri, you show me a side of your character I never assumed existed. My spineless student is seen to have a backbone—if not of steel, at least of tin. But you cannot frighten me, nor can *they*. I am involved with powers—"

"But they are not your powers! They are *his* powers. You do not hold the key! You did not heal Hintsanen! You do not gain information!

"Quite so; however—"

Yuri came to his feet and headed for the door, saying, "I will discuss this with Bazarov. He will decide!"

He slammed the door behind him.

Madderly noticed a faint smile on Golchov's lips, but the elderly man's hand trembled as he reached for a piece of sweet cake, and his voice fell momentarily to a whisper. "A young man, and therefore impetuous. You can see how complicated it is when science is mixed with politics."

Now his voice regained its old vigor. "You do not have that problem in your country, eh, Professor? But no matter. We will proceed without him. A very easy task, I assure you. In fact, much easier. Shall we have some sparkling wine to celebrate your arrival?"

He signaled to a serving woman. She filled the glasses and they drank. Outwardly, Madderly joined in the table talk. Inwardly, he reviewed the scene he had just witnessed.

What if this were an elaborate charade? What if the Reds orchestrated events to convince him they had attained ultimate psychic power? Mind control, the super weapon. And after he—an unimpeachable authority—spread the news, other nations would gravitate toward the orbit of this miracle-making power. Presto! The world became very pink.

Golchov was speaking to him. "Later, you will tour the Institute. I am truly interested in your work in telepathy. Would you mind a few tests? They are quite safe."

"Do I have a choice?"

The Russian formed his lips in a smile, but his eyes were humorless. "One always has a choice."

Antonich locked the door and pulled the shades. Golchov was a fool, a senile old man afflicted with egomania. If he wants to kill himself, that is his business, he thought, but he will not sign my execution order.

He reached for the phone. For once he wished to hear Bazarov's gruff voice.

The operator said, "Yes?"

Antonich hesitated, then returned the receiver to its place.

He could not call the Center, could not speak to Bazarov, not yet. To do so would be to admit the American had fooled him.

He slammed his fist into his palm.

It would do no good to warn KGB about Golchov. It would not salvage his own career. No, he had to take direct action. Bazarov had made him responsible. He must act accordingly.

He was on his feet now, pacing the narrow room.

Perhaps another talk with his misguided superior?

Perhaps action?

Hintsanen was willing to trade his daughter's life for his own health. *There* was a man who knew what he wanted and how to get it!

Antonich stopped in the middle of the room. Perhaps Golchov was lying? Yes, the old man was crafty. It was possible he was telling Madderly and the others they would not be harmed so as to keep them calm and gain information from them.

Antonich nodded. That was his own reason for being so friendly and reassuring.

And after they revealed all they knew, bang!

He frowned.

An interesting hypothesis, but at this stage nothing more. It did not offer him a way out of the trouble that would fall like a massive weight on his head when KGB discovered they had sacrificed two agents for nothing.

He shook his head.

"In the final analysis, it is up to me," he told himself. "I will protect the Soviet Union, of course; but since I am a part of that government, I must also protect myself."

The tests were of the standard sort. Madderly had given them as part of his own psychic investigations and had, in turn, undergone them many times.

There was the dice manipulation exercise in which the subject attempts to influence the roll by concentrating upon a particular number.

Another was the Zener card examination, the same used by an American astronaut during moon exploration. The subject sought to identify five geometric figures—square, circle, cross, star, and wavy parallel lines—as the administrator, sitting out of sight, turned the cards upon which they were printed.

And then there was the EEG—electroencephalograph—which analyzed and graphed brain wave patterns. Lastly was a blood serum test which provided information pertaining to the subject's genetic makeup.

Madderly still felt rather inhibited by the drug injected on the voyage from Finland. His efforts with the dice and cards were not good. As his failures accumulated, the administrator became more and more apprehensive. At last she removed her glasses and said, "You are not cooperating."

"I'm doing the best I can. Don't forget I was drugged."

"Professor Golchov will not be pleased."

"*I'm* not pleased."

She totaled the results and compared them with those determined by chance.

"How'd I do?" asked Madderly.

"Poorly."

"Well, it's not whether you win or lose, but how you play the game."

"I do not understand that expression. Remain here, please."

She showed the scores to a woman at the EEG. They looked at him with the same curious yet indifferent gaze one might view a guinea pig to whose soft flesh a drop of nerve gas had been applied.

They spoke briefly, then took him to the EEG and affixed electrodes to his scalp.

"Recline upon the table, please," one said. "Breathe normally. Allow your mind to relax."

The leads tickled. He wanted to scratch.

The operator spoke English with a German accent. "Good afternoon, Professor Madderly. You are familiar with the EEG procedure, yes?

"To begin, think of a pleasant scene, from the world of nature, perhaps. There is beauty which appeals to you, a harmony, if you like. Please close your eyes, relax. That is much better. Yes, and now into this pastoral scene permit someone to enter, a one for whom you have high regard. He or she is welcome in this place. You are happy to acknowledge her presence. You respond beautifully."

The hell of it is I *am*, thought Madderly. He was comfortable, relaxed. A lovely scene had captivated his mind.

And now the technician went further. She encouraged him to free his mind from his body, to allow it to soar, to accept responses from other consciusnesses. Into the snowy birch forest by the green sea came a figure in white more brilliant than snow.

Elina!

He held out his hand.

She moved away.

He called.

She stopped.

"Why?" he asked.

She touched his hand, said. "My father—you misjudge him—you have no right—what do you know of the pain he endured?"

"Your father betrayed us. Golchov will never—"

A message as clear, as distinct as a whisper, said, "I do this against my will. I do not wish to speak to you again."

The snow and birches vanished; the white figure disappeared. Madderly opened his eyes. The vision might be fantasy, a wish-fulfillment. But this was real. She was reaching out for him.

He moved his head slightly to the right. A window opened into an anteroom. She lay upon a table, undergoing an EEG test. Wires issued from her scalp like the terrible snakes of Medusa.

She said, "I hate you!"

He tried to tell her the truth. "They will never let us live. They cannot."

"Do not—I am through—with you—forever—"

She did not perceive his thoughts. Perhaps an image, a sign to show he meant no harm?

A dog, large, shaggy. Brown and white and very friendly. A collar around his neck bore his name—Madderly.

He projected the image. The beast sat before Elina and extended his paw. She knelt, took it in her hand, smiled. The dog barked. She patted its head. The collar caught her eye. She read the name on the collar. She laughed.

Did she understand?

Madderly looked again at the window for some sign.

A curtain had been drawn.

The technician removed the electrodes from his head. "That is enough," she said. "We have significant data."

Madderly nodded, but his thoughts were of Elina. What had just passed between them—did it mean that she, and not Katya, had sent the telepathic messages? Was there an affinity between them that drew them together as one?

Is this what Golchov suspected?

Yuri Antonich dealt the oak door a blow which would have made him wince in pain had he not been so angry.

No response.

He struck the door again, and when there still was no answer, he turned the knob slowly. The door was not locked. He peered in and called, "Professor?"

The study was empty.

An hour earlier he would not have dared to enter uninvited. But now the relationship between him and Golchov had changed. He would give the old fellow one last chance to do the reasonable thing, and if he refused, well, he—Antonich—was not going to be destroyed.

He stepped into the room and shut the door. The mahogany desk confronted him with its dictatorial power as though its owner were enthroned behind it. The bookcases intimidated with their bound volumes. An Oriental rug, a gift from the director of the Far Eastern Institute, warned his feet they were trespassing.

Antonich forced those same feet to walk up and down on the rug. "I have nothing to fear, nothing," he told himself. "I am in control of this situation. If all goes correctly, then *I* shall claim this room and its furnishings as my just reward."

These thoughts, so pleasant, reassured him. He set his shoulders a bit straighter and paused at the window to inspect the splendid view. From here one could see the Peter and Paul Fortress and the river. In spring, trees along the banks were green and sightseeing boats slowed while guides pointed to the Institute. Antonich visualized himself dressed in a handsome summer weight suit. He would throw open the window and wave a white linen handkerchief.

A treat for provincial folk. The very least an Institute Director might do for the people of the Soviet Union.

Such noble aims made Antonich proud. As he turned from the scene of his triumph, the decanter of brandy presented itself for his inspection. He stood on the brink of a new career. He filled a glass and saluted himself. Ah, *that* was brandy! Golchov knew how to enjoy life.

And so he knows how to preserve his life too?

A frown crossed Yuri's face, making his drink bitter. Was he really alone? It would be simple to hide a camera among the books—in fact—yes, there was a lens—no, his imagination.

He sat in Golchov's chair. The leather upholstery fitted him like a glove. It was cool, comfortable, elegant.

What else?

In for a kopek, in for a rouble.

He opened the desk drawer, shuffled the papers, saw Golchov's revolver. Nice to be warned your enemy is armed. Be clever to remove the cartridges. No use for the old fellow to risk shooting himself.

But before he could free the cylinder, there was a noise in the hall. Golchov!

Antonich came to his feet, closed the drawer, and jammed the pistol in his belt. He buttoned his coat and moved around the desk as the door opened.

Golchov was not alone. Madderly followed him. Seeing him, Golchov exploded. "What are you doing in my private study? Answer me!"

Antonich's knees shook, but the weight of the pistol at his waist reminded him of the problem he faced. "It is imperative I speak with you."

"Speak? I will speak! No one enters my study uninvited! I invited Dr. Madderly. I did not invite you!"

"But—"

"First you run to your KGB boss and now you come running to me! He is not impressed with your failure, correct? There is nothing I can do to help you. Go!"

"Me? You help *me*? cried Antonich. "You are the one who needs help!" He pointed at Madderly. "You would trust him, a spy, before me!"

"And you are not?" Golchov said. "Have you not reported my every move for years?"

"For the good of the project, of the nation!"

"And for the good of one Yuri Antonich,

don't forget that!"

"You have never liked me, never! You have done everything in your power to—"

Golchov took a step toward him. "Get out of this study and never return! *Never*, do you understand!"

Antonich clenched his teeth and brushed past Madderly. At the door he looked back and cried out, "Very soon this study will be mine!"

Golchov's scornful laugh pursued him down the hall like a swarm of angry hornets.

TEN

Golchov slammed the door and locked it, then faced Madderly and, taking a deep breath, managed a nervous smile.

"I apologize for that emotional scene," he said. "But, as you know, scientists are human and therefore as prone to violence as anyone."

"Antonich is dangerous."

"Yes, and foolish as well. A bad combination of traits. That is why we must talk. But first, a brandy?"

Golchov moved to the decanter. He saw the used glass on the table and growled, "The swine has been making himself at home!"

He smashed the dirty glass in the fireplace and filled two fresh snifters. "Sit there and I shall sit here, facing you. Shall we drink to science?"

Madderly sipped the brandy and tried to appraise his own position objectively. But at this stage there were too many unknowns.

"And how do you like my style of living?" asked Golchov. "It is above average for Leningrad but by no means the last word. A friend who heads the Novosibirsk installation has a twenty-room villa. Another is pampered with furniture from Paris."

Madderly smiled. "You should see the cubicle I call my office."

"But your research grants are generous, are they not?"

"KGB's information, if that's your source, is wrong this time. We spend almost nothing on psychic research. If it weren't for my teaching, I'd starve."

Golchov frowned. "There must be compensations."

"Sure, an occasional gold medal worth maybe fifty dollars."

"Our medals are iron. They chafe one's neck. But there are other rewards."

"A bullet in the back of the head?"

Golchov's brow wrinkled. "There are always certain hazards, regardless of the system under which one works."

"I'm not sure I want to hear any more," said Madderly.

Golchov placed his glass on the table and looked Madderly straight in the eye. "You are here because you wish to know everything. No need to deny it. I have Hintsanen's report, or did you forget? I know you plotted to come to the Institute for the purpose of spying on me. I know what you want—the technique we employed to gain top secret information from your President and from an associate of the Secretary of State.

"Of course, your plan was thwarted by Yuri's blunder. And now you are here, but in a very bad situation, one which promises an unpleasant conclusion."

Madderly said nothing.

Golchov continued. "I have decided to share my information with you."

Madderly placed his glass on the table beside Golchov's. "For what purpose?" he asked.

"For the obvious—to gain another viewpoint."

"Meaning?"

"Meaning, simply, I am in the uncomfortable position of being in possession of data which I cannot understand and which, consequently, I cannot treat scientifically by duplicating it experimentally."

Images swept across Madderly's consciousness and mixed with words uttered in anger by Antonich. That room again, and the creature on a bed of straw—the girl—Antonich's assertion that Golchov himself did not heal Hintsanen. . . .

Golchov emitted a short, bitter laugh. "It will do you no good to read my mind, Professor. It is almost as empty as Yuri's. I have no gift, no power. My fate is that of ordinary mortals. I am doomed to a consciousness determined by sensory impressions and nothing more."

Madderly said, "What makes you think I have an answer?"

"You have a gift. Perhaps you can see where I cannot."

Suddenly Madderly felt the same despair that he supposed Antonich must have known when he discovered he had been tricked. Golchov had not deceived him, true; but neither had he made a discovery in the sense that he himself had originated a method for psychic spying. At the moment, Golchov was in control of such a method, whatever it was, at least partially; however, the technique itself lay beyond Golchov's control.

"Well," said the Russian, "are you willing to try?"

"Why should I? Can you guarantee my safety and Miss Hintsanen's?"

"To be truthful, I don't know. I will do all in my power to secure your freedom."

"For what reason? Have you lost faith?"

Golchov shook his head. "I am beyond

politics. What we have accomplished here has given me a glimpse of a world made one and whole through a glorious spiritual union. The difficulty is that, as usual, science must be converted to technology, when then deals with material objectives, with one nation's attempts to dominate all others." He shook his head again. "I will not be concerned with such petty matters. Not when the discovery of all time is within my grasp!"

Golchov's words fell upon Madderly's ear. But a meaning implicit in a certain way he spoke fell upon an inner ear, and Madderly perceived that the professor was telling the truth but yet not all the truth. In his mind's eye an image struggled to make itself known, a human form, large and ominous.

"I have under my nominal control at this time an individual who possesses a gift of amazing proportions," said Golchov. "He is not without a reputation as a so-called warlock. In fact, to accomplish his ends he relies upon the most bizarre rituals of witchcraft—the coven, the black mass, even the letting of human blood."

"Magic, Professor, in the USSR?"

"No magic, of course. You know this, I know it, and so does Ragusa."

"Ragusa? He is your subject?"

"Yes. The power is his. Never mind how he came to the Institute."

"And he uses witchcraft? How? As a means of generating psychic energy?"

"Exactly. The rituals have an effect upon the others involved. It would seem that the mental energies they produce are put to use by him."

"How does Ragusa channel the energy?"

"I can only guess. He enters a trance-state and then he is able to place himself, so to speak, anywhere he wishes and observe what is taking place there, in the same way that Edgar Cayce, your famous American psychic, did."

Cayce's ability to make long-distance diagnoses of disease had been verified any number of times. All he needed to know was the address of the person he was to "examine." Then, although he had never been in that geographical area, he could make some sort of spiritual contact with the subject and observe not only his physical and mental state but his surroundings as well. Some seemingly miraculous cures had been thus effected by Cayce.

"The Cayce parallel explains the healing of Hintsanen?" asked Madderly.

"It would seem so."

"And the reading of the President's mind?"

Golchov smiled. "Politics. As you capitalists say, the bills must be paid."

"Or they turn off the power. Right. But have you developed a hypothesis to explain this Ragusa's power?"

"Any number! But all fall of their own weight. The most fruitful appears to be based on genetics, more specifically on the DNA molecule itself. To explain, perhaps we are dealing with a conscious state relating to forces beyond sensory perception, but which manifest themselves in sensory terms because that is the way the human brain functions, the manner in which its circuits are integrated. Follow?"

"Yes," said Madderly. "You of course are acquainted with the work of Cyril Burton. Well, this concept is directly related to Burton's theory that we fail to perceive some forces because our receptors are not sensitive enough. For example, so much stimulus is necessary to 'feel' a grain of sand dropped in one's palm. So much also to perceive radiant energy in the eye. But no one can 'feel' the photons which are the light we see."

"No one, excepting perhaps certain gifted persons," said Golchov.

Madderly nodded. "Like your Ragusa."

"Yes, and if we can determine a difference in his DNA, it may then be possible to synthesize it in the laboratory and, by injections, duplicate his power in others."

"Providing he cooperates."

"Yes, and it is not easy to keep him pleased. He has the temperament of a concert violinist. Would you like to see him?"

Madderly's heart leaped. He said nothing but his expression was enough for Golchov.

"I have scheduled another attempt to achieve a breakthrough. You may observe, if you wish. Perhaps you will see something that I have overlooked."

"And Antonich?"

"He will come to heel in good time, or else he will find other employment. My reputation is secure; my credentials are in order."

Madderly said, "All right, I'll observe. But first, I want to speak privately with Miss Hintsanen."

"That is easily arranged."

"We're on the same side," Madderly said, "whether you admit it or not."

Elina looked at him cautiously from across the small room provided for their meeting. Her head was bowed, her arms clutched defensively at her waist.

"I saw you on the EEG," he said. "Did you see me?"

She nodded.

"I received your message."

"Oh?"

"Yes, did you get mine?"

"I saw only a silly dog," she said.

"What was his name?"

"How should I know?"

"Think."

"Wait—it was on the collar—*your* name!"

"What did the dog say?"

"Nothing. Dogs cannot speak. Although. . ."

"Yes."

"He was very friendly."

"He didn't frighten you?"

"No. Should he?"

"Do I?"

Her lips trembled. She smiled. "That dog was you. I thought he was familiar."

"And friendly, very friendly."

"Yes."

"So you don't hate me?"

"You were cruel to my father!"

"He has placed us in danger."

"Professor Golchov has given his word! And, as my father said, we would still have been in jeopardy in any case."

"Jeopardy is one thing, betrayal another. And forget Golchov. He's not in control here. The KGB runs this show. They want us in prison. Or dead."

"But Golchov is an important scientist, and my father is powerful."

"Not in comparison to the secret police. And Golchov's function is to make discoveries for the Soviet Union. KGB will tolerate his delusions of superiority only so far. Revealing top secret information is too much."

"What can we do?"

"Escape."

"But how? We are in Leningrad. There is no one to help us."

He took her hand. "We'll help ourselves.

Trust me?"

"Yes."

"When and if the moment comes, do what I say."

"Very well. But my father, will you help him?"

"If I can without harming us. I sympathize with him. But he had no right to take the risk of trading our lives for his."

A knock at the door; after a moment, Golchov entered. "It is time," he said.

Madderly said, "Do you object to Elina's observing also?"

"For those who are squeamish the experience is traumatic."

Elina said, "I am a medical student. I have seen much."

"The decision is yours. Another pair of eyes will not diminish the effect. Hintsanen himself is invited."

They left the room and went down the hall, turned at a narrow passageway, and boarded an elevator.

"Is Antonich coming?" Madderly asked.

"Yuri has absented himself, so I do not know."

The elevator stopped its descent. They moved through another narrow hallway and came to a metal door. Golchov pulled it open and they passed through into still another hall which split off in two passageways.

"We must prepare for the ritual by changing into appropriate clothing," said Golchov. "Miss Hintsanen, your dressing area is to the left. Yours, Dr. Madderly, is to the right. Dr. Hintsanen has preceded you."

Yuri Antonich saw Golchov, Madderly and

Elina step into the elevator. So it is true, he thought. The old fool is determined to destroy the project!

His course of action was clear now. Golchov would have to be stopped, even if it meant killing him and the others. The pistol pressed against his stomach. It would not be murder. They were inviting this fate. It was almost as if they were committing suicide.

Yuri moved quickly to his own laboratory. He locked the door and checked his weapon.

"I am a scientist, not an assassin," he told himself. Golchov's insults, his accusations, came to mind and he slammed the cylinder. "But I am also a man!"

Hintsanen wore a black robe over his clothes. When Madderly entered the dressing area, Hintsanen was exchanging his shoes for felt slippers. Madderly took down a robe from a hanger and went to a locker. To Hintsanen, he said, "How do you feel? No relapse yet?"

"I am fine. No, better than that. I am *alive*," the Finn replied, smiling. "That is the most descriptive word. One cannot appreciate his life until he has almost lost it."

"Perhaps you've been deceived."

"Skeptical, Professor? Strange that you of all men should not believe."

"I'm a scientist, a professional doubting Thomas."

"I am sorry I have no wounds for you to examine."

"Sometimes there are wounds here," said Madderly, touching his head, "which can't be seen until it's too late." He slipped the robe on. "In the States we have a saying: there's a sucker born every minute."

"I have read of your P. T. Barnum. But frankly I see no connection. Look." He stood and turned around slowly. "You saw my previous condition. Now I am healed. What further proof do you need?"

"None. What you have proven to me is that your paralysis was psychosomatic. There was no damage to your nervous system. Perhaps you felt guilty for your wife's death."

"Psychoanalysis? Where is your couch?"

Madderly straightened the robe, then sat on the stool and removed his shoes. "So you're healed—for now, at least. But what did the cure cost? Did you make a deal for your soul?"

Hintsanen was amused. "Next you will claim I am Faust."

"Aren't you, in a way?"

A seriousness came into Hintsanen's tone. "You are difficult to understand. I have aided you, and yet you are angry because I got something for myself. Do all Americans share your idealism?"

"Do all Europeans share your lack of it?"

Hintsanen slammed his fist against the wall. He looked at his hand, flexed his fingers. "Yesterday I could not move. Now I inflict pain upon myself." He shook his head. "Do not forget I have been less than a man for too long."

Madderly put on the slippers. "All you say is true, but you may have traded Elina and me for whatever you got. I hope Golchov can keep his promise. Wouldn't it be ironic if you were healed in time to stand before a firing squad?"

"I have faith in Golchov!"

Madderly did not respond. After all, what could he have faith in? Wills? The United States government? Himself? In the long run, what exactly could a man depend upon?

Madderly picked up the black hood that went

with the robe and left the dressing room. In the hall Golchov and Elina waited. The Soviet professor said, "Cover your heads now. In a moment we will pass through that entrance." He indicated another metal door painted glossy black. "Within is a chamber where marvelous wonders are worked. There is one rule you must obey—you will not interfere, regardless of what happens. Do you understand?"

Towers said, "Sir, the Embassy."

Wills took the phone. "Go ahead."

"Message from D. C., sir, signed by Secretary of State."

What could Oscar Miller want? "Let's have it."

"Over the wire, sir?"

"I'm responsible. Shoot."

The clerk cleared his throat and spoke in a flat, unaccented voice: "Wills. Boss curious. NATO acknowledges delivery. Madderly? Support?"

Wills fleshed out the message in his mind. The President wanted to know what the hell was going on. So did he! Porkowski and Relling were gone. Did he need help? Sure—send a hundred, a thousand, psychics!

"Sir?"

Thing was to play it cool as long as possible. Just because he didn't know Madderly's fate was no reason to assume the worst yet, or if he assumed it, to pass on that catastrophic news to the big boys.

"A reply, sir?"

"Acknowledge reception and assure information to follow in twenty-four hours."

Wills hung up and looked out the window. Twenty-four hours. Who was he kidding? He was whistling in the dark and he knew it, but there was nothing else he could do. He felt a twinge of conscience at the probable fate of this likable young professor whom he had placed in such deep jeopardy.

At the foot of the lawn an expanse of bare earth was crusted with ice. Another couple of days and a stranger wouldn't guess that a few feet underground were three bodies, put there by violent death and buried with all the ceremony devoted to sweeping fluff under a convenient rug. In the spring, grass would grow there, and after a couple of years maybe a tree.

He glanced at the clock on the mantelpiece. Madderly and Elina had been gone almost twenty-four hours. Hintsanen had filed a flight plan for Stockholm, but hadn't arrived. With luck he'd crashed in the Baltic. But odds were he was in Leningrad, singing his head off and putting Madderly's feet to the fire.

He lit a cigar.

Still couldn't figure the kidnapping bit. No reason for it, none at all that he could figure.

Not that KGB didn't make mistakes. Everyone in the trade did, sooner or later. Pros expected them. Went with the territory. But Madderly, poor bastard, was an amateur! Maybe he pulled something that triggered the Russians, forced them into it.

But what?

The pills? No, they were props. Had to be something else.

Chambers had suggested they flash CIA. They had agents everywhere, surely in Leningrad. But doing business with those guys you didn't get something for nothing. It was chancy, like sending your kid sister to a cat house to borrow a cup of sugar.

Towers said, "What now, sir?"

Wills slumped on the sofa. "We wait."

"Here, sir?"

"This was their last point of contact with us. We'll stay put another day at least. What's the news on Sylvia?"

"Bad weather delay, sir. She'll arrive tonight."

"In time to be too late. Have someone drive her out."

"Will do, sir."

"And keep me posted on Katya. If she picks up anything, I want to know right away. Tell Chambers to have a look. Maybe she can slip her something to beef up her psychic powers."

"Sir, coffee's supposed to help. Read it in a newspaper article. It's the caffeine."

"That so?" said Wills, coming to his feet. "Let's get to the kitchen and brew her a few gallons."

The air was cold and damp. As Madderly's vision adjusted to the dimness, he became aware that he was in a large room. The stone walls were painted red. There were no tapestries, no altars, no arcane signs and symbols. A scattered pile of skins and furs lay on the floor within the circumference of a circle carved into the black stone.

The chamber was illuminated by two gas flames which shone weakly from fittings fed by pipes snaking across the ceiling.

"Our place is over there," said Golchov.

They moved to the left-hand wall.

"We must remain here," he said. "It is of utmost importancc that once we take our position we do not move until *he*, and he alone, indicates that the ritual is completed."

"*He* is Ragusa?" asked Madderly.

"Yes. Afterwards, if he is willing, you may speak to him about his work."

A bell rang—once, twice, three times.

"*Silence*," Golchov whispered. "The ritual begins."

A faint rumbling sent a tremor through the floor, and a section of stone wall opposite the door opened inward. A procession of red-robed figures passed through this square of blackness into the chamber. The first swung a smoking censer which fogged the air with camphor-scented vapor. Another figure bore upon outstretched hands a book bound in shaggy gray fur. A third struck a measured, hypnotic beat from a golden gong.

There were twelve in all. They moved about the chamber in a careful path weaving in and out of the inscribed circle, then formed a larger circle about it and stopped.

The gong sounded a quicker beat, the pulsating, urging rhythm of the heart, then suddenly ceased. But the cadence somehow continued in the flesh of those within the chamber. Madderly felt it throbbing in the pressure points of his throat, his wrists.

The robed figures knelt and pressed their foreheads to the glistening black floor.

The gas lights flickered, failed, then fought back the voracious darkness and shone again.

The pile of skins and furs in the center of the circle undulated, shifted, stirred, as though some palpable weight were being moved about upon them.

But there was nothing there, save the furs and the kneeling figures.

Madderly strained to see clearly.

The shadows were deceiving, yet the furs did move. And now, as he watched, two points of light appeared in the gloom several feet above the circle.

Two shining lights giving off a yellowish glow, and now a few inches below them another glow, a whiteness.

A figure materialized on the couch of furs.

Madderly saw the head take shape, watched the glowing lights become the eyes of the face, the whiteness become a curving smile of glittering teeth. The neck, massive, muscular, flowed into huge shoulders and broad chest. The arms were smooth and large.

The figure stood erect, his lower trunk, thighs and calves and bare feet coming into view as though a veil were dropped to reveal him.

Hintsanen whispered, "Ragusa!"

Madderly shuddered. The dream he had had at Elina's came into his mind. *This* was the creature he had seen, the one who seemingly transformed himself to beguile the young girl. A phenomenon that was as astonishing as pure magic was involved—the power of one masterful mind to overwhelm and beguile all disbelief from other minds.

Ragusa looked around the chamber. His eyes fell upon Madderly.

There was something in their glow, in their yellow depths, a ravenous craving, a monolithic hardness, calling to mind a primitive power. Madderly found himself somehow thinking of rough-cut pillars of stone set upright on bleak, lonely plains to gauge the coming and going of moon, sun, and stars since time began. And yet despair lurked in those yellow eyes also, like the soft pithy hearts of timeless oak trees yearning after lightning to strike them and burn them to dust.

He knew those eyes, their images of snow and of running wolves, of steppes and crawling things, of strange lights in manless forests, of night—and the darkness beyond night.

The eyes moved away from him. His head

spun. He blinked, moved his lips, found them dry, discovered his throat was parched.

What is he? Madderly wondered. Had Golchov discovered a prehistoric being frozen in ice? Had this creature come back to life like some forgotten monster whose natural enemies had long since perished?

The creature called Ragusa raised his arms and spoke a single word in a tongue—not Russian—unknown to Madderly.

The kneeling figures stood and cast off their robes.

They were seven women and five men—young, physically perfect. Very slowly they moved counterclockwise around the carved circle, their nude bodies shining, glowing.

A chill crept into the chamber. Elina shivered. Madderly held her hand firmly, as much for his own sake as hers.

Ragusa spoke again, and as his lips moved and his voice echoed from the stone walls Madderly inexplicably knew the words. "Let our ceremony begin," Ragusa said. "Let the power be increased. Let the life force and the death force commingle in one force and let that one mighty force be ours."

He clapped his hands. The circling figures stopped, their eyes frozen as though hypnotized or drugged.

Did the vapor contain some hypnotic substance? Witches often used narcotics to cloud simple minds and create illusions. Madderly inhaled deeply. The main ingredient was camphor, a powder commonly burned by covens to expel unsympathetic forces, but he also detected a faint bittersweetness that he could not identify.

There was a movement in the passageway through which the figures had entered.

Golchov whispered, "Do you feel it? The

power? He has not begun to generate his *real* strength, a force hundreds of times greater than any we have measured!"

Madderly recognized the power. In its own way it was as discernible as the camphor vapor. He had seen it in the dream. And Sylvia's coven, Katya, Natasha—they knew this Ragusa. Their force was similar, though not nearly as great.

Now other figures came into the chamber. Ragusa clapped his hands. They passed in a clockwise direction, their fine white bodies aglow with preternatural light.

Ragusa faced the passageway and spoke in words which echoed in Madderly's ears until they became knowable.

"Enter with your gift," he said. "Come into our presence that you may see and be seen."

A cold draft brushed Madderly's legs. A single figure slipped in through the door through which he and Elina and the others had passed, and moved to a position behind Golchov, who was so intent upon the circle that he did not notice this latecomer.

Who was it? Madderly focused his mind upon the stranger, but then Ragusa uttered a sobbing cry and four robed forms came through the square of darkness.

They carried an object—a person. She wore a silver robe. She was bound to a wooden cross.

They raised the cross, slid it upright into a slot cut in the floor. A grotesque shadow fell upon the opposite wall.

Who was she—her face—it . . .

Darkness hid her mouth, but the eyes . . .

Madderly knew them. Katya! No, she was in Finland. This was her sister, Natasha.

He was aware of Elina whispering, "What will he do to her?" But Madderly made no answer.

He projected his consciousness into Natasha's, he opened his mind to hers.

"I am from Katya, from your sister Katya," he told her.

Her eyes searched the chamber.

"From Katya and Stephan!"

Into his consciousness came her voice: "Danger—flee."

"I have come to help you."

"Too late—he knows we communicate—he knows all."

Ragusa slapped her.

Madderly leaped forward. Golchov blocked his way. "To violate the inner circle is death!"

Elina clung to his arm. He struggled to obey reason. Ragusa was too big, too strong. But his physical powers were the least of it. He could not be stopped that way—if at all.

"There is interference here!" Ragusa exclaimed. He grasped Natasha's chin, forced her to look into his eyes. "Do you still resist my power?"

"Good is the greatest power!" she cried out.

Ragusa threw back his head and laughed. "Good is a word. *I am power*! I am the power that has always been, will always be. You are mine, flesh and spirit. I will use you."

He released her, said, "The Book."

A girl—hardly more than a child—her hair a halo of golden curls, held the fur-covered volume open above her head.

Madderly recognized her—Sonya—the dream—she who knew Ragusa not as he was, but as he willed himself to be.

Ragusa turned the pages. They rustled like dead leaves blown by a cold wind across a dying world. He read, his voice the eternal call of the unknown, the cry one still hears on autumn nights as the moon crawls blood-red across the freezing sky.

"*Ushah, Melan, Zigran, Durash, Coptish*!"

"He summons the Powers," Hintsanen whispered.

Madderly knew the truth that Ragusa knew. These were only words, nothing more nor less. There was no magic in them, except that which came into the minds of those who heard them intoned. He knew the secret of the ritual, of all rituals. The power is within the individual, slumbering like embers covered by ash, waiting for a quick hot breath to return their color, their heat, lusting for fuel to consume and to be consumed.

Madderly knew this truth—yet his flesh crawled, his scalp tingled, and he was not surprised to see how the others in the chamber trembled, shook, how their limbs moved involuntarily, as an idea beyond words flowed into their beings even as air entered their lungs. It was a world beyond that communicated now—the other side—not beyond death but past the boundary of reason, the world of experience, of feeling, the universe of blood and fiber, in which the higher faculties were as lost as a blind man at midnight.

And at the same time, within his consciousness, he was aware of other, gentler words sung by the woman upon the cross. He echoed her last song with all his psychic power.

The chamber was hot, terribly hot. Heat poured from the naked figures around the circle. Sweat ran down Madderly's face and stung his eyes.

And the the heat diminished and the room grew cool. A vapor seeped from the floor and hung like a flimsy curtain between him and the circle.

He tried to reach Natasha again. But Ragusa's power was too great.

Natasha was silent, her song ended, her energy

subverted. A roar burst through Madderly's mind, a terrible ringing, snarling din that threatened his sanity. Yet Golchov and Elina seemed to hear nothing save Ragusa chanting the words that were scrawled in squat black shapes upon ancient pages.

The sound became pain. Madderly clapped his hands to his ears, cried out.

Ragusa mocked him. The yellow eyes looked away from the book and became open furnaces. His form doubled, trebled in size, and now his presence filled the chamber. Madderly felt himself pressed breathless against the cold wall—yet he knew—*knew*—nothing had changed—that still he stood between Golchov and Elina.

"The power is mine. All power is mine!" Ragusa proclaimed.

From between the pages of the book he drew a knife. The blade curved and glinted like an evil smile.

"All that is lacking is blood!" he cried.

"Blood, blood!" the others chanted, even Elina and Golchov. Madderly's own lips moved.

Ragusa gave the knife to the girl who held the book. "The animal is ready," he said. "The honor is yours."

She accepted the knife as though it were a sacred gift, to be cherished, to be worshipped. She pressed the blade to her lips, then held it before her in both hands and moved across the circle.

The edge flashed with the brilliance of lightning.

Blood sprang from Natasha's throat, like a red beast suddenly uncaged. It foamed over the black floor, ran into the grooved circle, filling it to the brim.

The roaring in Madderly's mind became a whine, shrill and shattering. And now before his staring eyes a glowing red haze pointed upward from the bloody circle. Shadows flitted like birds, like bats, within the crimson light.

"Now do they draw near!" cried Ragusa. "The power is upon us!"

He fell to his knees on the furs, his hands raised, the palms cupped upward. The light intensified. Shadows swirled. Shapes formed, broke apart, reformed.

"I am seeing a great, great distance," Ragusa chanted, his voice a monotone. "I am beyond a great sea."

His eyes were fixed, burning, unblinking.

"I see streets and people and monuments. There are great buildings made of marble that sparkle in the sun. I approach one building. A fence surrounds it. The lawn is white with snow. A window in a room above is open. I will—"

His eyes darted back and forth.

Anger came into his voice. "It is gone, gone! It has vanished because there is one in this chamber who seeks to destroy me. Fool!" He laughed. "Show yourself!"

He stood, pointed.

"I speak to *you*, Yuri Antonich!"

"What—*here*?" shouted Golchov.

The figure standing behind him pulled off his hood. There was the flash of gunmetal, the whine of Antonich's voice.

"Yes, I am here! Did you think you could do away with me?" He aimed the pistol at Golchov.

"My powers—the ritual!" exclaimed Ragusa. "Stop this madman!"

"Ritual?" cried Antonich. "It is an illusion—a clever trick! I will show you—see?"

He fired into the hazy light surrounding Ragusa. The deafening report pounded like an iron fist. Slugs struck the walls, ricocheted. One of the coven screamed in pain.

Ragusa bellowed, "I am no illusion. *You* are the illusion!"

Golchov leaped at Antonich. They struggled, fell. The pistol fired. A sudden force struck Madderly's arm and hurled him to the floor. For an instant all motions ceased. He saw Ragusa's burning eyes, Antonich pressing the pistol to Golchov's face, Elina tearing off her hood, Hintsanen falling.

The gun discharged again.

Golchov's face vanished in a quick red blur. Antonich sprang to his feet, the pistol ready.

"Powers, strike him down!" cried Ragusa.

Antonich hesitated. He glanced at Golchov's body. "It's over, finished." he said. "I control you now."

"No one controls me!" cried Ragusa. "And no one harms me!"

His eyes focused upon Antonich in all their intensity.

"My power is strong with blood!" he said. "You cannot resist. Throw down your weapon!"

"I am the new Golchov! Your work will continue without change!"

"Only if you put down your weapon."

These words came and went in Madderly's consciousness and he felt he was dying in this place, among strangers, among enemies. It was as though he were watching Ragusa and Antonich from afar, as though they were at some distance on a stage, and he was watching and—

Hands touched him, pulled him to his knees—a voice screamed into his ear—"Madderly! Madderly!"

Elina.

He saw her face. Was she watching this strange drama too?

"Madderly!"

He saw her lips moving, heard other voices,

saw the distance separating him from Ragusa and Antonich shrink until they stood before him, so close he could reach up and touch them.

The thing that struck his arm, that knocked him down, was gone—it was—no—the robe—more blood—

Crying—screaming—another voice—not Elina's—whispering—"I die but you may live-escape!"

Natasha, on the cross!

Yes, he saw her eyes. They moved once, then closed.

He came to his feet, quickly, easily. He sprang at Antonich, caught his arm, drove a knee into his stomach, tore at the revolver, wrested it from his fingers.

Now the full force of Ragusa's power bore upon him. It struck, pushed him back. Madderly regained his balance, leveled this pistol, heard his voice shout at Ragusa. "I shall destroy you!" He heard Ragusa laugh, reply, "No *man* destroys me!"

He looked at Natasha, saw the gash upon her throat, knew she had passed from this state of existence to whatever waited on the other side, knew that he might soon join her.

Ragusa moved—a giant spider maneuvering for the kill. Madderly aimed the gun, stepped closer, closer, until only the circle of blood separated them.

Ragusa taunted him. "So long as I remain within my place you cannot harm me. But I can reach you—with my eyes. You know my power. It is here, real, *alive*!"

Madderly's legs shook—from Ragusa's power or from loss of blood, he did not know which. He saw the pistol in his hand, really saw it for the first time, looming big—heavy—his finger on the trigger. Can I shoot him? he wondered. And then—then what would happen to Ragusa? Would he go away—perhaps to join Natasha?

But to his amazement, Ragusa spoke calmly. "I am going nowhere, Dr. Madderly, unless it is to the United States with you."

The beast was into his thoughts! Yes, he felt the insidious presence of those yellow eyes, felt them slipping behind his own eyes to make him see that which was not.

"You are surprised? Look about—what is left for me here? You will find me a powerful asset. But first I must have that weapon."

Ragusa's eyes blazed like an August sun.

"*Give it to me!*"

Madderly saw his arm extend; saw his fingers open. He closed his eyes and, summoning all his power, made his muscles obey not Ragusa but himself.

He squeezed the trigger.

The spell shattered like a mirror.

Splinters of icy wind spun through the circle, plunging the chamber into darkness, making a great shrill hiss that crescendoed into unbearable intensity. A burst of blinding light. Points of fire, whirling, blazing.

Ragusa vanished. Had he shot him? Had he missed?

Elina found Madderly. She pulled him after her. They reached the door, locked it behind them, ran through the hall toward the elevator. The building shook. There was a mighty roar of wind. Plaster fell. The floor cracked.

Madderly's arm throbbed. Fresh blood reddened his robe.

He tried to speak. "Your father—he—"

"The paralysis returned. He cannot be helped." She caught his arm, gave him her strength. "We must save ourselves."

The building quaked. Walls buckled.

Save how? Outside! But the cold—and his arm. Natasha's face appeared like a vision. Katya knew.

"We must get out!" Elina cried.

"Yes—but the ice—wounded . . ."

"There is a way. Trust me."

A star.

Madderly raised his eyes to its feeble glow. Snow caressed his face. Fingers, warm, soft, touched his brow, casting a shadow between him and the point of light.

A shade with substance—compassionate. He allowed his head to be comforted by the shadow. He was warm, safe. The pain in his arm was no more.

He told himself it was over, done for. He was dead.

But Elina? She touched him, held him so that the rocking and tossing did not cause pain. Rocking. . .tossing. . .a boat.

Yes—Elina—boat—and as they fled across the frozen river, she—

Madderly caught his breath. Salt—sea smell—cold. . .Now he half-remembered.

It was snowing on the ice.

He fell, slid.

She ran after him, fell, slid.

Images—coming back . . .

Ragusa—the Institute . . .

On the Neva ice there were flames. Walking on water—thought he would sink—fire melting ice—but no—it was the Institute ablaze—not the ice.

The cold, mercifully numbing his wound. Elina guiding, helping when he stumbled, pointing the way, saying, "Faith, have faith!"

A banging—shots? He moved, looked up for the stars, found the black cloud of sail cupping the wind. The deck heeled over. His feet rolled helplessly on the rough plank deck.

"What ship is this?" his voice whispered.

"Trust me," answered a voice like Elina's.

Over the ice he had trusted her. He was beyond the luxury of mistrust. His body deserted him, each foot running its own path, his will too weak to make them obey. There were lights on the river, sweeping the ice, and voices shouting, in Russian.

Elina waved, laughed, shouted back, said to him as he fell once more, "Wave. They think we are drunk."

He moved his good arm. The other was limp, lifeless.

They fled, she urging—her voice sometimes seeming to become Natasha's.

The sail caught the wind. The craft rose at the stern and darted ahead. The sea shook its hull. "We'll drown!" he cried out.

Holding him closer she said, "Not if we have faith."

He shut his eyes, buried his face in the musky fur robe wrapped about them both. He was warm, safe. A living heart beat in his ear.

Faith—yes, faith. And when he lost consciousness he knew the craft upon which he sailed would never slip below the icy waves.

Chapter 11

At last Wills slept, without benefit of Dr. Chambers' magic potions. Once he dreamed. An airplane. He was at the controls. In the co-pilot's seat was a young woman. She wanted to fly, she said, and so what could he do but take her up, up, and away?

They cleared the end of the runway, banked sharply left, and rose. He secured the landing gear. The craft climbed easier now. She smiled and opened a window to admit some fresh air and a piece of the hard blue sky. He removed his goggles, adjusted his cap to a jauntier angle, and lit a cigar.

He had just opened his mouth to inquire whether she preferred champagne or something else, when the plane shook terribly and went into a spin. Voices shouted at him from the sky. He fought the controls. The earth spun closer, closer—

"Sir—sir!"

Closer—

"Sir, wake up. We've got them!"

They clipped a tree and swerved up toward the blue.

"Sir?"

Wills rolled away from the hands shaking him. Couldn't even sleep, much less dream, in this goddam service.

"Sir, Professor Madderly and Miss Hintsanen—they're here, on the island!"

Wills opened his eyes to Towers' face. "Where?"

"At the lighthouse."

He stifled a yawn. "You've seen them?"

"No, sir, not exactly. Katya says they're here."

Wills checked his watch. "At seven-thirty?" He glanced at the window at the foot of the bed he sprawled across, still wearing his street clothes and shoes. Snow was falling. "In a blizzard?"

"She says so, sir. That's all I know."

"Anybody checking?"

"Thought you'd want to know first, sir."

"Okay, take a couple of the boys and for godsake don't get lost in the snow. I've got enough explaining as is without having to deal with the Defense Department."

"Right, sir."

"On your way out tell someone to fix a pot of coffee and wake up Sylvia."

Towers left. Wills closed his eyes for a moment and recalled the dream. Him, at the controls of a plane. Damn! And to think supposedly intelligent people believed such idiotic visions related to reality.

He laughed, swung his feet to the floor, stood, stretched, rubbed the back of his neck, and took a vow that if he got out of this mess with his scalp he'd never dream again.

The storm was over. A midmorning sun shone brightly on the new snow. All traces of the common grave by the wall were gone. The fir trees beyond the wall reached their green and white boughs toward a pure blue sky.

Wills and the others met in the drawing room.

For almost an hour Wills had questioned Katya and Stephan. It was a futile tug-of-war with emotion, a battle that not even Sylvia Week could win. From the bits and pieces spoken between outbursts, Wills surmised that something had happened at the Pavlov Institute and that Madderly and Elina had escaped and returned by ship to the island.

"What ship?" he asked, for the second time. "We have no boats in Soviet waters."

"Or none that you know of." said Chambers. "Maybe another party dealt himself in?"

That remark made Wills pause and take stock. It was always possible that other operations were at work. Yes, when it came to matters like this the national motto should be the Biblical injunction, "Let not thy right hand know what thy left hand is up to."

But no, this was too hush-hush.

"Let's take it from the top one more time," he said.

"Not now," Chambers said. "They're on the verge of a breakdown."

"Hell, so am I!"

Someone passed in the snow outside the window. Then there was the sound of shouting and Towers came into the room, his boots and trousers coated with ice.

"Sir, we've got them," he said. "Girl's tired but okay. Professor's been shot."

Chambers grabbed her medical bag and led them down the hall to the courtyard.

Madderly was strapped to a sled. His face was pale, his lips blue. She checked his pulse, then told the marines to carry him inside.

They placed him on a kitchen table. Chambers cut away the furs he was wrapped in and examined the wound. "He's not bleeding now," she said. "Got it in the upper arm. Good chance the slug passed through. I'll probe to be safe."

"This is no hospital," said Wills. "Give the guy something—I want straight answers."

"Not this time," said Chambers. "Talk to the girl."

"I plan to, but I need his testimony. Dammit, I've got a job to do. It's bigger than all of us!"

Chambers shook her head.

Bazarov experienced a feeling he had not known since Stalingrad, a dull metallic heaviness that called to mind the color green. It commenced in his mouth and flowed thickly down his throat into his stomach, settled, then oozed lower into his bowels.

Not since Stalingrad. . . but that disaster had been turned from defeat to victory. There was no such hope here.

His head hurt and his eyes smarted from the smoke. The winter sun made a valiant effort to shine, but the morning was nevertheless gray, overcast. There was the smell of smouldering wet wood, of combusted chemicals, or burned fabrics, plastics, and paper. The wind coming with the chill of winter across the icy river bore also the faint but unmistakable odor of charred human flesh.

He wiped his eyes with a handkerchief. What had gone wrong? In the middle of the night, Center had called to rouse him from a warm sleep with news that something was amiss at the Institute. When he told them he would see to it first thing in the morning, the duty officer read a direct order from the commander of the Leningrad garrison. Thirty minutes later Bazarov was on his way through the snowy night to the airport. He had tried to reach Antonich, but all lines to the Institute and University were shunted to a security switchboard manned by an army colonel whose orders were to say nothing.

Bazarov stuffed the handkerchief back in his coat pocket. Several men in white asbestos suits approached the piles of rubble and inserted long metal rods into the debris. Hose crews played streams of misting water over them from time to time, and rainbows formed in the arcs of spray when they passed through shafts of sunlight.

The fire marshal came across the frozen river, made his way up the icy bank, almost falling once. Stamping his feet so that his breath turned to smoky puffs, he said, "Colonel, the fire is now officially under control. My men are searching for survivors."

"Oh?" said Bazarov. "You believe persons could survive that inferno? Look, even the steel beams are twisted."

"We have rescued men from worse than this."

"I will not argue," said Bazarov. "But KGB wishes to know only about one fire—this one—and how it started. That is why I have been taken away from other duties and ordered here."

"Yes, Colonel. We can make no real judgment until the ruins cool and we are able to conduct a close investigation. However, we believe that vast quantities of volatile chemicals—"

"Yes, what else?"

"The building was very old. The basic structure was modified through the years. Many changes were made without consulting the local building committee and did not measure up to safety standards. There are basements and subbasements connected by tunnels, elevators, hallways, and ventilation shafts. Imagine a fire built upon a grate. As it burns, hot air rises and creates a suction, pulling in fresh oxygen to support further combustion. Thus . . ."

Bazarov listened to the marshal's detailed explanation. Fellow knew his job. Question is, do I know mine? What the devil really happened? Where were Golchov and that ass Antonich? Security reported at least two persons seen running down the frozen river.

"But of course," the marshal continued, "this does not give us a cause for this particular fire."

"Yes, the cause. Have you an idea?"

"I said the building was ancient. No doubt the gas pipes and the electrical wiring were faulty. Rats will eat the insulation off cables and even puncture gas mains. A pocket of gas, a single spark—boom!" He paused and drew a breath. Then, "But on the other hand. . ."

"Yes?"

The fire marshal looked both ways, moved closer, whispered, "Arson! Perhaps capitalist agents sabotaged . . ."

Bazarov shifted his gaze from the man's eager expression to the catastrophic scene across the river. Sabotage? What the fellow had in mind was plain. If the fire was caused by some weakness in the building, it was probable the fire inspectors would be reprimanded, perhaps demoted and punished. Let the "capitalists" take the blame, and then praise the heroic efforts of the fire fighters.

Sabotage was a tempting explanation and a good way out of a dangerous mess. But mention of sabotage would call attention to the KGB, and there would be a different sort of investigation. Bazarov had no choice.

"The building was not sabotaged," he said. "Of this the KGB is certain. The gas pipes and wiring were faulty. You will indicate this in your final report. Make no suggestion of sabotage."

The marshal frowned. "Comrade Colonel, the fire commission—"

"Comrade Marshal, KGB is positive. You

may have my word on it. Do you doubt me?"

"Of course not. It is—"

"Then the matter is closed, now and forever."

Bazarov walked away from the scene of destruction. As he rode back to the airport he roughed out his own official report.

Nikoyan and the others would be angry, but what could they do? The building was old and gas mains and electrical systems had a way of causing fires, especially in areas where explosive chemicals are stored. Golchov and Antonich whose charred bodies were easily identified, would be mourned as heroic scientists of the Soviet Union who gave their all, and so forth. Perhaps the older man would warrant a statue—no, a lab equipped in his name at some school would be more fitting. They would send a posthumous commendation to Antonich's parents. As for that Ragusa, who could know what might have happened to him. There was no trace of his body in the ruins.

It was snowing again. He watched the flakes swirl by the window. What really happened? No one would ever know, unless the two seen running on the ice were indeed survivors. An eyewitness said they reeled and staggered as though they were drunk. Maybe they were; maybe they had nothing to do with the Institute. Still, he would assign people to find them, and if they were Madderly and the Hintsanen girl—well—perhaps he would order a dirty trick. What was necessary would be done.

Shadows—moving on the walls—insects—climbing—falling—baring their claws and climbing again—their sticky webs—ready for victims—for capture.

Madderly tried to flee—but the webs—the claws—he kicked—something fell across his legs—the building, falling down—Ragusa—where was—

He cried out, "Elina!"

Her voice broke the awful spell. "I am here, with you."

He wanted to sit up, but his arm was on fire. "Where are we?"

Elina forced him to lie back. "We are safe on my island."

Safe, yes. He tried to remember. The circle, Natasha, Antonich and the gun—yes—Golchov dead—and he, he had shot Ragusa, or shot at him.

"Madderly?"

It was Wills' voice—he knew that. They hadn't killed him.

"I need some answers."

Elina said, "He is still too weak. He must have more rest."

"Time's running out," said Wills.

"I'm—I'm all right," said Madderly. "What do you know?"

"Very little. Elina told us about her father and about the death of Natasha."

"Katya—she's been . . ."

"She knew. Chambers gave Stephan something to make it easier. Elina told us you crossed the sea in a boat, said it was a sailing vessel manned by fur traders. She told them you were her lover, and her father discovered you in her room and shot you."

The star, the tilting deck and the sail overhead like a shadow—yes, it all came back now.

"And that's all she would tell us, period."

"I am concerned for you," Elina said. "They must make you well first so you can tell them."

Madderly recalled her voice summoning him to action, her hands leading him from the burning building, her strength supporting him down the frozen river. His fate and hers were bound together. He sensed the great concern she had for him. Suddenly, in spite of everything that had happened, he was very thankful Wills had sought him for this mission.

"I'll tell you what I know," he told Wills.

"Start at the beginning. Why did the Soviets pull that damn raid?"

"We brought it on ourselves because I was a little too clever."

"You? How?"

"The telepathy demonstration. I told Antonich the drug decomposed into amino acids which were assimilated within twenty-four hours. That put him on the spot. He needed a sample of the drug for analysis. The only way to get one was to kidnap us. They had equipment on the ship. But what happened here?"

Wills told him about Porkowski and Relling, about the appearance of the Chinese agent and the death of Gouzenko and Rostov.

For a moment Wills seemed contrite, but then he said, "So much for bits and pieces. You saw Golchov. What's the Soviets' big discovery?"

Madderly shook his head. "They discovered a man, not a discovery."

"They tricked us?"

"No. Golchov located a remarkable psychic with the ability to transcend space and project his consciousness to observe locations and individuals. That's how they were able to spy on the President and the Secretary of State. But Golchov was not able to discover the nature of this power, and so he could not duplicate it in the lab."

"Then the one with the real power is that Ragusa you raved about in your delirium?"

"That's right. Golchov was using him. And he was using Golchov."

"How?"

"Golchov gave Ragusa what he needed to apply his power. The Soviets had him under physical control, but I got the impression Ragusa was running the show."

"He conned them?"

"Not exactly. He wasn't a fraud. He had the power to create illusions in people's minds—a remarkably strong hypnotic gift. And he was also able to project his consciousness through space and report what he saw and heard."

"That's hard to believe."

Madderly looked to Sylvia Week for support, saying "He hasn't heard of Cayce."

Sylvia nodded. "Edgar Cayce's ability to observe subjects thousands of miles away was verified time and time again. All he required was their name and address. The Association for Research and Enlightenment at Virginia Beach has thousands upon thousands of documented instances. The Cayce phenomenon is real."

"But how?" asked Wills.

Madderly replied. "That's where the difficulty arises. No one knows. Cayce himself did not know. Golchov hypothesized that Ragusa's power was caused by a genetic factor which heightened his sensitivity to forces other persons cannot perceive."

"You mean Ragusa was a mutant?"

"In a manner of speaking—yes, his psychic power could be due to a mutation. All living things undergo constant bombardment by particles from deep space. In the vast majority of cases, these particles pass through us without any significant effect. But from time to time one strikes a gene and in some way alters the information it carries. Perhaps nothing tangible results immediately. But suppose the carrier of this affected gene mates with one whose same gene has been similarly altered."

Wills frowned. "That drops us smack in the middle of Mendel's bean patch. Confusing."

"Yes, and remember the time factor. It might require a hundred generations of breeding before the right genes come together to cause a discernible change in one individual. If Ragusa's—or Cayce's—power was created in this manner, the mutation may have occurred a thousand—or ten thousand—years ago."

"A bit of the hit-or-miss in there," said Wills.

"Precisely—which may be further proof that the theory is correct."

"Why?"

"Because there are so few psychically-gifted persons at any one time. The percent of the total population is miniscule."

"Okay," said Wills. "But Golchov had nothing—you're absolutely sure?"

"I'm not sure of anything, except that I'm not sure. Chances are his research records were destroyed. After seeing the poor relationship he had with his assistant, I doubt he kept copies."

"And Ragusa's dead, thank God."

"That's another thing we're not certain of."

"What? You shot him, didn't you? That's what you babbled in your delirium."

"I shot at him and I think I may have hit him. I might have killed him, but I can't swear to it."

Wills looked at Elina. "You were there. What about it?"

"It is as Madderly says. He aimed and pulled the trigger. But the chamber was smoky and poorly lit, and all was confusion. I did not see Ragusa leave; however, there were other doors than the one we used."

"Great, wonderful!" said Wills. "That leaves us not much better off than we were when we started. A cosmic mind reader running loose knowing we're after him."

Mrs. Week said, "Perhaps it's time we took stock. Exactly what does the government of the United States want?"

Wills pulled a cigar from his coat pocket, stuck it between his lips and stared at her over the tip, as though he were taking aim. "We want the usual—everything. We'll settle for the usual—all we can get."

"The present danger has been seen to," she said. "Also, Golchov has bequeathed us a working hypothesis which sounds plausible to me. I am inclined to believe that Ragusa perished by gunshot or in the fire; however, I realize the government cannot depend on my belief alone, so I suggest we take steps to protect the President."

"But how might that be done?" asked Elina.

"By creating a sort of psychic barrier to shield him from a projected consciousness."

"You've lost me," said Wills. "Do you mean exorcism?"

"No. Exorcism is a casting out of malign forces. What I propose is charging the area around the President's home with a positive force which will nullify and ward off projections like those of Ragusa—in other words, what might be called a blessing. It's probably unnecessary. Ragusa is most likely dead, and I doubt they have another like him. But why take chances?"

Wills fumbled in his pocket for a match. "You want to work a magic spell on the White House?"

"It's not magic," said Madderly, "unless all psychic phenomena are magical. But empirical tests have disproved that. It's just as Sylvia says—we create a field that insulates the President. It should work. We know how difficult it was for Ragusa to operate under the best conditions. The least interference should stop him."

"All right, let's say we do that and it does work. It's only good for the White House, right? I mean you can't protect every place the President goes."

"No, and we don't have to. The projective technique of Ragusa, and of Cayce, requires a fixed point of reference, a definite target. When the President travels he doesn't make his moment-to-moment itinerary public. He's only vulnerable when he's in the White House."

Wills found a match and lit his cigar. He broke the match in half and dropped the two pieces in an ashtray. "Can this be done quietly, without creating a scene?"

"Yes."

"If the media got wind of such happenings in the White House . . ."

A crewman of the jet that Oscar Miller had dispatched to bring them to Washington made his way aft and said to Wills, "Andrews Air Force Base in twenty minutes, sir. Also, this message for you."

Wills scanned the sheet of blue paper and told him there would be no reply.

To Madderly, Elina, and Sylvia, he said, "A few words from Brewster, our CIA link. Operatives in Leningrad report destruction of a building at the Pavlov Institute. Official line on the cause: faulty gas pipes and wiring."

He folded the note, placed it in an ashtray, and struck a match. The paper vanished in smoke.

"There was a PS concerning you and Miss Hintsanen," he said.

"Saying?"

"Not much—except our side made a few discreet inquiries along the waterfront, and guess what? No one saw you. So you must've perished in the fire."

"Which puts us in the clear," said Madderly.

Wills laughed. "Don't count on it. If they want you, they'll find you."

"That's a happy thought."

Wills was silent for a few moments. Then he said, "Our next problem is getting into the White House without alerting the media people. Since some of them know me, it would be best if we part company for a while and regroup inside.

"Suppose I make a grand entrance to draw their attention? Yeah. I'll borrow one of the boss's choppers and land on the lawn. We'll pretend Madderly's an invalid and get him a wheelchair, and you ladies can take him in with the other sightseers. Then Madderly can plead faintness, and Towers and Chambers will wheel him away for first aid and we'll all get together and do what has to be done."

Wills laughed softly. "I still think we're mad, but if it takes a touch of lunacy to put an end to bugging the President's mind, then I have to yield to superior psychic wisdom."

The cool air, the blue sky, the yellow—seemingly molten—puddles of sunlight on the snow, the lean strength of Elina's body helping him into the back seat of the car that met them on the runway—all these combined to give Madderly a pleasant sense of other-worldliness. He thought of a kite at the end of a fragile string whose existence depended upon an equilibrium of forces over which it had no control. A gust too strong, and the string would snap and down it would come, wheeling, plunging to ruin. But while it soared, every fiber sang.

Wills, Chambers, and Towers sped off in another car for the heliport beyond a distant row of hangars.

Madderly's driver, a young marine in civilian dress, took them through two security check-points and cleared the air force base. The plain, unmarked car joined the traffic flow on the highway leading into Washington.

But it did not go unnoticed.

A green pickup truck followed several car-lengths behind. From time to time the driver seemed to cup his hand to his mouth as though he were coughing. His fingers held a microphone. A whip antenna arched from the rear bumper to the side of the cab.

When the jet landed at Andrews, an operative with grease-stained hands who did engine maintenance for the Secretary's plane took a smoke break. He recognized Wills. Madderly and the others were unknown to him, so he followed his general instructions and called his wife to ask about the baby's cold. He passed on the tag number of the car. The pickup was in position in a few minutes, and even now a message was being transmitted from the Soviety embassy to KGB Center in Moscow. It would be decoded and sent along to the appropriate officers. One copy would be deposited in the already-full incoming basket on the desk of a Colonel Bazarov.

Eventually, he would read it, if more pressing matters did not require his attention.

The driver steered into the right lane, slowed and finally came to a stop in the slush by the curb. He engaged the blinker warning lights and went around to the right rear door. For a moment the wheelchair presented a problem, but with Sylvia Week's help he got it unfolded and then assisted Madderly in sliding from the seat into the chair. Elina shut the door behind them.

The driver said, "Can't park here, sir. Too heavily patroled. Mr. Wills said he'd call when you needed me."

Elina pushing the wheelchair, and Sylvia walking at Madderly's side, they passed through the gate into the White House grounds and came under the steady, searching gaze of the guards. A sign directed them to the area where tours originated. They found only a few people waiting.

A young woman introduced herself and said she would guide them and attempt to answer their questions. She smiled at Madderly, nodded to Elina and Sylvia, and asked them and the others to follow her.

After they passed another guard and entered the White House proper, Madderly moaned softly, then louder, and pressed his hand to his forehead.

Elina said, "Wait, please! He is not well!"

The guide rushed to Madderly's side. "There's an aid station beyond the elevator," she said. "Someone should be on duty."

Chambers and Towers were waiting behind the door marked with a small red cross. Chambers assured the guide that she would be responsible for this party of three, and that should Madderly feel better, she would have them rejoin the tour. The young woman thanked her and went back to the rest of her group.

When the door closed, Chambers said, "So far, so good. Wills has checked the situation with the President. Wills had quite a time with him but finally convinced him. The President says we do our thing in his office. Wills is having the area vacated and seiled off now. My instruction are that when we get to the office I take Madderly in alone for a few minutes, while the rest of us wait in the Administrative Assistant's office across the hall. We'll use a private corridor. No one will see us."

There were three corridors to be traversed. The first opened into the second through a door guarded by a silent man wearing a gray business suit. The third corridor turned to the left twice and ended at another door, the top half of which was glass. A uniformed guard watched them through the glass, and when they were close, the door swung open to admit them into the executive wing of the Executive Mansion. If there were a geographical nerve center of Washington, D.C., of the United States, of the Free World, this cluster of offices was it.

Elina, Sylvia Week, and Towers followed their instructions and went into a nearby office. Dr. Chambers pushed Madderly across a foyer and stopped before a closed door. She knocked once. From within, Wills said, "Yes?"

"Madderly," Chambers replied.

The door opened and Wills took charge of the wheelchair. Madderly found himself in the famous oval room elegantly carpeted and furnished with a huge desk littered with papers. Three leather chairs were arranged in front of the desk. Their upholstery showed the scuffs and cigaret burns of heavy use.

The President was seated behind the desk. He rose. He was a slim man, compactly and strongly built.

The President came across the room to greet Madderly. His smile was pleasant, even sunny, reassuring, as was his hearty handshake. "Welcome aboard, Professor Madderly," he said. "Good to meet you in person at long last. Hope the arm's not too painful."

Madderly said it was not.

"Good." He smiled again. "Don't want anything else happening to you. After all, we have a great deal in common."

"You mean you're into parapsychology?"

"A little—very little. But I don't mean that. We both have a Southern accent. It's not too common in this room."

Again the sunny smile. Then the smile vanished as quickly as it had come, and now the Presidential voice lost its folksy tone and became crisp and urgent. "Before you do anything, Professor, I want to speak to you for a moment. First, I've read Wills' report and I want to thank you for a job well done. I've dealt with those people myself and I know how difficult they can be. I have one question, though. Was there a connection between the death of my friend and the Soviets' gaining access to the information that passed between us?"

"To be perfectly honest, I don't know," said Madderly. "Ragusa's technique is explainable in psychic terms, so there's no need to introduce spiritualism. However, the fact that there were two deaths indicates there might be a connection."

"I see, or think I do," said the President. "All right. Second, I'm worried. Maybe this time we can attribute the Soviet breakthrough to chance. But what about the next time? They might be successful again, right?"

"It's certainly possible. They're spending millions on psychic research."

The President frowned. "That's the problem—research. We could supply funding, but not openly. Damn! You can imagine public reaction if it were known that we were in the Oval Office seriously discussing psychic phenomena. Left-wing, right-wing, middle-of-the-road, Protestant,

Catholic, Jew . . . they'd all be down here raising holy hell!"

He crossed to the window behind the desk and looked out at the snowy lawn. "Of course, there are ways of providing money. But that presents another problem. What would the country be getting in exchange for its tax dollars?"

He turned away from the window. "Don't read me wrong. I'm skeptical—hell, it goes with this job—but I'm not a nonbeliever. I've heard of Rhine and Stevenson—even heard about Ostrander and Schroeder. Damn interesting. And I don't doubt your experience with Ragusa. Or should I say *my* experience?"

As he spoke the President's mind opened to Madderly's consciousness. He perceived an attitude of sincerity.

"What it all boils down to is that old word, *trust*," said the President. "I'm asking you to keep this matter confidential and to be patient while I see what I come up with. I know this sounds like foot-dragging after what you've been through, but it's the best I can do."

Madderly nodded.

"I've looked over the CIA report of the fire at the Pavlov Institute. That should set the other side back at least one giant step."

"A lot of people died."

"Yes, ours and theirs. A tragedy."

Madderly wanted to reply that tragedies only happen on stages in the presence of sympathetic ticket holders. But the President was shaking his hand and saying, "Your expenses and medical attention and transportation will be taken care of, naturally. See Wills. On behalf of our nation, I thank you."

The President left through another door. A

moment later the others came in and Wills said, "All right, now what?"

At the top of the hill Madderly stopped jogging and took a breather. The golf course was still blanketed in the layer of snow that had begun falling the night before after he went to bed, and had stopped in the early hours, so that when he awoke it was to a clear sky and a world magically transformed.

As he walked in the powdery snow at the road's edge, Madderly tested his arm. The wound had healed nicely and now, after five weeks, there was only a slight tenderness from time to time to remind him of the pain he suffered during his and Elina's flight from the Institute. He was still a bit weak, but the daily runs prescribed by his doctor were rebuilding his strength. Wouldn't be too long until he was fit again.

Madderly left the road and took a short cut through a lightly wooded area. The snow felt good beneath his feet. He began jogging again and tasted the pine-scented cold air.

The forest in Finland was very much like this. Elina, what was she doing? In his mind's eye he saw her face. She smiled. Was she trying to tell him something? He had not seen her since they parted company at the White House, she to return to her country to attend to matters relating to her father's estate, he to come home to this place to recuperate. They had exchanged letters, and he had dreamed of her, but he longed to see her in person.

The way through the woods sloped downhill now. Madderly quickened his pace. Shadows made by his passing the trees reminded him of that last scene in the White House. Yes. Sylvia had formed them in a circle in the Oval Office, had pulled the curtains, had purified the air with a wispy cloud of smoke.

"What we are about to attempt," she had explained, "is neither complicated nor profound. We must think of ourselves as being akin to those living in this building, and we must consider them to be worthy of our affection. We are here to do a great good, to act positively, constructively. Our actions may have a pronounced effect upon mankind."

They held hands. They opened their hearts and minds. They gave to Sylvia Week whatever of the power they possessed, and they heard their voices speaking through hers, as she said, "We would that this place, sacred and dear, be blessed. Let not negative forces have entrance here. Let our strength stand as a shield, bright and beautiful, reflecting that which is malign back against itself, reducing it to its original nothingness."

In that moment, Madderly distinctly remembered, waves of light shimmered before him, and there was a sound as of clear water over bright rocks on a summer's day, of wind combing the branches of tall pines.

And had it worked—had the blessing succeeded?

Who could say? No further incidents had been reported. Perhaps Ragusa was seeking a new sponsor. Perhaps—

Madderly found himself upon the road leading to his house. His jogging was steady, strong, his breath forming precise puffs of steam in the cold, sunny air.

Around a bend, moving rapidly, appeared a massive gray limousine bearing DPL plates. As it approached and then passed Madderly, the sun glinted brightly on its rear window, illuminating what seemed to be an impassive, staring face with a pair of enormous yellow eyes. His mind reached inside the car but drew a total blank. In a moment, the light was gone, and Madderly, never breaking stride, saw that the passenger seat was completely empty. Self-hypnotic suggestion, he thought, or a trick of the light. And yet . . . The car vanished down the road.

All thoughts of what had happened left his mind. Now he visualized a car parked in his drive, still a considerable distance away. Yes, a sportscar. Blue. The tag number was blurred but he could make out the letters "EH."

There was a person in the car, waiting. The glare of the sun on the window hid her face. *Her*? He wondered how he could know that.

But then at last he reached a turn in the road and could see his driveway. There was the blue car! He increased his pace. The door on the driver's side opened and a young woman stepped out and waved.

Elina!

She ran to him, and when they met, he took her in his arms and held her close. Then he held her closer still—to be doubly certain she was not a visionary experience. She did not fade nor did she disappear. In fact, she hugged him back, closely and intensely. And then she kissed him tenderly.